KAVANAGH Q.C.
Blood Money

KAVANAGH Q.C.
Blood Money

Shirley Lowe

CORONET BOOKS
Hodder and Stoughton

First published in Great Britain in 1998
by Hodder and Stoughton
A division of Hodder Headline PLC

The right of Shirley Lowe to be identified as the Author
of the Work has been asserted by her in accordance
with the Copyright, Designs and Patents Act 1988.

10 9 8 7 6 5 4 3 2 1

A CIP catalogue record for this book
is available from the British Library

ISBN 0 340 70761 5

Typeset by Hewer Text Composition Services, Edinburgh
Printed and bound in Great Britain by
Mackays of Chatham PLC

Hodder and Stoughton
A division of Hodder Headline PLC
338 Euston Road
London NW1 3BH

PART ONE

Blood Money

1

'Mrs Meadows? It's bad news, I'm afraid. Your husband
...' The policeman's voice on the phone had been quietly,
reassuringly kind, as though he were explaining something
difficult and distressing to a very small, vulnerable child.
'... seems he took the bend a bit fast at Longmeadow
Road and lost control.'

'Nick? An accident?' Sarah had gripped the receiver so
hard that her fingernails dug painfully into the palm of
her hand. 'Is he all right?'

'They're operating on him now,' the policeman said.
'He's in good hands. Southbrook Hospital. They took
him straight there after the accident. I could send over
one of the lads to give you a lift there, if you like.'

'No. No, thank you.' Sarah had known instinctively
that she'd need time alone to come to terms with what
had happened and, even more, what she feared might
happen. 'No,' she had repeated. 'I'll be fine, thanks.'
She'd been surprised to hear her own voice; it sounded
perfectly normal.

Hanging up the receiver, she had been moved to tears by
the poignant sight of her gardening gloves on the table next
to the phone; it had been almost unbearable to realise that

3

while she had been out by the shrubbery planting hopefully for the future, Nick – only a mile or so down the road – had been careering towards oblivion.

She'd wiped her eyes with the back of her hand and forced herself to resist a powerful compulsion to jump into her Peugeot and race off to the hospital. She was in no state to drive and, she'd told herself firmly, there was a perfectly good minicab firm a couple of miles away in the village. After phoning them she'd gone upstairs, taken off her clothes, folded them meticulously and laid them out on the pale blue silk bedcover. Determinedly not looking at the 'his 'n' hers' cornflower-sprigged basins in the *en suite* bathroom, she had stepped into the shower, turned the gold dolphin tap to maximum and felt the pressure of the water gradually transform the turmoil in her mind into a sort of numb acceptance.

Relying on the minutiae of her everyday routine, she'd reached into the wardrobe for acceptable clothes, put them on, made up her face, grabbed her handbag and run down the wide staircase, shaking her head as she went, to dry her short blond hair. By the time she had locked up, set the burglar alarm and the minicab was halfway down the drive, her heart had stopped thumping and she was beginning to find that it was, after all, possible to breathe without gasping or retching.

And now, here she was, elegantly coiffed and clad, sitting in Out-patients waiting, waiting . . .

White-clad figures darted in and out of doors, trolleys trundled past, official-looking chaps with stethoscopes walked towards her and then passed by. Sarah got up and went over to the receptionist for the third – or was it the fourth? – time.

The receptionist sighed wearily. 'They've said they'll call down.'

Sarah said, 'Please . . .' and it sounded like begging.

'Oh . . . right, well, I'll have another try . . .' The receptionist was all too familiar with the look in Sarah's eyes, a look she nearly always found impossible to ignore. She picked up the phone and dialled. 'It's Reception again. Any news for Mrs Meadows? Uh-huh. Okay, I'll tell her.' Sarah gazed at her anxiously, trying to read her expression. The receptionist smiled. 'Everything went fine. You'll be able to see him in a while.'

'Thank God,' Sarah sighed. She smiled at the receptionist. 'Thank you.'

She went back to her seat and prepared to wait. Glancing around, she noticed a smartly dressed black woman rush out of one of the operating theatres – wasn't that where they had Nick? – talking animatedly into a mobile phone and struggling out of her white coat as she ran. Minutes later she saw the same woman dash back past Out-patients and into the operating theatre. She had put on her white coat and she was clutching a pager.

Sarah, feeling she could now afford to relax, slumped in her seat. A woman on a Tannoy was announcing an open day: 'We're raising funds for our dialysis unit and would like to welcome you all here next Saturday. Come and meet . . .' Sarah shut her eyes against the insistent voice and dozed off. When she opened them, she saw that the black woman, now dressed in a black skirt and a white angora sweater, was talking to the receptionist. They were both looking in her direction. Sarah watched curiously as the black woman came towards her.

'Mrs Meadows?'

Sarah looked up. 'Yes?'

'I'm Hilary Jameson. I . . . operated on your husband.'

Sarah was going to say, 'Oh, thank you, thank you,' but

something in the surgeon's expression stopped her. 'Well, he . . . he is going to be all right?'

'I'm so sorry,' Hilary Jameson said. 'I'm afraid he's dead.'

Sarah stared at her in disbelief. 'Dead? He can't be. They said . . .'

'I know. I'm sorry. It was a heart attack.'

Sarah fell back in her seat, trying to grasp the enormity of what she had just heard. 'A heart attack?' she said. 'I don't believe it.'

As the minicab drove away up the drive, Sarah stood and faced her glossy white house. It was a cared-for house like all the other Executive Homes around her, set in their secluded acres of Surrey shrubberies and manicured lawns. Sarah had found pleasure in pampering it ever since she and Nick had fallen in love with it some thirty years or so earlier. Now, the pink geraniums nodded cheerfully from the balconies, rare orchids were attempting a satisfactorily unusual second blooming in the conservatory, and the heavy brass on the front doors gleamed luxuriously. And yet it seemed to her an unwelcoming, empty house.

She went inside and into Nick's study. The pinkish glow of the evening sun flooded through the French windows, and she was surprised to find that she was shivering. She sat down at his desk and, crying softly, examined the happy, smiling faces in the photographs. Then she picked up a photo in a silver frame, showing Nick accepting some sort of award. He looked important, triumphant; more Nicholas, chairman, managing director and sole shareholder of Compcon Associates, than her Nick. She traced the outline of his face with a finger and then, suddenly, slammed the photograph down on to the desk. 'Damn you,' she sobbed. 'Oh, damn you, Nick Meadows.'

6

Shards of glass fragmented across the desk, the floor and Sarah. Unaware of the broken glass, she looked out of the windows into the calm of her garden. She gazed sightlessly at the old apple tree bordered by a circle of miniature pinks. All she could see was the troubled expression on the face of that surgeon – Hilary Jameson, wasn't it? – when she'd said: 'I'm sorry, it was a heart attack.'

'A heart attack?' Sarah said thoughtfully. 'Nick?' And for the second time that day, she said: 'I don't believe it.'

2

'How're you doing, love?' said the man at the station news-stand where Hilary Jameson always bought her *Evening Standard*.

'Okay,' Hilary said untruthfully. 'Thanks.'

He handed her the paper. 'Cheer up, love, it may never happen.'

But it had happened, Hilary thought, as she fished the return ticket to Surbiton out of her pocket. A man had died in her operating theatre. And what made it worse, she didn't know why. It was hard enough to come to terms with the death of any patient – a doctor is, after all, trained to cure, and any death, however inevitable, is a kind of failure – but this case did more than upset her; it worried her. What could possibly have happened in those few minutes while she was out of the operating theatre?

Hilary had made it a rule, for the sake of her sanity and her babies – three-year-old Alice and five-year-old Sam – to leave hospital tragedies and anxieties at the sign marked Exit as she left for home. But this evening she sat there on the train gazing at the front-page pictures of some superstar's fancy-dress party in her evening paper, and all she could see was the drama as it had unfolded in the operating theatre an hour or so earlier.

It had been an ordinary sort of day until Nicholas Meadows had been wheeled into surgery. She'd been on duty for about seventeen hours and she and her junior, David Cazalet, had performed seven, or maybe eight – Hilary couldn't quite remember – straightforward operations. Hilary had been thinking of going home; Alice had chickenpox and she longed to be there doing all the motherly things Lisa, her excellent nanny, was no doubt doing in her absence. But just as she was leaving the staffroom to get her coat, she'd had an urgent call from Out-patients. There had been a traffic accident. Suspected fractured ribs, and what looked like a torn aorta. The patient was leaking blood like a Thames Water pipe. Would she and her team please get along to Operating Theatre 3 now?

The ribs, Hilary decided, could be safely left until later. Priority number one was the patient's heart. He'd lost at least six pints of blood; David and Pat Linzey, the theatre sister, attached him swiftly and efficiently to a blood drip and a saline drip. As Hilary opened the patient up and began cleaning and suturing the jagged wounds in his heart, they had all studied the heart monitor anxiously. The blood was dripping steadily into a vein, and the monitor had begun to stabilise. Hilary remembered David checking the blood pressure monitor and looking up triumphantly. 'BP's going steady now,' he'd said. 'Jammy beggar. Looks like he's turned the corner.'

'More than he managed to do earlier,' Hilary had said, with a tired smile.

'Yes,' David grinned, 'shame about the motor.'

'Sorry?' Sister Linzey had queried.

'Steering column snapped on his chest,' David explained, and Pat Linzey had shuddered and groaned.

At that point, somebody's pager had started bleeping. It belonged to the anaesthetist. From what Hilary could gather from his end of the conversation, somebody – his wife? another surgeon? – wanted him somewhere else pretty fast. 'I'll be along as soon as I can,' he'd said.

This had triggered in Hilary's mind the sight of her small daughter's flushed, feverish face. She needed to be somewhere else pretty fast, too. She'd checked the heart monitor again. The rate was still reassuringly stable. Nothing could go wrong now. 'David,' she'd said, 'I'm a bit pushed for time. Do the closure on your own. Okay?'

'Sure,' David had said. It was routine procedure; he'd done it often.

Hilary could feel now the exhaustion, the ache she had felt in her back as she'd straightened up from the operating table. She had struggled out of her white coat, calling up Lisa on her mobile as she ran out of the theatre. 'I'm really sorry, Lisa. I'm just leaving now. Tell the kids I'll be home soon. Okay?' And she hadn't even got as far as the hospital gates before her bleeper had sounded and she'd heard Pat Linzey on her pager, a note of controlled hysteria in her voice. 'Mrs Jameson, please return to the operating theatre immediately. We're in trouble here . . .' Hilary had dashed back to find Sister Linzey handing David Cazalet the defibrillator irons. She had watched him place them on Nicholas Meadows's chest.

'Ready?' Pat Linzey had said.

David had charged the irons. 'Stand clear!'

Hilary had stared with horror and disbelief as the body jerked rhythmically and then went still. David Cazalet recharged the irons and for a second time the patient on the operating table was shaken by spasms and then became ominously lifeless.

Hilary had looked at David and then at the heart monitor.

11

It showed a flat line. 'What happened? For God's sake, what happened?'

David had ignored her. 'One last time. Charge!'

But there was no response. They had all turned desperately towards the heart monitor, willing it to move, to flicker, but it had continued to show a flat, unmoving line.

David had handed the equipment to Sister Linzey, who wheeled it away. His expression, as he turned to Hilary and answered her question, showed no emotion. 'He died,' he said. Then he'd thrown off his surgical gown and mask and walked quickly out of the operating theatre.

Hilary had taken off her own gown and, almost without thinking, picked up David's mask and dropped it into the waste container along with her own. As she had bent down there had been something on the floor which made her pause for a moment and look questioningly at the disconnected drips in the dead patient's arm. She tried to think now what had nagged at the back of her mind, and all she could come up with were the six empty blood bags laid out neatly on the floor.

As she walked towards Reception to talk to Mrs Meadows, she had found herself wondering what was so odd about empty blood bags in an operating theatre. And, with dread in her heart, she asked herself how she was going to explain to this poor woman, anxiously waiting to see her husband, that she would never see him alive again.

Lisa greeted her at the front door. 'It's good news,' she said. 'The temperature is down and Alice wants you to read her a bedtime story.'

Hilary took off her coat and hung it on the peg. 'What a relief. And Sam?'

'I told him he could stay up until you got home. He's

playing up something awful. After a bit of the attention, I dare say.'

Hilary smiled and the tension at the back of her neck eased and slipped away. Coming home invariably had this effect on her. Her flat – more of a maisonette, really, since it was on two floors of a rambling house just a road away from the river – was large and sunny and infinitely calming. She and Michael had bought it when they married eight years previously.

Sam came running out into the hall and threw his arms around her knees. 'Mum . . . will you give me my bath? Lisa says you will.'

'If Lisa says so, then of course I will.' Hilary kissed the top of her son's head. 'But first I must go and say hello to Alice, and have a bit of a wash and brush-up.'

Alice was no longer feverish, the livid chickenpox spots were calming down, and she was scratching one of them with evident enjoyment.

Hilary wrapped her arms around her. 'Don't scratch, my darling,' she said, 'or you'll have a horrible scar.'

Alice's eyes opened in alarm and then she giggled. 'It's nice when I scratch.'

'I dare say, but I am certainly not going to read to anybody who scratches,' Hilary said, firmly clasping Alice's hands together.

Alice shook her hands free and picked up a book from her bed. 'Read Babar,' she said, 'the one about the wedding. I like that one.'

Hilary rose from the bed. 'I'll be with you in a minute, my pet.' She went into the bathroom and stood under the shower, washing away all the hospital smells and problems. She thought about Michael far away in America and wondered if he was missing them all.

Their meeting had been such a curious coincidence that

they used to say they'd been destined for each other from the moment they were born. Before emigrating to England, both Michael's parents and her own had lived in the same small town in St Lucia, without ever meeting each other. And then, nearly thirty years later, a fellow medical student had taken her to a students' do at the School of Oriental and African Studies and introduced her to Michael. They'd had everything in common from the very beginning and both sets of parents were overjoyed when their children started going out together and decided to marry.

'A shared culture is more important than love,' her father had pronounced sagely.

'But we are in love,' Hilary had replied crossly.

And so they were. And so they might have remained if their careers had run along convenient, parallel lines. But, at almost the same moment, Hilary was offered the post of junior doctor at Southbrook, and Michael, after trying unsuccessfully to get a teaching post at an English university, got an offer to join the linguistics department at Syracuse University, in New York State. The pay had been brilliant and, for the first few years, he'd commuted back and forth to England for holidays and long weekends. When Sam and Alice were born he'd wangled extended paternity leave to be at Hilary's side. But, very gradually, the visits had become less and less frequent as they grew apart from each other. The fleeting meetings were no longer romantic reunions, but increasingly stressful, as they attempted to adapt to each other's unfamiliar lives and new needs. A couple of years ago, Michael, now a professor of linguistics, had been made head of department. He was too busy, he'd said, to come over for Christmas. This had been the moment when Hilary realised that the big commute could no longer continue. Either Michael would have to come back to England, or they would have to join him in the

14

States. She'd left the children with her parents, and gone over to discuss with him how they could best save their marriage and make a proper home for Sam and Alice. But, when she'd arrived, she had found that she was married to a stranger. A stranger, what was more, who had spent far too much of their precious time together talking in hissed whispers down the phone to somebody called Marie. They had separated by mutual consent. Occasionally, they spoke long-distance. Hilary reported on Sam and Alice's progress and they talked, in a desultory way, of getting a divorce. For some time now, Hilary had considered herself a single parent. As she read to Alice and tucked her up in bed, she thought that, perhaps, she was not making too bad a job of it.

She was sitting on the side of the bath, floating a duck towards Sam, when Lisa came in carrying the cordless phone. 'Call for you, Hilary. Somebody called Jellicoe.'

Hilary sighed. Mr Jellicoe was the chief executive at Southbrook, a stickler for rules, regulations and cost-cutting.

'Hilary?'

'Hello,' Hilary said cautiously.

'Could we have a word tomorrow morning? This Mead-ows business.'

'Well, I'm in theatre all day,' Hilary said. 'It'll have to wait.' Sam splashed her with water and squealed with delight. 'Hey, stop that,' Hilary said, and then into the phone, 'Sorry.'

'It's all right, we've got you covered,' Colin Jellicoe said coldly. Really, there was a time and place for high jinks and it wasn't when he was on the telephone to a subordinate. 'I'll see you at ten o'clock.'

'Right,' Hilary said, and switched off the cordless phone.

* * *

15

'What have I done?' Hilary asked as she walked into Colin Jellicoe's office the following morning. 'Exceeded my soap ration again?'

Mr Jellicoe gestured towards a seat on the other side of his desk. He was flanked by Geoffrey Beever, responsible for the legal side of Soúthbrook, and Pamela Erskine, chairperson of the hospital's NHS trust.

'Not this time.' Colin Jellicoe allowed himself a wintry smile. 'We've had a complaint from the Meadows woman. It looks as though we might have to go to trial. You know what that'll mean for patient care if it all goes pear-shaped, Hilary? We've got to make sure we're watertight on this.'

'Write out a statement,' Geoffrey Beever interrupted. 'Exactly what happened. Everything we need to know. Any errors . . .'

'I did everything I could,' Hilary said.

'Of course you did.' Mr Jellicoe got up, put an arm around Hilary's shoulders and led her out of the room. 'Don't you worry, Hilary. We stand or fall together on this one.'

He came back and looked thoughtfully at Geoffrey Beever and Pamela Erskine. 'Hilary's one of the best we've got, you know. I hope to God we don't have to lose her.'

'It's not a question of that, surely?' Pamela said.

'We can hardly renew her contract if she's found negligent. And if we were to lose, there might not be an intensive care unit for her patients anyway.'

'I beg your pardon?' Pamela was stunned.

'Four-million-pound overspend already this year,' Jellicoe said. 'I've deliberately been putting off the tough decisions, but this case may force my hand.'

Pamela Erskine bridled. She was good at that. 'Why haven't you told the trustees it could come to this?'

'Well, that's what I'm doing now,' Colin Jellicoe said reasonably.

Geoffrey Beever leaned forward. 'I understand Sarah Meadows is a friend of yours.'

'Vaguely,' Pamela said. 'Our husbands were. Why?'

'I can't believe she'd want to jeopardise lives,' Colin Jellicoe said quietly.

'I don't think she's capable of rational thought,' Pamela Erskine replied crisply. 'Her husband has only just died . . .' She looked at the other two, who gazed back at her stonily. 'Well . . .' she said. 'Well, perhaps . . . I suppose I could have a word . . . later, perhaps . . . it's too soon.'

Mr Jellicoe and Mr Beever smiled at each other. 'If you would,' Colin Jellicoe said.

3

James Kavanagh, Q.C., was looking rather pleased with himself as he walked down Middle Temple and turned into 5 River Court. He'd just won a case for the kind of client who wouldn't get through Customs without a full body search. Not guilty, the jury had said. Guilty as hell, James suspected, but that wasn't his business. His business was to represent the man in the dock to the best of his ability. He'd done that all right. Entering chambers, he passed through the clerks' room. Tom Buckley, the senior clerk, looked up as Kavanagh dropped a bundle of papers on his desk. 'Hello, sir. How did you get on?'

'Not guilty on all counts,' said Kavanagh.

Tom raised an eyebrow. 'What did he do? "Bung" the jury?'

Kavanagh looked at his senior clerk reprovingly. 'They saw the light,' he said. 'My client is a God-fearing man. He runs the only Baptist massage parlour in Birmingham.'

Tom chuckled. Kavanagh was a good man, in his book. No side to him, knew how to take a joke, and was the biggest earner in their set – a matter of some interest to Tom Buckley, since his salary was calculated on a percentage of the combined income of chambers. He handed him a letter.

Kavanagh glanced at the envelope and didn't even bother to open it. 'Don't say it's rent time again?'

' 'Fraid so, sir. Oh, something else. I've had Mr Ealand on the phone . . .' Kavanagh frowned disapprovingly. Timothy Ealand was the kind of solicitor who'd put his clients up to anything if there was a percentage cut involved. 'Quite so, sir,' Tom nodded. 'But he does put the butter on our bread, in a manner of speaking. Seems he's got a widow on the warpath. Negligence claim against the Southbrook Hospital Trust. He's sending the papers over first thing tomorrow. Wants to bring her in early tomorrow afternoon.'

Kavanagh sighed. 'If needs must, Tom.'

He went off to his office and Tom continued handing letters to Gary Potts, the office junior, who was slipping them into envelopes. Tom hoped that the right letter was meeting up with the right envelope. It was his view that Gary was a bit short on the grey matter, but he'd learn. 'And when you've finished that lot, Gary,' he said, 'there's thirty quid on your desk. Go and fetch a bottle of champagne. It's Mr Foxcott's birthday.'

'Thirty quid? How many bottles do you want, then?' Gary flicked through a few more letters. 'Here, this one's for Mr Aldermarten. Which one's he again?'

'He's a tall bloke, talks a bit like Prince Charles.'

Gary snorted. 'Oh, him! Buckets of aftershave. Fancies himself, I reckon.'

'Yeah, that's him.' Tom smothered a grin. 'Mind you, don't let the other governors hear you talking about him like that. Off you go, then.'

He looked up and saw trouble coming as Helen Ames strode over to his desk. She was a good enough barrister, Helen, but women in chambers . . . Tom didn't hold with them. Especially when they threw their weight around like this one.

'Tom, are you responsible for Mr Levison waiting twenty minutes in a room full of drug-pushers?' Her face was pink with annoyance. 'He is the director of a merchant bank, you know.'

'Should have felt at home, then,' Tom said, and grinned at her.

Helen did not grin back. 'Just don't let it happen again. Okay?'

Oh-ho, a proper ticking-off, Tom thought to himself. It didn't worry him. He was the one who brought in the work and allocated it out. Ms Ames would do well to remember that. And she was behind with her rent. He pushed back his chair, brushed down his suit and prepared to join the party in Mr Foxcott's office. Thirty quid. Gary should get a nice little vintage number with that; he could do with a quality tipple.

But it was still dainty cups of tea and birthday cake when he arrived. Mr Aldermarten was banging on about Byzantine churches and Mr Foxcott, inclining his head courteously but, Tom knew, not really listening, had his eye on a plate of vol-au-vents. Tom signalled to the waitress and she came over.

'Vol-au-vents?' Mr Foxcott put down his cup and saucer and helped himself to the pastry. 'Excuse me, Jeremy. How delicious.'

'Would you like another sandwich?' the waitress said, correctly gauging the greed of her customer.

'Well, do you know, my dear, I rather think I would.' Mr Foxcott smiled at her and took two.

He looked up as Helen Ames came over to him and handed him a wrapped parcel. 'Hello, Peter. Happy birthday.'

Foxcott took the present and put it down on the table. 'Oh, thank you, Helen. Oh, how kind.'

21

It would have been a nice gesture if he'd opened it, Tom thought, but there again, he reckoned Mr Foxcott held much the same views about Helen Ames as he did himself. A gentleman of the old school was Mr Foxcott.

He watched as Helen walked over to talk to Alex Wilson and Charles Beaufort. Tom smiled to himself as he remembered Alex Wilson's application. A. Wilson, it had said at the top . . . no clue there. And a first-class degree in law from Cambridge. Bit of a tragedy, Tom felt, that when she arrived for the interview she'd turned out to be both black and female. It surprised him when they'd taken her on. He suspected James Kavanagh's hand in that. He was a right old liberal, in his way. As for Charles Beaufort – he was the new boy in chambers. Seems he'd prudently left the navy before the defence cuts pushed him out. Tom found him a bit brash, but was prepared to give him the benefit of the doubt. Charles was a good man in the pub, and, Tom reasoned, he was probably finding it difficult to adjust from snapping commands at the lower orders to becoming the lowest in the chambers' pecking order himself.

He followed Helen as she joined Alex and Charles. He liked to keep his ear to the ground. Charles was telling Alex about the defence cuts. '. . . so I decided to jump ship and look for excitement elsewhere.'

'I shouldn't bank on getting much around here,' Alex said crisply.

'Hello, Charles,' Helen said. 'You're settling in fine, I see.'

Big smile, bags of charm. She's after something, Tom said to himself.

'It's such an attractive environment,' Charles said, giving her the eye.

Don't waste your time, old son, Tom thought. Aldermarten's been there, tried that, and came away with a flea in his ear.

'Now listen,' Helen Ames was saying, 'can you devil a brief for me? I'm up to my neck. You know about charter parties, I take it?'

Charles grinned at her. 'I've been to a few.'

Helen forced a smile. 'Right. Well, it's a bit tricky, but it's serious money. I'll bring you the papers.'

'Okay.'

Helen went off, presumably to get the papers, and Tom saw Alex narrow her eyes. 'What do *you* know about shipping law?' she said challengingly.

'I know it beats Bow Street magistrates,' Charles said with a disarming grin that failed to disarm Alex.

She looked even more displeased when Jeremy Aldermarten strolled over. 'Charles! Charles, my boy. You wouldn't fancy looking up some cases for me, would you? You see, my brief's just come in for tomorrow and I'm in a bit of a pickle.'

'I'm busy, I'm afraid,' Charles said, and nodded towards Alex. 'Alex is at a loose end.'

Aldermarten didn't even glance at Alex. Instead he turned to Tom. 'Strange . . . he's usually so keen.'

Ooh, dearie me, Tom thought, catching Alex's expression. There's going to be trouble, I can feel it in my bones. And he anticipated further trouble when Gary appeared in the doorway with several carrier bags. More carrier bags than you'd need for a couple of bottles of decent champagne.

'Da-da!' Gary exclaimed, holding the bags aloft.

'Oh, how's your new acolyte doing, Tom?' Mr Foxcott had appeared at his elbow.

Tom jumped. 'Gary? Oh, getting the corners knocked

off him. I think he'll turn out all right. His dad's a clerk up at Lincoln's Inn . . .'

'Familiar with the ropes, then,' Mr Foxcott said.

'Actually,' Tom said, 'I sent him out to get you a little something.'

Mr Foxcott beamed at Tom and at Gary as he handed him the carrier bags. He managed to keep on beaming as he pulled out the bottles and examined the labels. 'Well, well . . . Asti Spumante. How kind.'

Tom glared at Gary as James Kavanagh came over and pulled out another bottle.

'Oh, nice one, Gary,' he said. 'Plenty to go around.'

He's busting his gut, the old bastard, Tom thought to himself, but when Mr Kavanagh grinned at him he couldn't stop himself giving him a conspiratorial wink back.

Lizzie Kavanagh had arrived home from a fund-raising committee and prepared dinner. She'd put it in the oven and was waiting for James to come home. As a barrister's wife she'd done a lot of waiting over the years, and had fondly imagined that there would be considerably less of it when, nine years ago, James had taken Silk. He'd assured her that would be the case.

'Just you watch the briefs disappear as my charges go up,' he'd said. 'Who's going to pay Q.C. rates when they can call on a competent barrister at half the price?' He'd looked morosely out of the long drawing-room windows on to the green of Wandsworth Common. 'Won't be able to keep up this Georgian pile, for a start.' James had always been a pessimist. Lizzie had never directed him down a side road without him predicting gloomily that it was bound to be a dead end. And, once again, his pessimism had been ill founded. Kavanagh, Q.C., attracted more clients than he could handle, and his advice was sought after by all the best solicitors in the business.

Lizzie looked apprehensively at Matt, their eighteen-year-old son, who, it appeared to her, had spent weeks listlessly kicking the skirting boards or lying on the couch, half listening to very loud discordant music and waiting for his A-level results. She remembered going through the same exam result trauma with Kate, who was now up at Cambridge and – aside from an unfortunate affair with her tutor which, with a good deal of help from James and herself, had sorted itself out – seemed to be happily settled. On the rare occasions she came home it was a pleasure to have her around the house. You certainly couldn't say the same for Matt, Lizzie thought, however much you loved him . . . and she did love him a lot. 'Darling,' she said. 'Do turn that thing down. Dad will be home in a minute.'

Matt regarded her sullenly. 'So?' he said. Lizzie wished that James had more time to dispense advice on the home front. It saddened her that these days James and Matt seemed unable to communicate with each other without scowling and raising their voices. Lizzie hated rows. She turned away and was relieved to hear James's key in the lock.

He came in, waving a bottle of Asti Spumante. 'Present from Foxcott,' he explained, kissing Lizzie. 'Fancy a drop before dinner?'

'Lovely,' said Lizzie, who didn't like cheap champagne. 'I'll get the glasses.'

She fetched three glasses from the cabinet and put them on the table. Kavanagh poured out two and looked quizzically at the third. He spotted his son lounging on the couch, walked over, turned down the cassette player and moved Matt's feet aside. 'Still on the hod, Matt? Get your filthy feet off my furniture. You look like a Cairo navvy.'

25

Lizzie sighed with exasperation. She knew exactly where James was coming from. His father had been a small-time trades union official, and James had worked his own way up from a terraced house in Bolton, through university and his pupilage at the Middle Temple. He'd served behind the bar at the Kings Head when he was at Nottingham University and, after he'd been accepted at 5 River Court, he'd moonlighted nights as a minicab driver to pay the rent, constantly terrified that he might be spotted by a member of chambers, and chucked out for breaking the rules. Lizzie admired all that. She just couldn't understand why James didn't realise that having provided their young with a prosperous background, Matt and Kate had zero incentive to go out and stack supermarket shelves or whatever. 'I'm surprised you haven't set him up with a tin bath in front of the fire,' she said.

'Well, we can't have him skiving all through the summer, can we?' Kavanagh said in that equable tone parents use to rile their children. 'There'll be enough of that at university.'

'If he gets the grades,' Lizzie said.

'Of course he will,' Kavanagh said. 'God, Lizzie, you're more uptight about it than he is.'

'I am actually here, you know,' Matt said, getting up and leaving the room.

Lizzie and Kavanagh looked at each other. Kavanagh shrugged. 'What have I said now?'

'Come and have some dinner, darling,' Lizzie said. 'It's seafood pasta. Scallops. Your favourite.'

'I'm so glad you're going to be handling this, James,' Timothy Ealand said. He gave his client a deferential nod. 'Mrs Meadows is prepared to pay for the best.'

James regarded Ealand sardonically. He'd found, over

the years, that it was almost impossible to look at the plump, pompous solicitor in any other way. 'Well, don't rush your horses, Timothy,' he said. 'We haven't got a case yet.'

Sarah Meadows sat up sharply. 'But . . .'

James Kavanagh smiled at her across the desk and slightly raised his hand and his voice – an effective mannerism he often used to silence witnesses in court. 'Mrs Meadows, I have to be blunt. There's not a lot here on which to found an action for negligence. The hospital pathologist is adamant your husband died from a heart attack *after* the operation. It's not uncommon, you know. And the coroner agreed. I can't honestly see a judge disagreeing.'

'The coroner made his mind up before the inquest even began,' Sarah said. 'My husband had an air bubble lodged in his heart.'

'But it didn't show up at the post-mortem, did it?'

'Dr Clarke saw it. Haven't you read his report?'

Sarah looked meaningfully at Timothy Ealand who, stirred into action, nodded his head sagely. 'Our expert witness and he's quite adamant, James. If the surgeon had found the embolism when she operated on Mr Meadows's heart, she might have saved him.'

'But your expert witness didn't manage to convince the coroner, did he?'

Sarah sighed and Ealand, reflecting his client's concern, said: 'I have to agree with Mrs Meadows about the inquest.'

Sarah was convinced now that Kavanagh wasn't going to take her on. He probably thought she was one of those sad, vindictive widows hell-bent on revenge. Her jaw tightened and she straightened up. 'No one has told the truth from the outset. Not the hospital, not the surgeon, not the pathologist.'

Kavanagh looked at her curiously. Intelligent, head-strong, no fool – a bit like Lizzie, really, only blonde rather than brunette and probably a few years older; he was no good at judging women's ages. 'What made you think the surgeon was negligent, Mrs Meadows?'

'I *know* she was. You should have seen her face.' Sarah briefly closed her eyes. How tiresomely, intuitively feminine that had sounded.

James Kavanagh obviously agreed with her. 'So, it was just an instinct, was it?'

Sarah took a deep breath. 'Nick's heart was fine. He had a full insurance medical two weeks before he died. He was obsessed with his health. She *must* have made a mistake.'

'He was in a car crash,' James said reasonably.

Sarah gazed straight into the Q.C.'s eyes. 'Look, when I arrived at the hospital I saw Mrs Jameson leaving, hurriedly. Then they told me that Nick had survived the operation. I was waiting to go and see him, and she came running back. Now I didn't know who she was at the time, but I could see that she was upset. Then ten minutes later she reappeared and told me that Nick was dead.' She paused and said slowly, 'Even then I could tell that that woman felt sick with guilt.'

Timothy Ealand glanced at Kavanagh, trying to gauge his reaction to Sarah Meadows' eloquence. James looked down and fiddled with his papers. He glanced briefly at Ealand and then said to Sarah, 'Have you any idea what this action could cost you – emotionally as well as financially?'

Sarah misunderstood what he was trying to tell her. 'Oh, money's not an issue,' she said.

Timothy Ealand could see his Portuguese golfing holiday slipping away. 'Mrs Meadows understands the risks of litigation,' he said quickly.

Suddenly Sarah got up and faced Kavanagh. She was tired of listening to doctors, solicitors, barristers – professional people telling her how to think and what to do. 'Are you taking this case or not?' she said. She strode towards the door, followed by Timothy, hounding her anxiously.

Kavanagh went over and held open the door. 'That's entirely up to you.'

Sarah looked at him doubtfully. She instinctively liked and trusted him, and yet there was something rather arrogant about his manner; it made her feel foolish, which she knew she wasn't. 'Well,' she said, 'I think I'd better go and look elsewhere.' And then she couldn't resist delivering a parting shot. She knew it was childish but it made her feel a bit more in charge. 'Your dauntless reputation is obviously overstated.'

Kavanagh remained unruffled. He'd dealt with enough bereaved clients to know that there was nothing personal in her attack. He just hoped she knew what she was getting into. 'Mrs Meadows . . . I've given you my opinion. If you really want to pursue this, I'll help you in any way I can.'

Sarah looked at him steadily. 'I'm only asking for justice, Mr Kavanagh, not miracles.'

He put a hand on her shoulder. 'Sometimes they amount to the same thing.'

As Sarah Meadows walked out into the corridor, Timothy Ealand called out to her that he'd join her in a minute and did a neat step backwards into Kavanagh's office. 'She does know what she's doing, James.'

Kavanagh sat down at his desk and looked up at the solicitor. 'Yes,' he said thoughtfully. 'Yes, we could take them for one and a half, maybe two million, couldn't we?'

'It's a once-in-a-decade case, James.' Ealand was unusually animated. 'It's a plum.'

'Have they made you an offer?'

Timothy Ealand shrugged. 'Nickels and dimes . . .'

James Kavanagh looked at him with distaste. 'Oh? I thought money wasn't the issue?'

When the solicitor had gone, Kavanagh slipped out for a swift half of John Smith's at the Fox & Anchor. He felt the need to cleanse his palate. On his way back into chambers, he spotted Jeremy Aldermarten herding a small flock of clients into his office. 'Mr Jellicoe, Mrs Jameson, Mr Beever. Come this way, please.'

Kavanagh raised an eyebrow at Tom Buckley.

'Mr Aldermarten got the brief for the hospital in the Meadows case,' Tom explained.

'Oh. Might be in with a chance, then.'

Tom chuckled. 'Thought that bit of news might cheer you up, sir.'

They both looked at Jeremy Aldermarten's closed door. 'He may have the edge on charm, sir,' Tom said, 'but you've got it where it counts.'

Hilary Jameson, flanked by Colin Jellicoe and Geoffrey Beever, faced Jeremy across his desk.

'Right.' Jeremy Aldermarten looked at Hilary challengingly. 'So let's hear it again, to make it perfectly, perfectly clear. You assumed from the outset that the patient had died of a heart attack?'

Hilary felt she was already under cross-examination. 'Yes. I had no reason to think otherwise.'

Aldermarten flicked through his papers. 'But the plaintiff's expert says that death was caused by an air bubble.'

'Yes, I know,' Hilary said. 'He was at the inquest.'

'He says that the . . . the right ventricle was badly swollen.'

'I didn't see anything like that.'

'Now are you sure?'

'Well, as far as I can be. The heart looked fine.'

'No, you see, it's . . . it's vital that you try to remember exactly what you saw.'

Hilary had heard about this Q.C.'s single-minded persistence. 'It's like I said . . .'

'Was the heart swollen . . . yes or no?' Geoffrey Beever interrupted.

'Not that I noticed,' Hilary said.

Aldermarten had no intention of letting her off the hook. 'You see, it's imperative that you keep your remarks absolutely clear.'

'Just try and stick to "yes" and "no",' Geoffrey Beever said.

Colin Jellicoe sensed Hilary's impatience. 'Perhaps if Mrs Jameson had a moment to read Dr Clarke's report?' Jeremy Aldermarten handed her the papers, and Colin Jellicoe eased her towards the door and closed it behind her. 'She'll be fine,' he said confidently.

Aldermarten looked at him doubtfully. 'Do you think she'll be able to cope with a cross-examination?'

'Just needs a bit of careful handling, that's all.' Colin Jellicoe prided himself on his interpersonal skills.

'She needs to know her answers backwards,' Aldermarten said. 'And Dr Cazalet, too.'

'Don't worry about him. Solid as a rock.'

Aldermarten nodded and riffled through his papers. 'Now, I don't seem to have a statement from the . . . from the anaesthetist?'

Colin Jellicoe composed his features appropriately. 'I'm afraid we lost him . . . a few weeks ago. Heart attack, as a matter of fact.'

'Oh dear,' Aldermarten said.

Geoffrey Beever reached down into his case and took out a slip of paper which he handed to Jeremy Aldermarten. 'One last thing,' he said. 'We thought this might interest you. Slipped through the net on disclosure. Ealand's articled clerk must have been careless with the photocopying. A letter from the plaintiff's solicitors to Dr Clarke . . . their expert witness.'

Jeremy Aldermarten glanced at the letter gleefully but managed to convey an appearance of mild disapproval. 'How nice . . . Mmmm . . . how fortunate. But no . . . you do realise, of course, that this is a privileged document. I can't possibly use this in evidence.'

'No, no,' Geoffrey Beever said reassuringly. 'Of course not. Just thought it might give us one or two ideas.'

Aldermarten slipped the letter under his blotter. 'Well . . .' He rose to his feet and shook their hands. '. . . I await your instructions.'

4

James Kavanagh was sitting in his office studying a complicated diagram of the aorta and its assorted tubes in a vast medical tome. He ran a hand through his hair and closed his eyes for a second. During his years at the Bar he'd become an expert on any manner of esoteric subjects – the illegal cross-breeding of rare cattle in Clwyd had been a particular favourite, containing as it did elements of greed and fraud and sex – but the intricacies of medical cases invariably gave him a headache. There was a knock on the door. 'Come in,' he said gratefully.

'James . . .' Jeremy Aldermarten came in clutching a file and perched on the edge of Kavanagh's desk. 'Intent on ploughing on with this, are you? I mean . . . you must admit it's wonderfully ironical really, isn't it?'

'What?' Kavanagh said.

'Can't you see it? You, the bleeding-heart liberal being paid a fortune to attack the dear old NHS while I defend its crumbling ramparts on a pittance. It's not even your field. Far messier a game than crime, you know.'

Kavanagh took off his spectacles and sighed. 'What are you after, Jeremy?'

There was a steely look in Aldermarten's eyes as he said:

33

'Encouraging her to make a nuisance of herself won't get her anywhere . . .'

'Encouraging her?'

Aldermarten ignored the interruption. 'My clients are prepared to give her ten thousand pounds to go away. And that's a final offer.'

James Kavanagh put on his spectacles again and returned to his tome. 'They offered twice that three months ago, when we began this case.'

'If that's the way you want it . . .' Aldermarten jumped nimbly off the desk and, with a flourish, presented Kavanagh with a folder. 'Small gift, James. Mrs Jameson's personnel file. You're not strictly entitled to it, but I thought you might need a head start.'

Kavanagh waited until Aldermarten had left the room before eagerly snatching up the file.

He was grateful for his medical swotting when, later in the day, Ealand arrived with Sarah Meadows and Dr Clarke. He offered them coffee. As he cross-questioned Dr Clarke closely, he became uneasy about the doctor's inability to answer a question simply and to the point.

Eventually, he interrupted a polemic on the ineptitude of hospital pathologists. 'Right, Dr Clarke. But, post-operative heart failure was the most likely explanation, wasn't it?'

Dr Clarke shrugged dismissively. 'Hospital pathologists usually go for the obvious. They don't have time for detail.'

Kavanagh persisted: 'But your conclusion rests on, er . . .' He consulted his notes. '. . . pink froth in the artery?'

'Dr Salmon noted it in the initial post-mortem, but he obviously didn't know what to make of it,' Dr Clarke said. 'Coupled with the swollen heart, it leads only to one conclusion.'

34

'Presumably the body was not exactly in . . .' Kavanagh was careful not to look at Sarah '. . . pristine condition by the time you saw it?'

Sarah flinched and Dr Clarke said: 'It had decomposed a little, but the heart was still quite well preserved. I can be very precise about its dimensions. You can see from the photographs.'

Timothy Ealand took a batch of photographs out of his briefcase and pushed them across the desk towards Kavanagh.

Sarah recovered her compusure and said sharply to Dr Clarke, 'You told me he had the heart of a healthy man.'

Clarke nodded. 'Yes. It was remarkably good for his age.'

'And he shouldn't have died, should he?'

Clarke nodded again. 'I'm certain his death was caused by Mrs Jameson's negligence, yes.'

'Well, thank you, Dr Clarke,' Kavanagh said. 'I think that's all I need for the moment.'

Clarke waved as he left the room. 'See you all in court.'

Ealand nodded to the doctor and to Kavanagh and put an arm around Sarah's shoulders. 'Come along, my dear. I'll see you home.'

But Sarah hung back. 'Mr Kavanagh . . . you think I'm just being vindictive, don't you?'

Kavanagh shook his head and said truthfully, 'No . . . no.' He realised he had been frowning, and the reason was not Sarah Meadows but Dr Clarke. Jeremy was nobody's fool; it wouldn't take him long to puncture the doctor's brash self-confidence.

'If you had known my husband, you might think differently,' Sarah said. 'He was a whirlwind. You met him . . .' She stopped, remembering the day Nick had

35

caught her eye, and asked her to come into his office. He wanted to dictate a letter, he'd said. It was the most beautiful love letter and he'd addressed it to her. She took a deep breath. '. . . You couldn't help but be swept along. For it all to be taken away . . . it's almost as though he'd been murdered.'

Kavanagh smiled at Sarah and patted her arm.

Timothy Ealand stuck his head around the door. 'Sarah!'

It took less than three-quarters of an hour to drive back to Sarah's house. She was intrigued by Timothy's speedy, rather flashy style of driving and the abuse he hurled indiscriminately at any motorist bold enough to drive in front of him. She studied his profile, noticing the muscles in his jaw working convulsively. Why hadn't she noticed it before? Inside her staid Surrey solicitor was a tiny volcano waiting to erupt.

They swept up the drive. Timothy jumped out and opened the passenger door. 'Anything you need, just call. Okay?'

'Thanks, Tim,' Sarah said. As he swerved off, another car pulled up in front of the house.

'Sarah . . .'

Sarah peered inside the car. 'Pamela! What a surprise.'

Pamela stepped out. 'I was just passing.'

'Well, how nice . . .' And now I'll have to invite her in and offer her a drink or something, Sarah thought uncharitably. 'Do come in.' They walked through the hall into the drawing room. 'A drink? A cup of tea?'

'A glass of white wine, if you have it,' Pamela Erskine said. As Sarah went over to the drinks cabinet, took a bottle of wine out of the mini-fridge and reached for the bottle opener, Pamela put a restraining hand on her arm. 'Oh, don't break into a bottle on my account.'

Sarah firmly pulled the cork and poured wine into two

glasses while Pamela told her how brave she was being. They sat down facing each other on two matching sofas.

Pamela raised her glass. 'To you, Sarah.' She swirled the wine about and gave a wine buff's appreciative sniff and sip. 'And what are you planning to do with yourself? Nick never suggested you should get involved in the business, did he?'

Sarah shook her head. 'Heavens, no. Me in the computer business? He wouldn't even let me stay on as his secretary after we married.'

Pamela nodded sympathetically. 'Men . . .' She thought for a moment and then opened her eyes wide as though she had suddenly been struck by the most felicitous notion. 'I might be able to find you something. There's a real need for sensible school governors.'

'Maybe,' Sarah said cautiously.

'You mustn't let yourself get depressed, Sarah.'

Sarah looked at her in amazement. 'It does tend to be unavoidable when . . .'

'I know, I know,' Pamela interrupted quickly. 'But you must have someone close you can talk to? Someone to advise you?'

Almost as if she were talking to herself, Sarah said: 'People keep telling me how much I've got to be grateful for . . . as if Nick's money was all that mattered.'

'I don't know how you're coping . . .' Pamela put down her wineglass and came and sat next to Sarah. '. . . not with running a court case as well. Lawyers can be so manipulative, can't they? You must be a bit of a catch for them.'

Sarah got up from the sofa and looked purposefully towards the door. 'Please . . .'

Picking up her handbag, Pamela stood up. She faced Sarah, took a deep breath and plunged into the reason for her visit. 'We've worked so hard to keep going . . . on such slender resources, Sarah. We can still barely afford to keep our intensive care unit open. Your court case could send it over the edge.' She looked at Sarah pleadingly. 'I'm sure that's not what you want.'

Sarah backed away and raised a hand against such unsubtle emotional blackmail. 'I think you've said enough.' She had always disliked Pamela Erskine and took a certain pleasure in opening the front door and showing her out.

'I have to tell you, as a friend, Sarah, I hate seeing you being taken advantage of,' Pamela said, as she attempted a dignified retreat.

Sarah looked after her and snorted.

5

Charles Beaufort untied his brief and surveyed it with pleasure. 'So, my first Crown Court trial . . .' He read out the heading, slowly savouring each word. 'The Crown and Barrick. Wounding with intent . . .' After skimming through the rest of the brief, he looked across the room at Alex Wilson. 'It looks like you've already been involved with this guy. Anything I should know?'

Alex looked at him coldly and twiddled her pencil. 'I expect you'll take it in your stride.'

'Here you are, Charles . . .' Helen Ames burst into the room, loaded down with files which she dumped on Beaufort's desk. 'I need it by Monday. Seventy-five an hour. All right?'

'Great,' Charles said.

Alex glared at Charles and followed Helen out of the room. She made straight for Tom Buckley, who quickly picked up the telephone as she whirled towards him.

Alex, ignoring the phone call, slammed a fist on his desk. Tom jumped and put down the receiver. 'Am I being paranoid, Tom, or are all my cases going to Charles Beaufort?' she said. 'Mr Barrick, for example? I've already had a conference with him at Brixton.'

'Oh, yeah,' Tom said. 'Nasty piece of work, miss.'

'Oh, don't tell me . . . they wanted a man.'

'Er, something like that, yeah.' Tom couldn't understand why someone with all those degrees hadn't twigged the obvious. Your average con does not want to be represented by a woman who also happens to be black. Even the black villains would rather have a white bloke up front.

'So, my three years' experience didn't come into it?' Alex demanded.

'Well, I think they're just giving him a try-out. Know what I mean?' He foraged on his desk and held up a brief. 'How about a nice drink-driving in Camberwell?'

Alex snatched the brief and stormed back to her office. 'If you think I'm up to it,' she shouted at Tom over her shoulder.

Tom raised his eyebrows at Gary, who gave a sympathetic nod. 'Bloody prima donna,' Tom muttered.

Agreeable as it was to have the work piling up on his desk, Charles Beaufort hadn't reckoned to be still hard at it at 6.30. He had a serious date within the hour and was not best pleased when Helen Ames came in, cupping a mug of coffee in her hands, the way women do when they're planning a long, cosy chat.

'Hi,' she said, going over to sit at Alex's desk. 'How's it going?'

'Oh, it's coming along,' Charles said.

'Good.' Helen moved over towards him and slightly lowered her voice. 'Good. So, tell me, Charles, what do you make of this place? As an outsider coming in, I mean.'

'It has a certain Edwardian charm,' Charles said cautiously.

'Oh, yeah? It's full of pompous old common lawyers . . .'

Neither of them heard Jeremy Aldermarten come out of

his office, switch off the light, and walk towards them down the corridor. But Aldermarten heard them. Common old lawyers? He stopped outside their room and stood behind the half-open door, listening.

'I could be making serious money if I could just get my commercial practice properly off the ground,' he heard Helen say. 'I need the back-up. The problem is getting the right Silks. Kavanagh's a great advocate but he's happiest in the Old Bailey.'

'Jeremy Aldermarten seems like a good chap,' Charles said.

Jeremy's self-satisfied smirk was quickly erased as he heard Helen say: 'Oh, him. He's all right at what he does. Typical Temple . . . pretty average, really.'

Charles looked up at her. 'Foxcott?'

Helen shrugged dismissively. 'He's a bit of an old fart, don't you think? He's going to be on the Bench soon, anyway.'

Aldermarten retreated from behind the door and decided not to go home quite yet, after all. He walked back along the corridor and entered James Kavanagh's office without knocking.

Kavanagh looked up. 'Not another deal, Jeremy?'

'No chance,' Aldermarten said. 'It's that Helen Ames, James. The ingratitude. She was damn lucky we took her on.'

'I seem to remember you were very keen.' Kavanagh wondered if Aldermarten recalled Helen Ames's interview, when he'd had trouble raising his eyes above her extremely short skirt. 'What's she done to upset you?'

'Ever since she arrived in chambers she's done nothing but sow poison.'

'Do what I do,' Kavanagh said. 'Steer clear.'

Aldermarten, agitated, said, 'She's been conspiring, James. I overheard her with the new boy.'

'Charles?'

'Yes. She was inviting him to join some sort of clandestine ring she's organising. A sneaky little faction to keep all the best work for themselves.'

Kavanagh gave a sly smile. 'And she wasn't planning on including you?'

'No . . . well, come, I mean that's hardly the point, James. I mean, chambers is, you know, I mean it's a *family*. There's got to be trust.'

'And what do you expect me to do about it?' Kavanagh said.

'Talk to her,' Aldermarten said. 'You're closer to her than Peter or me. Well – and as it happens – you're the only one she doesn't regard as a toffee-nosed twit.'

James Kavanagh leaned back in his chair and laughed. 'You said it, Jeremy.'

Kavanagh always enjoyed the final bit of his journey home – walking alongside the common and seeing his house on the other side of the green. He felt a certain pride in having provided his family with such grandeur. It was neither large nor pretentious, which appealed to his puritan, socialist roots – like being in Wandsworth, rather than Chelsea and Hampstead, where his partners lived. And every evening he took pleasure in the knowledge that Lizzie would be there waiting for him. He'd never told her that; he wasn't a romantic sort of chap. Perhaps he should? He'd hated it when she'd been tied up with that EU-related aid agency and was constantly jetting off to Strasbourg. He'd never told her that either, but she must have guessed when she packed it in and took on the fund-raising job for the new hospital. Even all the hassle of Kate's abortive love affair with the tutor hadn't really impinged on his pleasure at having Lizzie home. The truth was that Lizzie mattered more to him than his children. He sometimes felt guilty about this, worried that it was unnatural, but he'd long ago salved his conscience by reasoning that one day Kate and Matt would leave home, and he and Lizzie would still be a strong unit. He crossed the common, smiling ruefully. At the moment, Matt appeared a pretty solid fixture.

He knew something was up the moment he stepped through the door and Lizzie ran over and clung to him. He could feel the tension in her body. 'Hello, love,' he said, a querying note in his voice.

She pulled away from him. 'It's half past eight. The A-level results came out at lunch-time.'

Kavanagh stifled a sigh. It seemed he'd travelled from one family drama to another. He patted Lizzie's shoulder encouragingly, only remembering later in the evening how much she hated what she called his patronising pat. 'Well, he's probably gone off with his mates.'

'But why hasn't he phoned?' Lizzie said, frowning with anxiety.

'Give him a chance,' Kavanagh said.

They'd just finished dinner in the kitchen when they heard the front door open and shut.

Lizzie leaped up. 'Matt?'

James continued reading his newspaper but, when he felt Lizzie glaring at him through the newsprint, he put it down and followed her out into the hall. Matt was taking off his jacket and, James couldn't help noticing, slinging it on to a chair instead of hanging it on the hook.

'Matt . . . darling,' Lizzie said. 'Are you all right?'

Matt had a piece of paper in his hand. He crushed it up in his fist and threw it on the floor. 'Leave me alone,' he said, and walked straight past his parents and out into the garden.

Kavanagh bent and picked up the crumpled paper. He straightened it out and read it. Lizzie held her breath and waited for his reaction. 'Two Es and an N,' he said heavily.

He gave the results to Lizzie and went after his son. Matt turned away as he approached. 'Come on, mate,' Kavanagh said. 'It's not the end of the world. You can take them again.'

'You shouldn't waste your money,' Matt mumbled.

Kavanagh put a hand on Matt's shoulder but he shook it off. 'You did your best.'

Matt looked at him. 'Why don't you say what you really think for once? May be you don't know what to say? You've never failed at anything.'

Lizzie watched sadly from the kitchen door as Matt ran past her without a word and disappeared into his bedroom. She linked her arm through Kavanagh's as he rejoined her. 'It's pretty bad, isn't it?'

Kavanagh nodded and sighed. 'Especially for Westminster.'

'But he can retake them?'

'Yes, of course he can retake them, and we can go through all this again.'

Lizzie looked up at him. 'Have we been negligent parents, James?'

'Oh, I'm told it's all my fault,' Kavanagh said. 'Would I have been a better father, Lizzie, if I'd been standing outside the Co-op selling the *Big Issue*?'

Lizzie squeezed his arm. 'Well, you are rather a hard act to follow, you know.'

They were sitting in the drawing room later. Lizzie was pretending to read and Kavanagh was attempting to go

44

top class. It'll cost, though.' And then he'd added, as though he were doing her the most enormous favour, 'I dare say I can help you out a bit with that.'

That was the last time she'd seen him. He hadn't helped her out because she had known, right away, that she was not going to have an abortion. She'd had Rupert, instead, who was the joyous plus factor in her life. The negative side was that her mother came, too. Helen's mother had been brilliant at the beginning, sinking her savings into a mortgage on a large house in Highbury which she had efficiently divided into two flats. She'd been recently widowed and was quietly delighted to find a role for herself. 'I'll have the ground floor, darling,' she'd said, 'and I can have the baby with me while you're working. You can have the top flat and when you get home you can collect your little one and the two of you can run upstairs and just shut yourselves away.'

But, of course, it hadn't worked out like that. Helen's mother was full of views about child-rearing and they did not coincide with Helen's. Rupert had to be potty-trained before he could sit up unaided, and cocooned in blankets when everyone else was complaining about a heat wave. He was far too young to go to playschool at three and the nursery school he went to at five didn't teach the children anything. 'Do you realise, Helen, that they spend all day messing about in the sandpit?'

She was always cooking nourishing meals which she wanted Helen to eat with her, and when Helen refused she'd act all buttoned up and hurt, as though Helen had thrown the plate of lamb stew in her face. She popped upstairs a lot to 'help out' or 'have a little chat', and what she wanted to have a little chat about most evenings was the whereabouts and irresponsibility of Rupert's father.

'That new school uniform is going to cost you a fortune, Helen. Three different styles of shirt, can you believe? He should be contributing. It's his child, too, you know.'

Helen hadn't told her mother, because she knew it would precipitate further rows, that she had never told Matthew about his son. She'd tried, she had thought it only fair that he should know about Rupert and that Rupert should have a father. All the time they had been together she had never been to his home – they'd always gone out for lovely meals and to the cinema or the theatre, and then he'd come back to her flat. 'You're so lucky to be in central London,' he was always saying. She'd known he lived somewhere near Blackheath, and after Rupert was born, she'd tracked him down. A child had answered the phone. 'Daddy isn't home yet,' he'd said. 'Shall I get Mummy?'

Helen had discovered that the real reason Matthew Friend couldn't afford to have a child was that he already had two, and a wife to go with them, and she wasn't about to ruin some other woman's life by going after child maintenance. She'd manage by herself. It hadn't been easy and it wasn't getting any easier. Only this morning her mother had popped upstairs to inform her that the washing machine had broken down. 'It's a twenty-nine-pound call-out charge before they start, Helen, and heaven knows what they'll want for the new parts.'

And, as she pointed out to Tom Buckley, he still hadn't paid her for the fraud case she'd won two months ago for a famously wealthy insurance company.

Fortunately, Helen was unaware that just along the corridor she was the subject of discussion between the senior members of chambers.

Peter Foxcott was examining the contents of a Waterford crystal decanter with some pleasure as James Kavanagh came into his office. 'Sherry, James?'

Kavanagh accepted the sherry, sensing that the situation

felt more like a committee meeting than an idle social occasion.

'We were just remarking, James, that Ms Ames seems to have developed quite a gift for upsetting people, especially Tom,' Foxcott said. Jeremy Aldermarten, across the room, nodded eagerly.

'Well, she certainly speaks her mind,' Kavanagh agreed.

Peter raised his glass in salutation and took a sip. 'We think, perhaps, Five River Court isn't *quite* right for her, after all.'

'You brought her in in the first place,' Kavanagh said, wishing beer or at least whisky were on offer instead of this elegantly dry thimbleful of sherry.

'She looked good on paper,' Foxcott said.

'And in a cocktail dress,' Kavanagh remarked unkindly.

Foxcott nodded. 'I confess, I was swayed by rosy first impressions.'

'A younger, more informal chambers would suit her much better,' Aldermarten said. 'Somewhere with chipped mugs and potted plants.'

Kavanagh grinned. If only Jeremy would listen to himself sometimes. 'You can't just sling someone out.'

'Well, I seem to remember you were all for not letting her in,' Aldermarten said.

Foxcott sat down in the leather chair behind his desk – as though, James thought, he were settling in for a comfortable nap. 'We're a clubbable set here. One either fits in or one doesn't. Don't you agree?'

Aldermarten and Kavanagh sat and faced him from across the desk and James said, 'We are barristers, Peter, not freemasons. To be fair, she's bringing in more work than the rest of the juniors put together.'

'And that excuses dishonesty and scheming?' said Aldermarten.

Kavanagh felt a sneaking sympathy for Helen Ames. She was as much of an outsider as he had been when he'd first arrived at River Court from Bolton via Nottingham. He shrugged. 'She's trying to get ahead of the game. Good luck to her.'

'Another thing, Peter,' Aldermarten said, suddenly beginning to enjoy himself. 'She considers *you* a bit of an old fart.' He turned to Kavanagh. 'Rates you, though, James.'

Foxcott, who did not relish being described as an old fart, nodded genially at Kavanagh. 'Then maybe it ought to be James who speaks to her?'

Kavanagh returned to his office, put away his papers, locked up and wandered along the corridor to Helen Ames' room. 'I was wondering if you'd care to join me for a drink at the wine bar?' he said.

'Well,' Helen said, 'I'm just clearing up.' She guessed that James was not seeking her out for the pleasure of her company. If it had been Jeremy Aldermarten, now, she'd have been wary. 'Thanks,' she said. 'I could do with a drink.'

The wine bar was just around the corner. Kavanagh settled Helen at a discreet table and fetched two large glasses of chilled house white, which he happened to know was an agreeable Chenin Blanc.

'This isn't very easy . . .' he said, as he sat down and handed her her drink.

Helen raised her eyebrows. 'God, it's not going to be embarrassing, is it?'

'No, no,' Kavanagh said hurriedly. He cleared his throat a few times. 'I've . . . er . . . been asked . . . Peter asked me to have a word with you . . .'

Helen was rather amused by his discomfiture. 'Oh yes?'

'It seems you've ruffled a few feathers.'

'Mmm.' Helen smiled at him. 'Well, perhaps if you'll

tell me who these sensitive little creatures are, I can tread more carefully.'

Kavanagh moved on to firmer ground. 'It would help if you paid your rent on time.'

Helen looked at him frankly. 'James, I've got no husband, a bloody great mortgage, a kid and an ageing mother to support. I'll pay the rent.'

Kavanagh was tempted to commiserate, to confide in her about his own early struggles. The shared room in Camden Town, the minicab, the senior partners who had closed middle-class ranks against the young upstart. Wisdom overcame temptation. 'Look,' he said, 'no one's deliberately getting at you. You just can't afford to upset people. You know how quickly a bad word gets around Temple.'

Helen sighed. 'I try. Look, I'm endeavouring to make a successful career for myself. There are so many women in the second division of this profession. Well, I'm not going to be one of them.'

'Then start doing yourself some favours,' Kavanagh said. 'Even if you don't like the rules, you've got to learn to play the game.'

He ordered them both another drink and commenced instruction.

'Rule number one . . . keep on the right side of the senior clerk. Cross him and he can starve you of briefs . . . even force you out of chambers. Rule number two . . . go out of your way to charm the senior partners . . .'

By the time he'd got to rule number ten, 'Keep up to date with your rent, that's the simplest way they can nail you . . .', Helen was laughing.

'Okay, okay, James,' she said. 'I think I've got the picture, thank you. Watch this space, as they say . . .'

8

Sarah had demanded a meeting with Timothy Ealand. She had gone to his office and faced him with the accusation that he had instructed Dr Clarke to slant the medical evidence. Timothy had refuted it with such blustering vehemence that she was convinced he was lying.

She'd asked him frankly about her chances of winning and he'd as good as told her that she would be wise to cut her losses and run.

'I'm not making a move until I've spoken to Mr Kavanagh,' she said.

Timothy had sighed, but he'd picked up the phone and made an appointment for them both to meet with Kavanagh the following morning.

He'd just driven her home, they were getting out of the car, and Timothy was assuring her that he'd pick her up at ten o'clock the next day, when a man pushed past him and slapped an envelope into Sarah's hand.

'Mrs Meadows?'

Sarah looked at him, bemused. 'Yes?'

Ealand intervened. 'What's this?'

'Well, I haven't come to tell you you've won the pools,' the man said.

71

Timothy snatched the envelope and opened it. 'Good God, he's serving you with a writ.'

'A what?' Sarah said. 'What is it?'

Timothy read the warrant slowly; it was one of the worst bits of news he'd ever had. 'It's from your husband's company. They seem to be saying he died owing them money.'

'What?' Sarah said, disbelievingly.

'Rather a lot, actually,' Timothy said. 'Seven million.'

Timothy took the precaution of phoning Kavanagh before the meeting. 'Bit of bad news, I'm afraid,' he said. 'Um . . . there's no easy way to say this, James. If we lose, Sarah might have problems paying our fees.'

'What?' Kavanagh wondered if he'd misheard.

'Well, it seems that Nick Meadows was guaranteeing his company's debts with his personal assets. The bank's called them in. She's a busted flush, James.'

Later that morning, Kavanagh looked at Timothy and Sarah, as they sat together on the other side of his desk, and thought that although Ealand looked disturbed, Sarah seemed remarkably unaffected by the news of her sudden poverty. 'And you never had any idea?' he said.

'He would never discuss money with me,' Sarah said. 'Working-class pride, I suppose. It's ironic, really. Money was the one thing I always thought I could trust him with.' She gave a slight giggle. 'I certainly couldn't trust him with much else.'

'How will you manage?' Kavanagh asked her.

'Well, you never know,' Sarah said cheerily. 'Someone might even give me a job. Do they still use shorthand?' She put her hand on Kavanagh's. 'Don't worry, I don't expect you to make any promises.'

72

'Do you think he *knew* he was in trouble?' Kavanagh said.

'Even if he did, I don't think he would ever let the thought of defeat enter his mind.' She looked challengingly at him. 'That's what makes a man successful . . . isn't it?'

Timothy Ealand glanced from one to the other. Dear God, he said to himself, they're going to continue with this pointless charade.

Walking up the ramp into the hospital, Hilary bumped into Colin Jellicoe. She knew she'd have to be in court the following morning and she was anxious about Mrs Peters (pneumonia with complications) in Ward 3 and old Mr Jackson (senile dementia and no nursing-home beds available) in Ward 6.

'Hilary? I thought you'd be glad of a night off,' Jellicoe said.

'There's a couple of patients I want to check up on,' Hilary said. 'Nothing wrong with that, is there?'

Jellicoe stepped in front of her, almost blocking her way. 'They're in very capable hands. Shouldn't you be getting back to those children of yours?'

Hilary looked at him coldly. It was the first time he'd shown any interest in her children's welfare. 'They're with their nanny.'

'I think tonight they should be with their mother, hmm? She's got a hell of a tough day tomorrow.'

'They might be seeing a lot more of her in future,' Hilary said. 'Isn't that right?'

'Oh, it won't come to that,' Jellicoe said, almost pushing Hilary back down the ramp.

The protagonists had taken their seats in court and Jeremy Aldermarten was questioning the hospital pathologist,

73

using a far gentler tone than the one he'd employed when harassing Dr Clarke.

'So, Dr Salmon, you were left in no doubt that a post-operative heart attack was the cause of death?'

Aldermarten knew he'd have no trouble with Salmon. He was a stolid staff man who knew his job backwards and was familiar and at ease with court procedures.

'None at all,' Dr Salmon replied. 'The heart was beating normally throughout the operation. That would not have been the case if there had been air lodged inside it.'

The judge leaned forward. 'As a hospital pathologist, you must encounter cases like this all the time?'

'Of course,' Dr Salmon said. 'Sometimes several a week.'

'What was your opinion of Mrs Jameson's surgery?'

'It looked like a first-class piece of work, my Lord.'

Hilary sighed with relief as James Kavanagh put on his spectacles and picked up his case notes.

'Let's look at your notes, shall we, Dr Salmon? That's the date you made them, is it ... the, er, fifteenth of September?'

'Yes.'

'The day after Mr Meadows died?'

'As I recall.'

Kavanagh removed his spectacles which Sarah had come to recognise as a sign that he was on to something. 'But Mrs Meadows was unable to see the body shortly after seven p.m. on the evening of the fourteenth because it had been taken away for post-mortem.'

'I must have looked at the body briefly on the evening of the fourteenth, and then again the following morning.' Suddenly, Sarah realised, the pathologist was looking less sure of himself.

'So the cause of death was not immediately obvious to you?'

Dr Salmon shifted his feet. 'That's not what I said.'

'But most hospital post-mortems take less than twenty minutes,' Kavanagh said. 'Am I right?'

'Broadly speaking,' Dr Salmon conceded.

'But this one took much longer. You looked at the body the next morning because you were worried by the pink froth and the swollen heart.'

'No. I was just being thorough. This was obviously a sensitive case.'

Kavanagh leaned forward and said agreeably, 'You were doing what my learned friend accused Dr Clarke of doing. You were looking for the most convenient explanation.'

Mr Justice Fulbright sighed. 'I think River Court rivalries are best settled before a jury, don't you?'

During the afternoon Sister Linzey was called to the witness box. Sarah had never seen her before, and thought she seemed uneasy.

'When did you first become aware that something was wrong?' Jeremy Aldermarten asked her.

'After closure,' Sister Linzey said carefully. 'Er, the anaesthetist had just left ... he'd been called away to another patient. Mr Meadows was doing well, then he suddenly arrested.'

'Do you know why that was?'

Sister Linzey shook her head. 'No. But it's not unknown with open-heart surgery.'

'And there was nothing you could do?'

'Dr Cazalet and I tried cardiac massage.'

'So, despite your best efforts, you failed to revive him?'

'Yes.'

'Thank you, Miss Linzey.'

Aldermarten sat down and the judge nodded to James Kavanagh, who rose and faced Sister Linzey.

'What is your own opinion of Mrs Jameson?' he said. 'On a personal level?'

Sister Linzey seemed fazed by this unexpected line of questioning. 'She ... well, she just gets on with things. She's a bit of a stickler around theatre, but she stands up for herself against the management.'

Hilary felt rather than saw Colin Jellicoe glaring at her. She kept her eyes on Pat Linzey.

'Why should she have to do that?' Kavanagh said.

'Well, they're always cutting back and economising,' Sister Linzey said. 'Complaining about the way we get through supplies.'

'How many hours had she been at work?'

'I think she and Dr Cazalet were both on a one-in-three. Mrs Jameson had definitely been on call the previous night.'

Sarah's eyes widened in amazement as Kavanagh said quietly, 'So ... about seventeen hours, would you say?'

'Yes.'

'She must have been exhausted.'

'She never let it show in her work,' Sister Linzey said loyally.

'Presumably she was very eager to "knock off" as soon as possible?'

'No. She was always very meticulous.'

'But she was dictating her notes more than ten minutes before Mr Meadows arrested?'

'She only left Dr Cazalet to do the closure,' Sister Linzey insisted.

'So,' Kavanagh said slowly, 'for the final stages of the operation, the principal surgeon wasn't present?'

Sister Linzey looked around anxiously. 'That wasn't a problem.'

'Leading counsel have been known to leave their juniors

in the lurch on occasions,' the judge remarked. 'They seem to get away with it.'

Kavanagh smiled dutifully. 'But Mrs Jameson wasn't racing off to attend another case, was she?'

'No.'

'She just didn't feel like hanging about.'

'No,' Sister Linzey protested. 'It wasn't like that. There was a reason. She had to get home. One of her children had chickenpox.'

Hilary felt Mr Jellicoe throw her another meaningful glance. She waited, full of foreboding, to hear what Pat Linzey was going to say next.

'Chickenpox?' Kavanagh remarked to the court in general. 'Not exactly on a par with open-heart surgery, is it?'

'I think that's enough excitement for the day,' Mr Justice Fulbright remarked, and the Clerk of the Court stood up and called out: 'Court rise.'

James Kavanagh was feeling slightly more hopeful as he rounded the corner of Wandsworth Common. He'd found one chink in their armour and he was certain now that there had been some sort of cover-up. He confidently expected to break their story. Lizzie always said he was a pessimist; that was true enough, generally speaking, but in court he knew he had to be an optimist.

He whistled cheerily as he fished out his front-door key and then stopped in his tracks. There was Matt, crossing the road, slinging a couple of bags and his favourite guitar into a car. He recognised the car. It belonged to a friend of Matt's who, Kavanagh vaguely remembered, was called Pete. He watched as Pete stuck his head out of the car window and shouted to Matt: 'Hey, Matt, it's your old man.'

Kavanagh hurried across the road. 'Matt! Matt, what are you doing?'

77

'I'm going to stay with Pete for a bit,' Matt mumbled. 'He's got a flat up in Notting Hill.'

'Well, what about your college applications?' Kavanagh said. 'You might get a place somewhere.'

'Yeah,' Matt said on a sarcastic note. 'Yeah, right.'

Kavanagh looked at his son in amazement. 'You mean you were just going to take off without telling us?'

Matt scowled. 'Oh, come on, don't make such a big deal out of it, Dad. I don't need the hassle.'

He climbed in next to Pete and, as the car started to pull away, Kavanagh called through the window, 'Well, what's the address of this place?'

'I'll give you a buzz, Dad. Okay?' Matt turned to Pete. 'Come on, let's go.'

Kavanagh knew Lizzie was at a meeting. He groaned out loud. He'd have to tell her and it would hurt her almost more than he could bear.

Hilary hadn't felt like going straight home after the court rose. Listening to Pat Linzey quoting her rehearsed lines, she'd begun to suspect a conspiracy. Perhaps if she went back into the operating theatre she might get some sort of clue about what was going on.

She switched on the light and went over to the operating table. She could almost see Nicholas Meadows's body lying there. He had been all right when she left, hadn't he? She had covered all the possible eventualities?

The door creaked and she turned to see Pat Linzey standing there. 'Mrs Jameson,' she said, 'I'm sorry, I . . . I was only trying to help.'

Hilary didn't reply. Pat Linzey, clearly upset and unable to stop herself, spoke in a rush. 'It wasn't my fault . . . honestly . . . I haven't told anyone.'

Hilary turned to her. 'Told anyone what?'

And Patricia Linzey told Hilary what had happened in the operating theatre that night, after she had left to go home to Alice.

Hilary went straight around to Colin Jellicoe's office. Luckily he was still there, with Geoffrey Beever.

She stormed in without knocking. 'How dare you implicate me . . . put me in this position?'

'No one is asking you to tell an untruth,' Colin Jellicoe said.

Hilary paced up and down the room. 'What exactly are you asking me to do?'

Geoffrey Beever sounded eminently reasonable as he said quietly, 'The point is, Mrs Jameson, you can only give evidence of what *you* saw.' Hilary sighed. 'Miss Linzey had her opportunity in the witness box.'

Hilary turned and walked out of the room without looking at either of them.

Geoffrey Beever felt himself sweating with anxiety. 'Can we rely on her?'

'Two small children, a mortgage and a nanny,' Jellicoe said. '*And* we're not asking her to perjure herself.'

9

David Cazalet was absurdly handsome; the young doctor on the cover of all those old-fashioned women's romances. His manner in the witness box was casual and relaxed, almost to the point of arrogance. As if the witness box were his stage, Hilary thought, as she watched his performance. And performance it definitely was, complete with hand movements and voice projection.

Hilary had passed him in the corridor on her way to the courtroom. 'Oh, best of luck, Hilary,' he'd called out to her. She hadn't replied. It's like being part of some awful competitive team, she said to herself. A notion that had been reinforced as she was ushered into her usual seat between Mr Beever and Mr Jellicoe on the left side of the court. Us and them. She'd looked over to the right-hand side of the court where Sarah Meadows was sitting next to her solicitor. She knew it would have been inappropriate but she'd wanted to smile. Anyway, Sarah had turned away.

'The operation passed off very successfully,' David Cazalet was saying to Jeremy Aldermarten, who nodded approvingly. 'I was very impressed with the quality of Mrs Jameson's work.' Hilary was unable to suppress a snort of irritation, which caused Geoffrey Beever and Colin Jellicoe to exchange anxious glances over her head.

'So why do you suppose Mr Meadows suffered a heart attack?' Aldermarten asked.

'It was hardly surprising. The blood loss would have put his heart under enormous strain.'

'And what more could possibly have been done to prevent it?'

Cazalet shrugged his shoulders. 'Nothing. He was receiving the best treatment Southbrook Hospital was capable of giving him – from one of its best surgeons.'

Beever and Jellicoe smiled in agreement; Hilary raised an eyebrow. Aldermarten thanked his witness and sat down.

James Kavanagh removed his spectacles and studied the witness for a moment or two, which seemed to Sarah (and, she guessed, David Cazalet) at least five minutes. 'How many operations had you attended during the day Mr Meadows died, Dr Cazalet?'

'Seven . . . I think,' David replied.

'That's a gruelling shift. You must have cursed your luck when an emergency came in?'

'It was just another patient. Another challenge.'

James looked at him as though he didn't believe a word of this gung-ho attitude.

'So you went along to theatre with the same enthusiasm and energy you'd had at nine a.m., did you?'

David smiled easily. 'We were in good spirits, yes.'

'And Mrs Jameson was full of the joys of spring too, was she?'

'I've got the message, thank you, Mr Kavanagh,' Mr Justice Fulbright interrupted.

'Well,' Cazalet said, 'it *was* the end of a long day.'

Kavanagh inclined his head, as though grateful for this small measure of agreement. 'So there you were, in theatre, faced with an unconscious, middle-aged man who had already lost six pints of blood. You must have been very worried about his survival?'

The judge looked up from his notes and at Cazalet as he said: 'Of course.'

'The situation couldn't have been more stressful, could it?' Kavanagh continued. 'The two of you, dog-tired, facing a man about to expire, needing a highly dangerous operation on his main artery.'

Cazalet said: 'We didn't have much time to reflect.' Timothy Ealand gave Sarah Meadows a knowing nod; one point to them.

'What was *your* role during the operation?' asked Kavanagh.

'I was just a second pair of hands. I did what Mrs Jameson asked me to do.'

'You were able to see the heart clearly throughout?'

'Yes.'

'Did either of you notice anything unusual about it?'

'No. Mrs Jameson was perfectly happy with the patient's progress.'

Kavanagh gazed slowly around the court and then focused on the young man in the witness box. 'But the man's heart was swelling up like a balloon. It must have been very difficult to overlook that?'

The judge gave Cazalet another sharp look as he said: 'It appeared perfectly normal to me.'

'So, as far as *you* were concerned, everything went swimmingly, did it? Or maybe you were in such a hurry that you turned a blind eye? Mrs Jameson couldn't get out of the door fast enough, could she?' Kavanagh laughed disbelievingly at such callous behaviour and shook his head. Sarah thought that if someone had laughed at her like that in the witness box she'd have seen it as a chill warning.

'She didn't exactly leave me in the lurch,' Cazalet said, looking slightly less suave. 'I am perfectly capable of closing an incision.'

'Yes, but you shouldn't have had to, should you?'

'I'm sure she wouldn't have left if she'd thought there was the slightest risk of something going wrong.'

'As it turned out,' Kavanagh said slowly, 'she made a fatal miscalculation, didn't she?'

Cazalet hesitated, tossed his head and looked over at Hilary. 'That's something you'll have to ask her.'

David was asked to stand down and Hilary was called to the witness box. They passed each other *en route* but each avoided catching the other's eye.

Aldermarten put her at her ease with a series of stock factual questions, then said: 'Apart from the torn aorta, were you aware of any other injuries sustained by Mr Meadows?'

'He had several fractured ribs, but I didn't see any rupture to the lung or any sign of an embolism. When I left the theatre his heart was performing well.'

'Thank you.'

Aldermarten sat down and, once again, Kavanagh rose to cross-examine. 'When you set to work on Mr Meadows, you had already been at work for seventeen hours and done seven or eight operations,' he said. 'Wasn't it irresponsible of you to operate in that condition?'

'Exhaustion becomes a way of life,' Hilary said.

'Especially for a single parent,' Kavanagh remarked. Sarah noticed Hilary's slight wince. Ouch, she thought, that was below the belt; she even began to feel sorry for the surgeon. 'So you had no misgivings . . . about your ability to act competently?'

'I didn't have time to have misgivings about anything,' Hilary answered flatly. 'The patient was bleeding to death.'

'You automatically assumed his main problem was loss of blood?'

Hilary glanced at David Cazalet as she said: 'He was in shock. We were squeezing blood into him as fast as it would go.'

Kavanagh raised his voice and said harshly, 'The truth is you put everything down to that tear, and when things still weren't right after you'd fixed it, you just crossed your fingers and hoped for the best.'

'Nonsense,' Hilary retorted.

'All you cared about was clocking off.'

'I left him in a perfectly satisfactory condition.'

She's telling the truth, Sarah said to herself. Why can't James see that? Why does he keep on at her?

'A grossly distended heart was satisfactory?'

Hilary began to lose her temper as Kavanagh had hoped she would. 'I'm telling you the truth. The blood loss alone nearly killed him. If there had been that much air in his heart, he would have been dead long before we got to him.'

Mr Justice Fulbright sighed. 'We've been over this ground before, Mr Kavanagh.'

Kavanagh nodded at the judge and changed tack. 'Sister Linzey says that you've had a few run-ins with the management about their economising?'

'Yes. When we run low on the basics I'm expected to account for every last item.'

'Waste not, want not,' Kavanagh observed.

'Waste not or look out for your job,' Hilary retorted. 'I'm afraid money was often considered more important than the treatment.'

Kavanagh nodded and riffled through his notes. 'Open your file, Mrs Jameson. Can you find your operation notes there?'

Hilary located them. 'Yes.'

'So who was with Mr Meadows in his final minutes in theatre, after you'd left?'

'Just Dr Cazalet and Sister Linzey. Then another doctor came to help with the resuscitation.'

'And from what you have told us, once air gets into the blood, death is virtually instantaneous.'

'More or less,' Hilary said.

'Well then, let's see how it might have got there, shall we?' Kavanagh couldn't see them but, behind him, he could almost feel the combined team from Southbrook Hospital sitting up and holding their breath. 'We'll start with the basics. At the end of the operation there were five tubes going into Mr Meadows's body. Two drips into the arm, a CVP line into his neck measuring the pressure in his veins, a urinary catheter and a chest drain?'

'Yes,' Hilary agreed.

Kavanagh removed his spectacles. 'So – if a large bubble of air was to get into the bloodstream at this stage, it must have been via one of those tubes.'

'If you accept that was the cause of death, yes.'

'Well, air couldn't have got in through the catheter because that's just connected to the bladder, isn't it?'

'Yes.'

'And the chest drain is merely there to stop fluid building up, it doesn't go into the bloodstream?'

'No.'

'What about the CVP line? Did you check that?'

'There was nothing wrong with it. The records will show it was working normally.'

'That just leaves the two drips. Did you check them after Mr Meadows died?'

Hilary closed her file and said: 'No, I had no reason to.'

'Because it's not something a surgeon usually concerns herself with – it's nurse's work?'

86

'Mostly, yes.'

'So, if either of them was faulty, and somehow letting in air, you wouldn't have known?'

Geoffrey Beever and Colin Jellicoe exchanged glances and watched Hilary anxiously. 'The chances of that are so remote,' she said.

'Was the bag changed at all while Mr Meadows was in theatre?'

'Yes. A fresh bag was connected a few minutes before I left.'

'So, it wouldn't have been changed again?'

'No. I remember seeing it still about a third full when I came back to theatre.'

'And you are sure that the saline drip was working normally?'

'Yes.'

'Then that just leaves the blood drip, doesn't it?' Kavanagh said. 'Was that set up in the same way?'

'Yes, virtually identical.'

'And when was the last time the blood bag was changed?'

'About the same time as the saline.'

Kavanagh paused and studied his notes. Sarah suspected he was doing it for effect, alerting them all to the importance of what he was about to say. She waited expectantly. 'He'd gone through a lot of blood, hadn't he? He'd lost more than six pints.'

'Yes.'

'How long does one of these blood bags take to empty?'

'His levels were nearly back to normal by that time,' Hilary said. 'He'd stopped bleeding, so the flow rate was quite low. Maybe about twenty minutes.'

'Can you remember how much was in the blood bag when

you came back to theatre? Didn't you have to account for every last bag?' He glanced towards Colin Jellicoe. 'Must be very expensive stuff, blood.'

Hilary hesitated. Beever and Jellicoe tensed and the judge leaned forward and smiled kindly at Hilary. 'Please try your best, Mrs Jameson.'

'It had been disconnected,' Hilary said. 'I assume it must have been empty.'

'Assume?'

Hilary saw the six blood bags on the floor. She knew now why the sight had worried her so. 'Actually,' she said, 'I think it had been put on the floor with the other empty bags.'

'If your timings are right, it should have been about a third full . . . like the saline.' Kavanagh paused and then looked directly at Hilary Jameson. 'Mrs Jameson, what happened to all that blood?'

'I don't know.' There was a note of desperation in her voice. 'I wasn't there.'

'Well, there can't be that many possibilities, can there? One bag and two people? It might have been faulty. Er . . . maybe Sister Linzey made a mistake. I'm sure that's easily done when you're tired.'

'No!' Hilary insisted.

'He was your patient. He was ultimately your responsibility.' Hilary nodded agreement. 'You must have demanded an explanation. And what did they say?'

'Nothing.'

'You were happy with that, were you? You were prepared to risk taking the blame for a slapdash nurse's mistake?'

Hilary reacted angrily, as Kavanagh hoped she would. He'd had her down from the start as a decent woman. Not someone who would be prepared to let a nurse go to the wall for somebody else's error. 'It wasn't her fault,' Hilary cried. 'I should have been there.'

'How did Nicholas Meadows die, Mrs Jameson?' Kavanagh asked quietly. 'It wasn't just a heart attack, was it? One of your colleagues was to blame.'

'I didn't see, I wasn't there,' Hilary said desperately.

'But you're the only one who will tell us, aren't you?' There was a brief electric silence in the court. 'What is more important to you, Mrs Jameson – a human life or your professional loyalties?'

Hilary looked over at Sarah, and then at the judge.

'Be very careful about your answer,' Mr Justice Fulbright said.

Kavanagh was watching Hilary as she turned and looked coldly at Colin Jellicoe, Geoffrey Beever and David Cazalet. 'It's easy for them,' he said. 'They don't have a man's death on their conscience.'

Hilary looked over again at Sarah, who held her gaze. She sighed and then she spoke, falteringly. 'We had been told . . . not to waste blood. Supplies were running low. I didn't know what happened until last night . . . Sister Linzey told me. Dr Cazalet was in a hurry. He was probably exhausted. The last of the blood was hard to squeeze in. As the bag empties it collapses . . . there's no air inside so the blood just runs around your fingers . . .' She faltered.

'And what did Dr Cazalet do, according to Sister Linzey?' Kavanagh prompted her gently.

There was desperation and resignation in David Cazalet's expression as he stared at Hilary. 'He injected a syringe of air into the top of the bag so he could force through the last of the blood. It was crazy . . . for the sake of a few drops. I'm sure he wasn't meaning to . . .' Hilary broke down and, putting her hands to her face, started to sob. Through her tears, they could just hear her say: 'He must have accidentally squeezed air into the line . . .'

'Mrs Jameson, did you volunteer this information to your superiors?' Mr Justice Fulbright asked her.

'Yes, I did,' Hilary sniffed, attempting to compose herself. 'Last night.' For a second she looked accusingly at the group sitting on the Southbrook benches. 'I was told not to say anything.'

There was a subdued murmur in the court and David Cazalet, Colin Jellicoe and Geoffrey Beever kept their heads down as everyone turned to look at them.

As Hilary stumbled from the witness box, she saw, through her tears, that Sarah Meadows was smiling. And she realised that she was smiling at her.

James Kavanagh nodded to Sarah and to the judge, and sat down.

in a clear but nervous voice, 'I'm sorry. I don't know much about the law, my Lord, but I do think that both sides have damaged each other enough.' She sat down quickly.

The judge regarded her disapprovingly and said: 'You will receive a measure of damages, even if they are only for one penny. Give it to charity if you wish.' Colin Jellicoe laughed aloud, and the judge froze him with a look before turning to Aldermarten. 'You will agree to an order for costs, Mr Aldermarten?'

Aldermarten gave Kavanagh a sly smile. 'At the legal aid rate, my Lord,' he said.

The court rose and David Cazalet hurried past Pamela Erskine, who had been sitting next to him, and attempted a quick getaway. Hilary stepped in front of him, just as he was about to dart out of the exit. 'I hope you can live with it,' she said. 'You probably can.'

Colin Jellicoe, standing behind her, put a hand on her arm. 'If only he'd had the guts to speak up at the time. Unforgivable.'

Hilary shook off his hand. 'Yes,' she said.

'I had to put the hospital first,' Jellicoe said. 'You must understand that. I couldn't gamble with people's lives.'

'You were quite prepared to sacrifice me,' Hilary said coldly. ' "Sorry" would have been something.' She walked briskly out into the corridor where Sarah and her solicitor were shaking hands.

'Thank you,' Sarah was saying.

Timothy Ealand's expression was blank. 'Goodbye, Sarah,' he said, and walked quickly away without a backward glance.

Kavanagh came through the door and, removing his wig, went over to Sarah. She reached up and kissed him on the cheek and then clapped a hand to her mouth.

'Oh, I'm sorry. I never *believed* . . . I'm not sure how to react.'

Hilary stepped towards them. 'I just wanted to say how very sorry I am,' she said to Sarah. 'Maybe if I'd stayed he might have . . .'

'No, no,' Sarah silenced her hurriedly. 'No, you weren't to know.' At that moment Colin Jellicoe, Geoffrey Beever and Pamela Erskine came out into the corridor and pretended not to see them. 'Mrs Jameson,' Sarah said anxiously, 'they will have you back at the hospital?'

Hilary shrugged and straightened her shoulders. 'It feels like the right time for a fresh start,' she said. 'I might even go to America.'

As Hilary left them, Sarah said: 'She's right – it does. But what?'

'What about a doughnut across the road for a kick-off?' Kavanagh suggested.

'That sounds tempting,' Sarah said. 'But I'm not sure that I can afford to eat out.'

Kavanagh nodded. 'That was an expensive gesture you made in there. I hope you won't regret it.'

'Oh, it was never really about money,' Sarah said. 'That won't bring Nick back. It was the principle.'

Kavanagh grinned at her. 'My treat, then,' he said.

'You won?' Lizzie said. 'I can always tell, almost before you've got through the door.'

'That's because you've got magical psychic powers,' Kavanagh said, kissing her. 'Yes, we won. Sarah Meadows was right all along. You know, I wasn't really sure until we had that theatre Sister on the stand. I just knew she wasn't telling us everything.'

'Whisky?' Lizzie went over to the drinks tray.

'A large one,' Kavanagh said.

Lizzie poured out the drinks, they sat down and Kavanagh filled her in on the day's happenings. When he'd finished, Lizzie gazed pensively into her whisky. 'And Hilary Jameson? Will she be all right?'

'There'll be dozens of hospitals waiting to snap her up,' Kavanagh said. 'Loaded with qualifications, a woman of integrity, and not a stain on her character.'

'I wish Matt was here,' Lizzie said.

'Lizzie . . .' Kavanagh said. 'Don't . . .'

'Oh, it's not just that I miss him, that I'm worried about where he is and what he's doing,' Lizzie said. 'It's what he said to you . . . all that stuff about ruining "a promising little career".'

'It doesn't matter,' Kavanagh said truthfully. 'Really.'

Lizzie took a long gulp of whisky. 'But I hate it when he goes for you like that,' she said. 'I want him to know what you do, what you stand for . . . he doesn't understand . . .'

'Of course he doesn't,' Kavanagh said. 'He's far too busy rebelling to think what he's actually rebelling against.'

Lizzie came over and kissed him. 'I think the reason I love you is because you are a very wise man.'

James held her close for a moment. 'And a very hungry one,' he said. 'I've had nothing to eat all day except a doughnut.'

11

The following morning, Peter Foxcott phoned through and invited James to join him for coffee. As he came into the room, Jeremy Aldermarten waved the Cona pot aloft. 'Ah, see the conquering hero comes.'

Peter handed him a cup. 'It's Djimah, James.'

James looked suspiciously into the cup. 'Do I detect a whiff of sour grapes?'

'No, James,' Aldermarten said. 'That's the coffee. It's Ethiopian.'

Foxcott sniffed the aroma of the coffee in his cup appreciatively. 'You know, we still haven't resolved our little problem with Ms Ames.'

Aldermarten nodded. 'No, indeed. She completely cut me dead this morning. Didn't even give me the time of day.'

'Perhaps she was preoccupied,' Kavanagh said. 'She is a working mother.'

'If only she brought more of her maternal qualities into chambers,' Foxcott said.

Aldermarten laughed. 'Well, what do you recommend? Breast-feeding in the clerks' office?'

'I just wish she was a little more amenable,' Foxcott persisted.

'I do think . . .'

There was a knock on the door and Helen Ames walked in.

'Fascinating case in the Court of Appeal yesterday,' Aldermarten remarked to the room.

'Yes, extraordinary,' Foxcott said quickly.

Helen poured herself a cup of coffee and came over to them. 'Jeremy, I have a favour to ask you.'

'Oh?' Aldermarten looked worried.

'One of my solicitors is looking for a first-class Silk to appear in the Companies' Court. I hope you don't mind, I said you might be available. You see, he really doesn't want to have to settle for second best.'

Aldermarten swallowed. 'Yes, yes, of course, of course, I'd be delighted.'

'Oh, good,' Helen said. 'Oh, Peter, Tom said you wanted a word.'

'Yes . . .' Peter looked around for an ally. 'There was one matter . . .'

Aldermarten stepped forward. 'No, no, no, it wasn't that important, was it, Peter?'

'No,' Foxcott said doubtfully. 'No, I suppose not.'

Aldermarten smiled agreeably at Helen, who smiled back.

'Well, if there's nothing I can do help . . . ?' Helen beamed around the room. 'I'll be off, then.' She sidled up to Kavanagh on her way out. 'How am I doing?'

'Splendidly,' he said.

Aldermarten waited until Helen had left. 'There's really no need to go out of our way to create bad feeling, Peter.'

Foxcott stared at him, open-mouthed.

'That's what I admire about you, Jeremy,' Kavanagh said. 'Your infinite capacity for forgiveness.'

'Well, I do like to think, as a senior man in chambers, one can rise above petty point-scoring. Don't you agree, James?'

'Oh, absolutely,' Kavanagh said.

Aldermarten put down his cup and wandered off. Foxcott turned to Kavanagh. 'What on earth was all that about?' he said.

PART TWO

Mute of Malice

12

The young defendant kissed his mother, embraced his solicitor – almost hugged his counsel. 'Oh, thank you, thank you, Mr Kavanagh. I can't tell you how grateful . . .'

James Kavanagh smiled broadly and patted his arm. 'No, no, young man. You're innocent. Don't waste your time thanking people.'

Over the years, he'd been a part of so many dramas outside the Law Courts. More often than not there were tears, recriminations and abusive threats to sue everyone, including the judge. This was an unusually happy scene. He waved to the solicitor. 'You see, it does sometimes turn out all right.'

He looked around for Alex Wilson, his junior, who had been submerged suddenly by a crowd of people shoving and jostling their way up the steps. She was there, behind a pillar. Kavanagh put his arm around her shoulders to guide her down towards a taxi, but they were pushed back by the angry crowd, shouting and catcalling and waving their fists.

'What's this all about?' Kavanagh said. He looked up at a small group who had emerged from the courts and were standing at the top of the steps, where he and Alex had been standing only a few moments ago.

Flashbulbs were popping. 'Look this way, Mr Beddoes!' reporters were shouting. 'Will the pensioners get their money back, Mr Beddoes?' A very large solicitor was attempting to block the questions. 'My client has a full answer to all the charges brought.'

'Of course,' Kavanagh said. 'It's Miles Beddoes.'

Alex nodded. 'The Palanquin Investments fraud.'

At the back of the group they each spotted, at the same moment, Jeremy Aldermarten, looking extremely pleased with himself.

Kavanagh grinned at Alex. 'It's Jeremy's crock of gold,' he said.

'Are you innocent, Miles?' one journalist called out. 'How does your wife feel about it, Mr Beddoes?' shouted another.

'The pensioners have not been betrayed,' countered the large solicitor, 'and will, I'm certain, eventually be fully compensated . . .'

'Your old pupil-master's in seventh heaven,' Kavanagh remarked to Alex as they finally reached the pavement.

Alex yelled for a taxi and thought how much she preferred working with James Kavanagh than for Jeremy Aldermarten. She'd been assigned to him as his pupil for her first year in chambers, and whenever she'd displeased him in some way – failed to produce a relevant paper at the right time, or avoided an encircling arm in a taxi – he'd been quick to point out her good fortune in being accepted at River Court. 'I don't think anyone could call me a racist, my dear Alex, but it is quite unusual for a traditional set to open its door to a young . . . er . . . ethnic woman.' Aldermarten had also made it clear that if it hadn't been for Kavanagh the door might very well have been slammed in her face.

Alex was small, but she was purposeful. She managed

Aldermarten looked at Mr Justice Way uncertainly. 'Your Lordship is too kind,' he murmured.

He sat down, but found himself stirring uneasily as the judge continued to eye him thoughtfully. 'Mr Aldermarten?'

He stood up again. 'M'lud?'

'Why are you wearing that wig?'

Aldermarten put a hand to his wig. It seemed to be in place. Was there something wrong with it? Had he, perhaps, put it on incorrectly or was there, unknown to him, some gross insect perched on his head? 'Well . . .' he stammered, 'it . . . it's the only one I have, m'lud.'

Mr Justice Way chuckled. 'What *are* you talking about?' Aldermarten looked around the court in desperation. What in heaven's name was going on? Either he was going mad or Mr Justice Way had a serious problem. 'M'wig, m'lud,' he said.

'Do we have time for that?' the judge snapped. 'I don't think so. Get on with it, Mr Aldermarten.'

Aldermarten stumbled on for the remainder of the sitting, in spite of frequent interruptions from the Bench. He determined to discuss the matter with Peter Foxcott when he got back to Chambers.

'You haven't forgotten, then?' Lizzie Kavanagh said, as her husband came through the front door.

'Forgotten?' Kavanagh kissed his wife.

'About going down to the Coach House,' Lizzie said. 'You're nice and early. We'll be there in time for supper.'

Lord Probyn, Lizzie's father, had bought the Coach House twenty or so years earlier, as a family bolthole, just after he and Lizzie's mother were divorced. Lord Probyn . . . Kavanagh grinned to himself, remembering his surprise and his own father's outrage when they'd discovered that his future father-in-law had a handle to his name. Alf Kavanagh, Hon. Sec. of the Bolton branch of the TGWU, had reacted to the hand-engraved wedding invitation as though he'd been posted an insult. 'You'll not be expecting your mother and me then, Jim,' he'd said. 'They're not making fools of us.' But, of course, they'd come to the wedding and, of course, Lord Probyn and Alfred Kavanagh, bluff men both with similar reactionary views on how to put the country to rights, had bonded like Araldite as the drink flowed.

The Coach House was tucked away down a country lane several miles outside Cirencester. Kavanagh remembered now that he'd promised Lizzie they'd go there this weekend. Pity. He'd been looking forward to a quiet weekend, the two of them, and feet up in front of the rugger match on Saturday afternoon. England versus France at Twickenham. He looked wistfully at the television. 'Of course I haven't forgotten,' he said.

Lizzie, busily stowing food into a freezer bag, correctly interpreted the look. 'We do have to go, you know. See and be seen, stand by Angela, all that.'

'Of course,' Kavanagh said. Angela and Lizzie had been brought up together in the same small Gloucestershire village. Angela in the Old Rectory, where she still lived, Lizzie in the big house next door. They'd been friends ever since. Angela was Miles Beddoes's sister. 'Bit of a coincidence,' he said. 'Alex and I were leaving court today when Miles and Gemma were being pilloried by the press and damn near assaulted by the baying hordes.'

Lizzie stopped packing. 'Oh, poor Gemma. You will come to church with us, won't you? Just this once. Well, this is the last time we're going to be down for ages. I mean, even Father won't come. Angela and her family need all the support . . .'

'I never go to church when we're down there,' Kavanagh

said. 'Look pretty obvious, wouldn't it, going now? I just think they'd prefer not to be gawped at.'

'Okay,' Lizzie said. 'We can have a picnic after . . . on the way home.'

'I'll make the sandwiches,' Kavanagh said.

Lizzie accepted this concession graciously. Kavanagh was not a good man in the kitchen. 'Just don't bother with the hard-boiled eggs,' she said.

They were halfway down the M40 when Lizzie pushed a tape into the cassette player and they were instantly engulfed by a barrage of raw, futuristic sound. 'Oh God!' Lizzie said. 'One of Matt's . . .'

Kavanagh winced. 'Turn it off, for heaven's sake.'

Lizzie pressed the off button. 'He did phone . . .'

'I know,' Kavanagh said. 'You told me.'

'He is all right . . . he and Pete . . . they're going to some pop festival this weekend . . . Reading, is it . . . ?'

Kavanagh gripped her hand. 'Don't ask me, love. I'm a Snoop Doggy Dogg man, myself.'

13

Edgar Beddoes, chaplain to the cadet corps, led his colour party down the aisle of the university chapel. Lizzie, sitting next to Angela in the third pew, whispered, 'He's wearing his medal on his cassock. It doesn't seem like Edgar, somehow. The flags, the guns, all that regimental paraphernalia . . .'

'It isn't,' Angela whispered back. 'I think he hates it.' Edgar was her tall, fair brother. Miles was the shorter, darker one. Edgar was the brother who always got to play the angel in the school nativity play. When she and Miles had fought together, Edgar had made peace. If they had got into trouble for some childish naughtiness, Edgar knew how to defuse parental rage. Ever since he'd returned from Bosnia four years ago, as sweet-tempered as ever yet curiously detached from their world, she'd watched anxiously as he'd tried to find a niche for himself.

'Oh, God our help in ages past . . .' The organ boomed, and the choir swung gratefully into the old favourite at full throttle. Angela glanced around the empty pews. Hm, she said to herself, they've heard Father preach before.

The Reverend Matthew Beddoes was on his usual form. His eyes blazed at the small congregation of students, lecturers and elderly villagers as he urged them to make room for God in their minds. 'There are those with minds abroad or coddling mischief . . .' Angela looked at Lizzie and rolled her eyes. '. . . and to them I say, welcome the devil into your heart, he will make you feel complete.'

After the service, Lizzie and Angela strolled together through the churchyard.

'So, Miles didn't turn up to give them all a thrill,' Lizzie said.

Angela raised an eyebrow. 'Are you surprised?'

Lizzie thought of their shared childhood. Miles had always been the leader, full of anarchic plots, ready to challenge authority. 'He doesn't usually run away,' she said.

'Perhaps he thought your father might be here,' Angela said. 'He helped Miles a great deal, you know.'

'They help each other in the City,' Lizzie said.

'Miles wouldn't have got where he did in such a short space of time if your father and Gemma's father hadn't given him a great deal more than help,' Angela said. 'Trust, confidence, support. Well, Lizzie, he's let them all down.'

There was the sound of a horn from the lane outside the church. Lizzie looked over to see Kavanagh leaning on the car. 'Must go, Angela,' she said. 'See you soon.'

They kissed. Angela waved at Kavanagh and Lizzie said: 'You'll let me know, won't you, if there's anything I can do.'

Angela walked slowly back towards the Old Rectory and the ghastly ritual of Sunday lunch.

She found Gemma in the kitchen, lifting a heavy roast out of the top oven of the Aga and putting it into the bottom oven to rest. 'Dad'll be happy you're down for a Sunday,' she said. 'Now he can carve something up. Where are my brothers?'

'Shooting . . . birds,' Gemma said, moving over to the

sink to top sprouts. 'Too much to hope Miles might do the decent thing, I suppose?'

'Confess?' Angela picked up a knife. 'Here, let me help with some of those.'

Gemma pushed a pile of sprouts towards her. 'No, bump himself off.'

Angela gave her sister-in-law a sideways glance. 'That's a pretty dreadful thing to say.'

'Yes, isn't it,' Gemma said, straightening up and dusting down her apron. 'I do, however, mean it. He's a crook, Angela.'

'Is he?' Angela sighed. 'Yes, I suppose he is.'

Gemma went over to the stove and took out the roast. 'With him gone, we might all eventually live it down. My father had a good name in the City.'

'Miles won't do any decent thing,' Angela said. 'Of all of us, only Edgar ever has done.'

'Oh, Yugoslavia,' her father said. He'd come in to oversee his lunch and overheard Angela's last remark.

'Bosnia, Father,' Angela said.

The Reverend Beddoes picked at the meat with his fingers. 'I suppose I'll be expected to carve it, if I can recollect how.'

Angela looked over at Gemma, who was putting the sprouts on. 'What he's saying is, I won't cook meat. Well . . .' She turned to her father. 'I'll carve, if you like. I won't do more than hack chunks off any old how, though. No silly sacrificial nonsense.'

'Well, then, I'd better try,' her father said. 'The creature died, after all, Angela. One ought to show gratitude.'

Angela's irritation at this remark evaporated as she saw that Gemma was standing by the Aga, holding her head in her hands.

Through the muffled thickness of her oven gloves, Angela

113

heard her say, 'I worry about the children . . . the boys. I don't give a damn about . . . us . . .'

Angela went across to comfort her. The Reverend Beddoes deliberately turned away from the two women and gazed out of the window as he sharpened his carving knife with brisk rasping strokes.

Gemma blew her nose and sniffed. 'I'm all right.'

Angela placed a sympathetic hand on Gemma's shoulder and then went to get the water jug.

Her father put down his carving knife as she was running the tap. 'At least I don't need to do evensong. Edgar kindly offered. So . . . bottle of wine?'

'Never stopped you before, Father,' Angela said. 'You and old Canon Jolly. Now there was a sympathetic man. One could talk to him. A real priest.'

'I miss him, the old soak,' the Reverend Beddoes said. 'And his good ordinary claret. Mint sauce?'

Gemma reached for the mint. 'Miles won't be happy without it,' she said.

While the others were in church, Miles went to the gun cupboard and took out two rifles and a shotgun. He polished them lingeringly with the palm of his hand, laid them on a chair and looked around for Edgar. Where the hell was he? He'd finished marching around with his little troop of cadets at least half an hour ago. Miles had seen him from the window, leading them out of the chapel. 'Edgar,' he called, 'what are you doing?'

'Coming,' Edgar called from upstairs.

Miles went up to Edgar's small bare room, and found him loading clothes and schoolboy trophies into a box which he was depositing in another room, already full of his belongings.

114

'I'm making space in which I might . . . breathe better,' Edgar explained. 'Emptying it of the clutter.'

'Well, come on,' Miles said, 'or it will be lunch-time.'

'Yes, yes, yes, yes,' Edgar said. He looked out of the window at the countryside, at the framed medal hanging on the wall, and at the book lying on his bedside table – *Regeneration* by Pat Barker. He followed Miles downstairs. 'Here,' Miles said, 'you'd better have this.' He handed Edgar one of the rifles and tucked the other under his arm, leaving the shotgun on the chair.

As they walked down the lane towards the woods, Miles took a large envelope out of his pocket.

'What's that?' Edgar said.

'My last chapter.' Miles shoved it in the postbox.

Edgar laughed. 'You're not still hoping to have it published?'

'Why?' Miles challenged him. 'Don't you think I can write . . . ?'

'Well, actually, now you ask . . .'

'Didn't all get firsts, you know.' Miles threw a playful punch at his brother. 'You're in it.'

They followed the path into the wood. Edgar grinned. 'Thanks for nothing.' And just look where my first has got me, he thought. Padre to a university cadet corps and not even any good at that. 'They're chucking me out, the university. They're right, of course . . .' He paused and added quietly: 'I seek . . . need a new ministry, Miles.'

'Yeah, well, join the club,' Miles replied.

He strolled on as Edgar stopped and groaned. 'Oh . . . you.' He sighed. 'Your trial coming up. Me . . . again.' He beat his forehead with the flat of his hand. 'Me, me, always me.' He caught Miles up and placed a hand on his shoulder. 'How are *you* bearing up, Miles? Oh dear, I can't help, can I?'

115

Miles wished old Edgar weren't so OTT about everything, but he hugged him tightly, anyway. 'No, oh no, no. This is the big one, Edgar. "Financial whizz kid hits skids", eh?' He chuckled. 'No, no, no. It's the Scrubs for me. The Scrubs.'

'There are others,' Edgar offered. 'There's a *Good Nick Guide*, I believe.'

'Yes,' Miles said, and he seemed to Edgar to be resigned to his fate. 'I'm sure.'

'Look,' Edgar said, 'I really don't understand money things. You were doing so well, everyone was amazed. What did you do?'

Miles looked at his honest, upright brother – probably the only person in the world he'd ever flatter with the truth – and said evenly: 'I took a lot of money, rearranged it into bank accounts I controlled – some in Switzerland, some Gibraltar and other hidey-holes.' He gazed steadfastly at Edgar. 'Pensions.'

'Ah, pensions,' Edgar said.

Miles shifted his rifle in his hands. 'I could finish it – here and now. Leave Gemma and the kids with some money, at the very least.'

'Don't ask me to condemn,' Edgar said quietly. 'I can't. I saw what real crime is.'

'Ah, yes. But you're golden.' Miles smiled in a way Edgar found irritatingly patronising. 'You fought for Christ.'

'Mention that in your book, do you?'

Miles laughed and looked up at the sky. 'Rooks!' He stepped on to a fallen tree stump and aimed his rifle. 'Missed. Wait for them to come back. They always come back, rooks.'

'One always comes home, I suppose,' Edgar said.

'What, even if not wanted or someone is waiting with a gun?'

'People do.'

'Yeah,' Miles said bitterly. 'And I'm bloody tired of it.' He gestured towards Edgar's rifle. 'Wouldn't care to help me out, I suppose?'

'Me?' Edgar backed away. 'Isn't it *you* who prides himself on helping me?'

'I've done my best,' Miles said. 'Aren't you grateful?'

Edgar thought for a moment. 'Mmm, sometimes.'

'Got you a gong and a mention, didn't I? That helped, didn't it?'

'I'm not sure. Yes, you know it did.' He grinned at Miles. 'Thoroughly dishonest, though . . . to be honest.'

Miles chuckled. 'Only we know.'

'Until your rotten book comes out,' Edgar said.

'Oh, do cheer up, Padre,' Miles said. 'It may never happen – not with my spelling.' He looked up, spotted a rook and raised his gun.

'Hold still, hold still.' Edgar handed Miles his rifle. 'Here, have mine. There's just one left up the spout.'

They heard the rifle shot in the kitchen. Gemma put the vegetables into tureens and gave the mint sauce a stir. 'Must be on their way back,' she said.

A few minutes later Edgar came through the kitchen door and laid a rifle down on the table. 'I should have left it there,' he said wearily.

Angela and Gemma gazed, mesmerised, at the barrel, which was covered in a mahogany-red sticky substance. 'What's that?' Angela said. 'Blood?'

Edgar stared at her. 'Where is Father?'

'And where's Miles?' said Gemma.

Angela looked around. 'Father? Probably gone down to the cellar.'

Edgar's expression was blank. 'He's dead,' he said. 'I just

117

shot him. Dead. Miles, I mean.' His head was spinning as he came towards them. 'I killed him. Dead.' The door to the cellar was open. As Edgar gazed down into the murky darkness there was a movement, the flicker of a shadow on the wall. Edgar's legs buckled under him and he fell to the ground.

Edgar was lying on his bed in the Old Rectory. But he could hear the gunfire, the rumble of tanks, the smell of death . . .

The bodies, piled up carelessly on top of each other in a dank cellar . . . a breaker's yard of human debris . . . limbs contorted, faces anguished, resigned, terrified, surprised . . . hundreds of faces. He had stood at the top of the steps and, slowly removing his helmet, looked down on the pitiful sight. The stench had been unbearable – he could smell it now. Somewhere an arm moved, somewhere else a baby cried and was silent. It was too awful to contemplate . . . or to forget. Edgar knew he would never get that sight and that smell out of his head.

He opened his eyes, looked curiously around his room and saw the medal framed proudly on his wall. He closed his eyes again, quickly.

And then . . . coming home to the cadet corps, the training exercises . . . the smoke-filled fields . . . bombs exploding around their heads. Were the tanks really crashing through the familiar bracken of Oxfordshire or was he still in Bosnia?

There had been a girl, too young, too small in her army fatigues and her heavy tin hat. She'd turned to him, frightened. 'I'm not sure if I can hack it, Padre,' she'd said as they bumped over the countryside in a jeep. Later they'd been in a dugout together. She'd told him she was lonely. 'Sometimes I just sit and stare at the wall, you know.' She was appealing to him for help. 'I have to say . . . I do cry a lot, Padre.'

He'd wanted to say something comforting about God's all-embracing presence, the healing nature of time, the fact that she'd soon forget all this and get a normal job and live a happy, fulfilled life, but he'd been too damaged himself to help her. Instead, he'd picked up his binoculars and looked through them intently, as though he were studying the mock battle going on in front of them. And all he had seen through those binoculars was a man dying from gunshot wounds in a small village in Bosnia, and a cellar full of bodies.

14

Tom Buckley, the senior clerk, strolled into River Court, took off his coat and slung it on the peg. 'Morning, Gary,' he said to his junior. He picked up the morning paper and wandered off towards the clerks' office.

Gary was collecting the post as James Kavanagh came in. 'Morning, Gary.'

'Cold enough for you, sir?' Gary said.

They were stopped in their tracks as they heard Tom shout: 'Bloody hell!'

'What's Tom shouting about?' Kavanagh said.

Gary shrugged. 'You know Mr Buckley, sir.'

Tom sat down in his chair and gestured despairingly at the newspaper. 'Nice little fraud tickle, that,' he said to Helen Ames, who was standing behind him, looking through the pigeonholes. 'I was anticipating years of steady.' He handed her the newspaper.

Helen read the headline: 'Palanquin Chief Death Shock'. 'Not like you to back a loser, Tom.'

Tom sighed. 'I don't know what this country's coming to. No moral fibre. I mean, where would we be if every flash client decided to top himself sooner than face the music in court?'

Helen dropped the newspaper on to Tom's desk and went over to check on the planner board. 'Undertakers?' she suggested.

'Skint is where, Miss Ames,' Tom said. 'I do hope it doesn't become a trend vis-à-vis the financial classes.'

Helen laughed and wandered out. Funny the way that one's lightened up, Tom said to himself. These days she's almost human.

'Tom?' Kavanagh queried from the doorway.

Tom held up the newspaper. 'Our chap Miles Beddoes is dead.'

Kavanagh took the newspaper from him and read the lead story. He looked at Tom. 'Does he know?' Tom shook his head. 'I'll break the news, then.'

He went off and Tom lit a cigarette and flicked through the briefs on his desk. 'Right,' he murmured. 'Better find Mr Aldermarten something else to keep him off the streets. Something . . . sticky.'

Peter Foxcott poured Jeremy Aldermarten a cup of coffee. One of the problems about being the senior member of chambers was that people kept bringing him their problems, as it were. He'd listened to Aldermarten's disjointed tale about Mr Justice Way's strange behaviour in court and, frankly, he'd been unable to make head or tail of it. 'Would you say a joke?' he hazarded.

'Well, it's an odd sort of joke,' Aldermarten said.

They both turned when there was a knock on the door and Kavanagh came in.

'James knows him, of course,' Foxcott said. 'Good morning, James.'

'Morning,' Kavanagh said, keeping the newspaper under his arm. 'I think it's colder.'

'Do you, James?' Aldermarten said.

Foxcott poured him out a coffee. Kavanagh took a sip and walked over to Aldermarten. 'Definite chill in the air. Has it not reached your regions yet?'

Aldermarten looked at him curiously and Foxcott said: 'You know Mr Justice Way, don't you, James?'

Kavanagh nodded. 'Oh, I most certainly do.'

'An old friend?'

'Yes,' Aldermarten interrupted eagerly. 'That's right, I know he is, Peter. Now, that's why I mentioned him to you.'

'What about him?' Kavanagh said.

'What do you think of him?' Aldermarten countered.

'Well . . .' Kavanagh shrugged. 'Sensible. Always helpful. Likes a joke. Doesn't ask daft question like . . . who Snoop Doggy Dogg might be.'

Aldermarten nodded and then thought for a moment. 'Who . . . who *is* Snoop Doggy . . . ?'

'There you are, Jeremy.' Foxcott sat back in his chair, relieved that the matter seemed to be cleared up. 'Way J is a very good judge, very well liked.'

Aldermarten was still anxious. 'Should I have laughed, do you think? Nobody else did.' He turned to Kavanagh. 'He asked me why I was wearing a wig.'

'Well, that's it, then,' Kavanagh said. 'If you can take a joke.'

'I can take a joke,' Aldermarten said defensively.

'Good chap,' Kavanagh said, enjoying the moment. 'Here's another one for you.' He handed Aldermarten the newspaper. 'Your client shot himself.'

Aldermarten gazed at the headline in horror. 'Oh, Lord.'

The telephone rang and Kavanagh pointed to it. 'Is that your accountant?'

'Now, now, James, that's just cheap,' Aldermarten said.

*　　*　　*

Back in his office, Kavanagh phoned Lizzie. He hardly knew the Beddoes boys himself, but they were part of Lizzie's childhood and she and Angela had always been very close. He didn't want her to be upset by the sudden sighting of a tabloid headline.

'Oh my God, how dreadful . . . and just when we were having our picnic, and it was all so sunny and lovely,' Lizzie said when he told her. 'Suicide?'

'So they say.'

'I'll ring Angela . . .'

Lizzie was amazed at how calm Angela sounded. She described how they'd heard the shot, and how Edgar had walked into the kitchen like a walking statue and dropped the gun on the table next to the joint. 'All covered with blood, Lizzie . . . Miles's blood. And then Edgar told us – Gemma and me – that he had killed Miles . . .'

'He what . . . ? He couldn't have,' Lizzie said. 'Not Edgar.'

'Yes, right,' Angela said. 'But that's what he said. "Miles . . . I killed him . . . dead . . ." Something like that; I can't remember the exact words. And then poor Edgar wandered about the kitchen a bit and fainted clean away.'

'And your father?'

'Oh, pottering about down in the cellar seeking the perfect claret,' Angela said. 'When he arrived on the scene we left Edgar lying there and rushed out into the wood to check on Miles, who was, of course, horribly dead.'

'Oh, Angela . . . and what about Gemma? Is she all right . . . I mean, as right as she could be . . . ?'

There was a cold note in Angela's voice as she said: 'Ah, Gemma . . . she's called in the police, Lizzie. She shouldn't have done that. She was only saying, while we were doing the sprouts, that she hoped Miles would do the decent thing

124

– family shame . . . her father's reputation . . . the effect on the boys . . . you know, all that. Well, he did do the decent thing, didn't he? There was no need for the police.'

'But why . . . ?'

'It's Edgar, you see. We got him up to bed and he came round, all right, but he won't speak. Won't say a word. Just looks at us in a blank sort of way and then turns his face to the wall.'

There was a silence at the other end of the line. 'Angela . . . ?' Lizzie said. 'Are you still there?'

'I never liked Miles,' Angela said quietly, almost as though she were talking to herself. 'But you don't have to *like* the people that you *love* in a family, do you? Or where would that leave . . . Daddy? Edgar, however, is different. We all liked him, loved him. Gemma, too. I reminded her of that, but she just looked hard and not at all like herself and said: "Yes, but Edgar said it. You heard him."'

'And your father?' Lizzie said. 'How's he taking it?'

'Egotistically,' Angela said, and Lizzie could almost see her friend's ironic smile. 'Goes on as if nothing had happened. By the time the ambulancemen had arrived and then the police . . . well, the joint was ruined, of course. Gemma had taken off in the car, I was shattered . . . and worried sick about Edgar. You won't believe this, Lizzie, but while I was clearing up in the kitchen, Daddy came in and he didn't say anything about Miles . . . or Edgar . . . or even was I all right. He just lifted a saucepan lid and said: "Back to greens, are we? Greens and beans?"'

'I believe it,' Lizzie said grimly. 'Shall I come down? I can be there in an hour or so . . .'

'Bless you, but really not necessary. They've taken Edgar into custody . . . his solicitor, the chap who was Miles's solicitor, is with him there, now. He says it's bound to go to court. So Daddy and I are coming up to see James the day after tomorrow.' She paused for a moment. 'Will you do something for me, Lizzie . . . well, two things, actually?'

'Of course.'

'Try and persuade James to take us on – and then have lunch with me after the meeting.'

Phew, this is a tricky one, Sergeant Spiridion thought. He and Inspector Judd must have been in the interview room half the night looking across the table at this bloke who wouldn't say a bloody word and his fat solicitor, who kept falling asleep. And who could blame him? He'd felt like nodding off himself more than once. He stretched and eased his shoulders as his inspector came back into the room.

'Has he said anything yet?'

The sergeant checked his watch. 'No.' He leaned towards the tape. 'Inspector Judd enters at ten twenty-six.

He wasn't sure if he really needed to go to the bog or just needed to get out of the room. He tapped the inspector on the shoulder. 'Look, I'm just gonna . . .'

The inspector nodded and said into the tape, 'Sergeant Spiridion leaves at ten twenty-eight.' He put his elbows on the table, and leaned forward with an encouraging smile. 'It's all right, Edgar. Your solicitor, Mr Dartwood, is here. We've sent for a doctor for you. We'll wait. We can . . . we have . . . patience.' He thought Edgar was taking it all in, the way he looked sort of questioning, but there was nothing . . . no response in the eyes; they were looking beyond them all, far away. 'We have to question you, you see. You were the only one there. You know what happened. Do you want anything at all . . . ?' The inspector felt a flicker of hope as Edgar opened his mouth. He was trying to speak. The inspector could see a flutter in his throat. But, no luck. Edgar closed his mouth again. 'If you want anything . . .

just write it down . . .' He pushed a piece of paper and a Biro across the table, which Edgar ignored. '. . . anything at all.' He sat back in his chair and chanced a light-hearted remark which brought nil response. 'You a clergyman and nothing to say? I don't believe it.'

They were there all day, the four of them. Plastic cups with dregs of coffee littered the table. Inspector Judd put out his twenty-fifth cigarette – he'd counted the butts in the ashtrays to pass the time – and coughed. He really must give up, he thought, reaching for his pack of Marlboros. There wasn't a sound in the room except for the solicitor's snoring. It was heavy and rhythmic, so damned soporific that even Edgar Beddoes had stopped staring into space, fallen forward on to the table with his head on his arms and nodded off. He woke up and rubbed his eyes, though, when Spiridion came in and sat down again next to the inspector. 'I think that's my fastest slash ever,' he said. 'Olympic.'

Inspector Judd nodded briefly (he didn't hold with that sort of talk in front of outsiders) and looked wearily at his watch. 'Sergeant Spiridion comes back in at twenty-one thirty,' he recorded. The solicitor yawned and then fell back again into a deep sleep. Is he . . . ? Can it be . . . ? Inspector Judd held his breath as Edgar pulled the piece of paper towards him, picked up the pen and began writing, very slowly. Judd and Spiridion glanced at each other, wide-eyed with hope. The inspector leaned down towards the tape. 'Mr Beddoes writes . . .' His voice alerted the solicitor, who suddenly woke up and reached for the piece of paper. Spiridion got there first. On it there was just one word, written in shaky capital letters. The inspector sighed his relief into the tape. 'Yes . . . "GUILTY".' He glanced at Edgar, who had slumped back in his seat. 'Well, that's good, isn't it, Edgar?' There was another pause while nothing happened. 'What?' the inspector said. 'Not even a nod?' They all stood up and stretched, except for Edgar. He remained sitting in the chair. He was tentatively opening and shutting his mouth, but he made no sound.

Tom Buckley knocked and stuck his head around James Kavanagh's office door. 'Got Mr Dartwood in Reception, sir. And his clients. The Beddoes business.'

Kavanagh, who was on the phone to Lizzie, put his hand over the mouthpiece. 'Right, Tom, wheel them in.' He removed his hand. 'They've just arrived. Yes, I will. Yeah. 'Bye.' He was just replacing the receiver when Mr Dartwood, Angela and her father appeared in the doorway. 'Angela,' he said, 'Lizzie says the Ivy at one fifteen. All right?'

'Oh, good, perfect,' Angela said.

Kavanagh was just about to invite them to come in and sit down when Jeremy Aldermarten appeared and proffered a hand to Matthew Beddoes. 'Hello,' he said. 'Um, Miles was my client. I'm so sorry.'

Matthew Beddoes shook his hand grudgingly. 'Mmm, yes,' he said, looking Aldermarten up and down critically.

Aha, Kavanagh thought, he's lost one Beddoes brother and now he's after the other. He glared at him. 'Mr Beddoes, Miss Beddoes, this is Mr Aldermarten, who is no longer involved and will not linger.'

Alex appeared, clutching a large file. 'Oh, and this is Alex Wilson,' Aldermarten said, as he began unwillingly backing out.

Matthew Beddoes smirked. 'Is she his devil?'

Aldermarten, embarrassed, shot his cuffs and adjusted his tie. 'Huh, yes, well, we don't use that term any more in these days of political correctness. Not wise.'

Alex, who had been called all sorts of unpleasant things

in her time, including 'stuck-up black bitch', gave a slight smile and put the file on Kavanagh's desk. 'You'll need these, Mr Kavanagh.'

Kavanagh nodded to her, put on his spectacles and looked over at Angela. They were all still hovering around the doorway; he wished to God they'd come in and sit down so they could get on with it. 'Angela, I'm sorry, I'm afraid you can't stay.'

Angela was surprised and somewhat put out. Was this some kind of archaic men-only Middle Temple rule?

Alex went over to her. 'It's just that you could well be a prosecution witness,' she said, 'so we're not allowed to talk to you. Can I get you a coffee or something while you're waiting?'

They went off together and Matthew Beddoes turned to Aldermarten and boomed: 'I was once chaplain to the Devil's Own Inns of Court Yeomanry.'

'Oh, really,' Aldermarten said. 'Did that conflict . . . spiritually?'

Matthew chuckled. 'Devils, indeed. Hardly. More likely the Guards' Cavalry. Bum-boys to a man, a surgeon told me. Abnormally high incidence of a filthy disease of the rectum, he said.'

Mr Dartwood raised an apologetic hand in Kavanagh's direction. Kavanagh grinned. That'll see Jeremy off, he said to himself.

Aldermarten reversed swiftly into the corridor. 'Well, duty calls,' he said.

Alex returned and went to sit beside Kavanagh, and Mr Dartwood and Matthew Beddoes took their seats on the other side of the desk. The vicar wasted no time. He folded his arms, sat back as though he was here in charge of the meeting and announced: 'My son admits his guilt.'

'How?' Kavanagh said. 'If he can't or won't speak.'

'Can't. Dartwood tells me you call it a "visitation". That he's been struck by the hand of God.' Matthew snorted. 'Believe that and you will, without doubt, believe anything, by God.'

Kavanagh pursed his lips and frowned. Alex recognised the expression. He's not going to take on this case, she said to herself. The vicar's blown it already.

'And what do the doctors say?' Kavanagh asked the solicitor.

'It's all there . . .' Mr Dartwood took a document out of his briefcase and dropped it on to Kavanagh's desk. 'And he, er, made a statement – well, he wrote just one word, actually. "Guilty." That's all. Look . . . I'm sorry, I was tired.'

Kavanagh smiled sympathetically. 'Of course. Now . . . er, Mr Beddoes, as a preliminary, there will be a little trial at which a jury will be asked to decide whether . . . um, Edgar . . .'

'That's rich,' Matthew Beddoes interjected.

Kavanagh ignored him and continued, '. . . is mute of malice . . .'

'Doesn't even know his name,' Matthew snorted.

'. . . or mute . . .' Kavanagh persevered.

'What sort of lawyer is it can't remember his client's name?'

Mr Dartwood put out a hand to silence his client, but Matthew shook him off.

'. . . by visitation of God,' Kavanagh finished.

'Ring out, base bugles . . .' Matthew Beddoes cried, in resonant pulpit mode.

Mr Dartwood collapsed back in his chair. Up all night . . . stuck in a cubicle reeking of cigarettes, followed by a grim day of the same . . . nothing to eat except stale police canteen sandwiches, and now this . . .

'Whatever the outcome, the plea will be not guilty . . .' Kavanagh knew he wasn't going to finish this sentence either, as he saw the appalling vicar draw breath.

'No decent angel would go near either of them.'

Alex wondered how long it would be before Kavanagh lost his temper. He was not renowned in chambers for suffering fools gladly, and this one was a real idiot. She was full of admiration when Kavanagh continued speaking in a reasonable, measured tone.

'It will be all the better for Edgar's defence if a jury doesn't think that he refuses to speak, is mute of malice. It's difficult. He shot his brother and said so.'

'The fatal wound was found to be equally consistent with suicide,' Mr Dartwood said. 'But, in the absence of a suicide note and the existence of an admission of guilt, they have a case.'

'Why?' Kavanagh turned to the solicitor. 'What motive?'

'Well, the police suggest one. Both of them were with the UN in Bosnia and Edgar was attached to Miles' regiment. Miles hoped to publish a book to cash in on his notoriety. And in it, I understand, he deflates Edgar's heroism for which he was decorated.'

There was a further eruption from Matthew Beddoes. 'Hero? Huh. They're none of them heroes these days. They call them heroes as soon as they're booted and badged. He got a mention in despatches . . .'

Kavanagh had had enough. He leaned forward across the desk. 'Why are you here, Mr Beddoes?'

Matthew leaned back and grinned. 'I'm paying. I am quite rich, you know. Something you "peak quotation Judases" like to hear, don't you?'

Mr Dartwood closed his eyes. Alex held her breath.

Kavanagh got up and strode over to Matthew Beddoes. 'Well, you *won't* be paying *me*.' He opened the door and

131

turned to the solicitor. 'I don't want to take this case, Mr Dartwood.'

'These are for you, sir.' Gary Potts handed Aldermarten a foolscap-sized brown envelope and a large carrier bag and went out, leaving the door half open.

Aldermarten eyed the bag eagerly. He put it carefully on his desk and went over to the door. Glancing up and down the corridor, he came back in, made sure the door was properly shut, and darted back to his desk. Sitting down, he opened the carrier with mounting excitement and lifted out a wig box. He opened it, took out the wig and, holding it up, admired it from every angle. It was a splendid wig, one which, surely, even Mr Justice Way would find acceptable? He tried it on and it fitted to perfection. He checked with the small hand mirror in his top drawer and was more than pleased with his reflection.

Taking it off – he didn't want anyone to come in and catch him wearing it – he restored it to the box and slit open the brown envelope.

The title on the front page read 'Afterword'. It was the final chapter of Miles Beddoes' book. Jeremy flicked idly through the pages, not even noticing the handwritten note on the final page. 'Ah, *vita brevis*,' he murmured to himself philosophically. Replacing the manuscript in the brown envelope, he tossed it on to a pile of box files, labelled 'Crown versus Beddoes', which were lined up on a shelf next to his desk.

He went through a few papers, checked his post and looked around to see if there was anything else needing his attention. He was just flipping open the wig box to give his new purchase another admiring glance when his eye fell on the Beddoes files . . . there were at least half a dozen of them taking up good shelf room. He piled them up, and rang for Gary.

'Bring a trolley to my office, Gary. I've got a load of files here that could well go into the archives.'

Minutes later, Gary wheeled in the trolley and loaded the files on to it. Aldermarten held open the door, and Gary was just about to push the trolley along the corridor when Aldermarten spotted Matthew and Angela Beddoes and their solicitor coming towards them. Quickly, he gestured Gary back into his office. It wouldn't do for them to see him disposing of the dead relative's effects, as it were.

He stood in the doorway as they passed. Angela Beddoes seemed worried. 'Can he do that?' she was saying to Dartwood.

'No, he has to take the case if you insist. But, er, will you if he doesn't care to? Perhaps better not.'

Oho, Aldermarten said to himself, so Kavanagh's turned them down. Might be in with a chance there, then. He watched them as they went down the stairs. 'All these stairs,' Matthew Beddoes was announcing in a loud voice. 'Place is like a Shepherd Market brothel.' On reflection, Aldermarten felt sympathy with Kavanagh's reluctance to get involved.

'Mr Aldermarten?' Tom Buckley had something in his hand which looked to Jeremy like a brief.

'Tom.'

'I've got this for you, sir. Immoral earnings and arson.'

'Ah, mmm,' Aldermarten murmured. 'Hot crumpet.' He was rather pleased with this witty play on words, but his smile faltered as Tom said, 'Mr Justice Way, sir.'

Aldermarten groaned. 'Oh, no. Way J. Oh, well . . . I shall try to make a spoon of it.'

Tom grinned at Gary, who was still in charge of the trolley. 'What shall I do with this lot, sir?' he said.

Aldermarten was now at his desk, opening the brief. He waved a hand casually towards a corner of the room. 'Oh, just leave them there, Gary, for the time being.'

'I say, Mr Buckley,' Gary said on his return to the clerks' office, 'Mr Beaufort was right.'

'Surprise me,' Tom said. 'What about?'

'You know what was in that box that come this morning?' Gary jerked his head in the direction of Jeremy Aldermarten's office. 'The hatbox-shaped thing that come for 'im?'

'I dunno,' Tom said. 'An Easter bonnet, maybe?'

'Not far wrong, Mr Buckley,' Gary said. 'A new wig. I saw it. And what Mr Beaufort said when he got back from court the other day was that Mr Aldermarten had acted very fidgety and strange about his wig because he thought the judge was being rude about it. We had a laugh about that, me and Mr Beaufort.'

15

'Hi, Angela!' Lizzie jumped up from the banquette to greet Angela, who, led by a waiter, was weaving her way through the tables towards her.

'Lizzie.' They kissed warmly.

'So, how did it go?' Lizzie said.

'Quite unbelievably awful,' Angela said.

The waiter whisked napkins on to their laps and Lizzie passed Angela the menu. 'I'm having the fishcakes,' she said.

'Sounds perfect. Make that two fishcakes,' she said to the waiter. 'And God, I need a drink.'

'House white?' Lizzie said.

Angela looked up at the waiter. 'And a bottle of the house white, please.'

'Awful?' Lizzie gazed at her friend anxiously. 'Oh dear. What did James say?'

'James? Oh, no. No, Father. Father.'

'Where is he? Did he go to his club?'

'No,' Angela sighed. 'No, I put him on the train. If he went to his club he'd attack somebody, then come back exultant that he'd bashed a bishop, or worse. He was intent on going to where they preach at lunch-time on Tower Hill.'

'To preach?'

'No.' Angela grinned. 'To heckle those he hates who do. I wasn't at the meeting this morning . . .'

'Because you might be called for the prosecution?'

'Exactly. But, while we're on the subject of heckling, Mr Dartwood said your husband could hardly get through a sentence without Father shouting something offensive at him. And he came out of the meeting chuckling, looking so damned, irritatingly pleased with himself.'

The waiter came over and poured out the wine. Angela took a sip, and then another. 'Delicious. Lizzie, your husband doesn't want to take us on. And, you know, I don't blame him, not one bit.'

'Oh dear.' Lizzie put down her wine glass and looked at Angela anxiously. She was so pale in her grey suit with her streaked blond hair tucked neatly behind her ears, and the pallor in her cheeks almost translucent from, Lizzie guessed, lack of sleep, as well as grief and anxiety. 'I haven't wanted to interfere but . . . should I?'

Angela shook her head. 'It's all right, we'll find someone. Lizzie, Edgar is determined on his own guilt. All that can be done is to ask for clemency, or whatever it is one does. Though why Edgar should expect it, I don't know.'

Lizzie thought of good, kind Edgar in the dock. 'But you must try.'

'To be fair, Edgar doesn't expect it,' Angela said. 'He simply awaits his fate.'

It was one of those travel programmes that makes you glad you're staying at home. Straw-roofed huts, each with their own veranda and all mod. cons, clustering on a golden beach under palm trees; black men dressed up as waiters scurrying from hut to hut with trays of drinks ludicrously decorated with hibiscus flowers. And in the background, the crash of waves vying with the brash nasal twang of the English upper classes.

James Kavanagh shuddered. His idea of a holiday was getting away to Ipswich and sailing his elderly *Nicholson's Sloop* down at Pin Mill. He settled comfortably into the armchair, poured himself another glass of wine, flicked off the sound with his remote control and, after a period of pleasant contemplation, decided that, all things considered, renovating his boat was almost more pleasurable than sailing her. He thoroughly enjoyed cleaning up the mellow mahogany, resurrecting the old brass, and the many happy hours spent chatting with fellow fanatics at the ships' chandler's.

He looked at his watch. Eight o'clock. Lizzie should be home by now. Once that wouldn't have worried him, but ever since it had happened he'd felt a frisson of foreboding when she was unexpectedly late. It seemed to him now so long ago, but it was actually only a couple of years. He'd been too wrapped up in a complicated Jockey Club enquiry to notice that Lizzie was drifting away from him. While he was working late at chambers and coming home with his head full of equine anxieties, Miles Petersham had been available, charming and attentive. Kavanagh winced, feeling again the pain that had seared through him when he'd discovered they were having an affair. His Lizzie, who mattered more to him than anything else in the world. But, of course, he'd never told her that, hadn't really felt it necessary. What made it worse was that Miles, renowned for his skill in sweet-talking a jury, had been a friend of his. The wounds had healed, but he and Lizzie were careful with each other now, aware that what they had was delicate and precious and could easily be destroyed. He sighed with relief as he heard her key in the front door.

'I'm home, darling.' She came in and flung off her

pillar-box red jacket and ran a hand casually through her dark, curly hair. The vibrancy of her personality matched her colouring; it never failed to give him pleasure. He turned off the television and poured her out a glass of wine.

Lizzie took it and said: 'Meeting with the big boss of Cromart International.' She knew James would want to know why she'd been held up and equally she knew he wouldn't ask. 'I went to see him after Angela ... oh, darling, I think his company's going to sponsor a new kidney machine.'

'You've scored again,' Kavanagh said. 'Lizzie Kavanagh, the Great Persuader.' They grinned at each other, and Kavanagh followed her into the kitchen. 'I don't like your friend's father.'

Lizzie, busying herself with the chicken and baked potatoes she'd put into the oven on the timer, said: 'You're always telling me you're not supposed to like, just defend. They are friends, James.'

'Not friends of mine,' Kavanagh said, getting out the cutlery and placing a candle in the centre of the table.

'Of mine. You know them and they've asked for you.'

Kavanagh sat down. 'They don't need me, Lizzie, to plead mitigation, which is what it'll boil down to. Any competent barrister can do that.'

Lizzie tipped a pack of frozen petit pois into a pan, set them on the hob and turned to him. 'Will you think about it?'

'There's no point to it, anyway,' Kavanagh said. 'How long before we eat?'

'A couple of minutes,' Lizzie said. 'Isn't there supposed to be a motive for someone accused of murder?'

'Well, there is a motive floating. Miles was writing a book, their deeds heroic – not so heroic, it seems, on Edgar's part – in Bosnia. I haven't seen it. Yet he did get a medal . . .' He paused. 'What was said when he did, Lizzie? When he got his medal. Do you know?'

They were interrupted by the phone. Lizzie picked up the receiver. 'Hello . . . ? It's Angela,' she hissed at Kavanagh.

He took the chicken from the oven and began carving it. Lizzie chatted for a while and then put down the phone and came over to strain the peas. 'She wanted to know if I'd spoken to you.'

'Well, you have,' Kavanagh said. 'Is she all right?'

Lizzie sighed. 'I suppose.' She went over to the fridge to get out a bottle of water. It was a large fridge, stacked with food. 'There's too much for the two of us,' she said sadly, 'but I can't get out of the habit.' She came back to the table with the water and the vegetables. 'Do you realise that when Matt gathers up his pot plants and CDs, takes up his videos and walks, they might never come back and live with us again?' Kavanagh fetched a loaf of bread and a box of matches and lit the candle. 'Oh, candle. Nice,' Lizzie said. 'Kate and Matt, I mean.'

Kavanagh served up the carved chicken and they sat down opposite each other. 'These days you'd hardly know the difference,' he said. 'Where is he? Still with Pete or cohabiting elsewhere?'

'Who knows?'

'Poor chap,' Kavanagh said. 'Oh, then there's going to be trying to find a job, and trying to find a place he can afford. Just to think about starting again, being thrown into all that . . .' He shuddered. 'It's terrifying, isn't it?' He looked at Lizzie. 'I had a sudden urge for my pension last week. It came on me.'

Lizzie laughed. 'I'll believe that when I see it.'

Kavanagh munched for a moment and then said: 'Your

friend Angela is a prosecution witness, you know. She shouldn't be involved. *Can't* be involved. You ought not to really, love, so do be careful what you say to her. I would rather . . .'

'But surely it doesn't matter if you've avoided taking the brief,' Lizzie said.

'Well, no, no, that's true,' Kavanagh said pensively. 'Who've they got?'

Lizzie refilled his glass. 'Well, I said I'd keep trying with you.'

He smiled at her. 'I can't turn it down . . . I'm not allowed to. Your friend, that crazed old bugger in the dog-collar, got up my nose. When I think what he's had and what my father hasn't had, Lizzie . . . rude old sod. Well, you can tell Angela I've changed my mind.' Lizzie looked at him, surprised. Kavanagh chuckled. 'Well, you know me. Anything to keep Jeremy's hands off a case.'

16

'Well, here I am again,' Colin Dartwood thought. He settled his weight, as best he could, on a hard chair in the prison interview room behind James Kavanagh and Alex Wilson, and they all looked hopefully across the table at Edgar Beddoes. He could see that Beddoes wasn't going to say anything. During the long watches with the policemen he'd become an expert on the subtle nuances of Beddoes' expression. Fraud cases were notoriously tricky, but he wished to God he'd still been representing the dodgy plausible brother instead of the doggedly silent one. It was Dartwood's view that Edgar Beddoes felt guilty because he was guilty. He'd probably had a rough time in Bosnia and shooting his brother – the noise, the mangled flesh, the blood and so on – had revived that traumatic experience. Motive? The manuscript, of course.

It was lying on the table now. Kavanagh glanced at it and cleared his throat. Poor old Kavanagh, Dartwood said to himself, he doesn't know what he's in for . . .

'Edgar,' Kavanagh began, 'I'm told you understand but don't choose to talk, indeed can't talk. Is that correct?' He looked at Edgar, who looked back at him. 'Are you trying?' Edgar's expression didn't change. 'The doctor has said there is nothing wrong, physically wrong. Your condition is simply aphonia . . . that is, you can't speak.' He waited for a reaction which didn't come. 'Your brain isn't damaged and you are equipped to talk but you don't, or won't. Nor will you write any more . . . or can't. Nor will you nod . . . or shake your head . . . or won't. Can you make any noises?' Edgar turned away sharply at this. 'I don't mean to offend you,' Kavanagh said gently. 'Now, you will stand trial for the murder of your brother on the evidence of your own reported words. This . . .' He gestured towards Alex. '. . . this is Alex Wilson. She will read what the police say you said. Alex?'

Edgar looked blankly at Alex as she picked up the statement and read: ' "He's dead. I just shot him, dead. Miles, I mean. I killed him. Dead." '

'Did you say that?' Kavanagh said. 'It seems to me you might have done.'

Alex noticed the slightest flicker in Edgar's eyes. She reached forward and put her hand on Edgar's, which was lying motionless on the table. 'It's all right, Edgar, really. You don't have to try. We understand.'

Edgar jerked his hand free.

'It's all right, Edgar, keep calm,' Kavanagh said patiently. 'We know that you can't talk.' He gave a small smile. 'It would help us if you could. It would help us to defend you. You don't want to be defended?' Edgar just stared at him. 'Did you kill your brother?' Edgar continued to stare. 'You see, if you plead guilty we've still got to say something on your behalf in mitigation. Well . . . we would like to know what to say . . .' He nodded to Alex, who pushed a piece of paper and a pen towards Edgar. 'Alex has offered you paper, if you want to write something.'

Edgar gazed at the paper and then pulled it towards him. He picked up the pen in his right hand and then switched it to his left. They watched him trying to write, concentrating as though he were a small child attempting joined-up writing for the first time.

'You managed to write "Guilty" for the police, Edgar,' Alex said.

Edgar looked at her for a moment and then screwed up the piece of paper and tossed it over his shoulder.

Kavanagh sighed. 'Don't worry. It's all right.' He and Alex stood up and collected their papers together. 'We'll come and see you again, Edgar. We've asked a doctor to have a look at you. Talk to you.'

They went out, followed by Colin Dartwood. As they left the room, Edgar threw his head back and shrugged his shoulders, easing the tension in his back.

He looked up again as a tall man with dark hair strode into the room and held out his hand. 'This is Edgar, is it?' he said. 'Jolly good. My name is Cole and I'm what you might call a shrink.'

Edgar didn't take the proffered hand. He looked down, further down; down into a dark basement. He saw hands lying across legs, flung over decapitated bodies . . . and faces, with dark sockets where the eyes should have been. Edgar closed his own eyes against the fearful sight.

Jury service . . . who needs it? Dave Adams thought as he sauntered into the jury room. He got himself a cup of coffee from the machine and looked around. There was another black guy, youngish, early thirties, about his own age, sitting in the smokers' section. Dave lit up and went over.

'Bugger this for a game of soldiers,' he said, sitting down. 'They can count me out.'

'You gotta do jury service, man,' the other guy said.

'I got other things to do. You wanna do it?'

143

'I don't *wanna* do it.'

Dave shrugged. 'You do it, then. You ain't got other things to do, maybe.'

'I got plenty of things to do,' the other guy said.

'Yeah?'

'Come on, it's forty pound a day, man.'

Dave drew deeply on his Silk Cut. 'Don't need it. I earn more than that. Bit of this, bit of that, it soon adds up . . .'

They both turned as the chief usher, who looked to Dave suspiciously like his fat Aunt Mary from Brixton, came out of a door marked 'Chief (P)Usher'. Dave grinned and gestured at this comical piece of graffiti.

'Williams?' she called.

'Here.'

'Shankar?'

'Here.'

They watched the chief usher move around the room with her clipboard and Dave's companion jerked a thumb in her direction. 'She's got the list.'

'Sissons?'

'Here.'

'Adams?'

The other guy laughed out loud and dug Dave in the ribs. 'You might get the murder.'

'Yes,' Dave said unwillingly.

'Justice calls,' the chief usher said.

Dave sighed, dropped his cigarette into the coffee cup and followed her into court.

Down in one of the cells below the courtroom, James Kavanagh, Alex Wilson and Colin Dartwood were facing Edgar Beddoes across a different table.

Edgar, spruce in his cassock and dog-collar, was as uncommunicative as ever.

'Do you understand what this is all about, Edgar?' Kavanagh asked him.

'I have told him, Mr Kavanagh,' Colin Dartwood said.

'Yes,' said Kavanagh. 'Well . . . I'll tell him again.' Edgar raised an eyebrow. Whether in query or resignation, Kavanagh couldn't tell. 'You will be asked how you plead – guilty or not guilty. If you say nothing there will be a small trial, before the big trial, when a jury will be asked to decide whether you are mute of malice or mute by visitation of God. You have been examined by doctors who will say that you haven't spoken, cannot. Whatever the jury decide, the judge will order that you are to plead not guilty so that you may face a proper charge for murder with a defence. But . . .' He paused meaningfully. 'All this may be avoided if you speak. Are you going to . . . ?' They all looked at Edgar. He opened his mouth slowly several times and then closed it and folded his arms on his chest. 'Very well. We'll do our best.'

Colin Dartwood opened the cell door and they all went out into the corridor. Alex looked back at Edgar and smiled, but he was gazing up at the ceiling.

Colin Dartwood said: 'In the nineteenth century, those mute of malice were pressed under weights until they either died or pleaded.'

Alex nodded. 'Yes. Every law book I've read enjoys that footnote. I don't think he'd say anything even then, do you?'

Just outside the courtroom they found Dr Cole, complete with briefcase and a sheaf of papers. Kavanagh went up to him. 'Dr Cole, thank you for your medical report and thank you for coming. I'll have Alex warn you when we're getting near to wanting you.'

He and Alex went into the courtroom, where the jury were being sworn in. 'Neville. Radcliffe. Merlus. Kidd. Shankar. Adams.'

Dave reluctantly took his seat. 'I'm here.'

'Anybody here whose religion does not let them swear?' said the clerk.

Dave grinned. 'My mum count?'

The chief usher appeared at his side and in a voice that reminded him even more of his Aunt Mary said: 'Now, you just stay quiet and listen to what he says.'

The clerk was instructing the first juror 'Stand and read the card,' and the juror had begun 'I swear . . .' when Dave noticed Edgar being led into the dock. Could it be? It bloody was. He could hear the first juror droning '. . . try the defendant to give a true verdict according to the evidence', and he thought he'd better get a move on. He gestured to the chief usher, who came over, glaring at him disapprovingly.

'What is it now?'

'It's just that . . .' Dave took another quick look at Edgar. '. . . oughtn't I to say . . . if it's Mr Beddoes' trial . . . I know him. He saved my life.'

'You sure?'

''Course I'm sure. He saved my life.'

Dave watched eagerly as the chief usher went over to the clerk, who whispered to the guy sitting on the bench, who asked somebody else if they would stand this juror by. Phew, Dave said to himself, saved by the bell, or, to put it more correctly, by the good old padre. A grey-looking bloke in a wig then told him to 'Stand by for the Crown', some poor sod called Williams was called in to take his place, and the chief usher led him out of the courtroom.

They walked together down the steps leading into the main lobby. 'Well, that's right, isn't it?' Dave said. 'Bloke saves my life, I'm bound to find him not guilty, aren't I?'

'How did he save your life?' asked the chief usher.

Dave flipped a cigarette from the pack into his mouth

and looked at her knowingly. 'He just did. Can I go now?'

'I'll tell you when you can go.' She consulted her clipboard. 'Yes, you can go. Services not needed. We've got enough.'

'Right,' said Dave. 'Where do I parade for pay?'

'In the post,' the chief usher said. 'What do you think this is, the DSS?'

Miss Haddon, Q.C. for the Crown, had presented her case and, for the benefit of the jury, was going through the medical evidence again, with her expert, Dr Trevis.

'My understanding is that Edgar Beddoes has not suffered injury, or wounding, his brain is not damaged, his condition has no basis in physical impairment, but is more likely to be the result of an emotional shock of some kind which has resulted in aphonia or lack of speech?'

Dr Trevis nodded. 'That is my view.'

Kavanagh leaned over to Alex, sitting behind him, and whispered, 'Warn Dr Cole.'

Alex hurried out and found Dr Cole still sitting on the bench where they had left him earlier that morning. 'Dr Cole? They're almost ready for you now.' She gestured towards the courtroom.

Dr Cole picked up his briefcase and went in. Alex was about to follow when she was stopped by the chief usher, who put a hand on her arm and said in a motherly tone, 'Are they treating you all right, my dear?'

Alex smiled at this gesture of black solidarity. 'Yes, thank you.'

'What are you up for?'

'Crown versus Beddoes,' Alex said.

'Really?' The chief usher linked her arm in Alex's and

led her towards a quiet corner. 'I can tell you something about that . . .'

When Alex returned, Kavanagh was questioning Dr Cole in the witness box. 'Dr Cole, you have examined Edgar Beddoes?'

'I have.'

'Can he talk or is he shamming?'

'Physically there is no reason why he should not talk.'

Alex tiptoed across to Mr Dartwood, whispered in his ear, and handed him a piece of paper. Edgar gazed impassively from the dock.

'He is refusing to speak?' Kavanagh asked.

Alex returned to her seat, and Colin Dartwood crept out of the courtroom as quietly as his bulk would allow.

'His brain is refusing to allow him to speak,' the doctor said. 'He's not aware that that is the case. He is simply unable to speak.'

'Why?'

'He doesn't want to. He has a powerful reason not to wish to speak or communicate in any way.' The jury gazed at Edgar with mounting curiosity as the doctor continued. 'So powerful that he has no control in the matter. He cannot nod and now he cannot write, which is unusual in such a case. Often the urge to write is strong.'

'Has he been struck dumb or not?' demanded Mr Justice Carteris from the magistrates' bench.

Dr Cole turned to him. 'In a sense he has, and in a sense he has not. I'm sorry, I cannot be clearer than that.'

'Seems clear enough to me, Dr Cole,' Kavanagh said, causing Mr Justice Carteris to give him a sharp look and Miss Haddon to snigger.

'The shock of his brother's death has triggered something,' Dr Cole said slowly and thoughtfully. 'It's brought something back that is very shocking, something that he cannot talk about, something he has never been able to talk about.'

'And do you know what that might be?'

'No.' The doctor shook his head. 'It's very deep. I would need time.'

'Now,' said Kavanagh, 'how does he feel about being on trial? How does he view the situation he finds himself in?'

Dr Cole glanced briefly at the dock, where Edgar was sitting back with his arms folded, almost as though he were watching a performance being enacted for his benefit. 'He's amazingly unconcerned.'

Kavanagh also glanced at Edgar. 'Indeed. And yet he wrote "Guilty" on a piece of paper.'

'I have to say that he appears to have no guilt whatsoever about the death of his brother. But . . .'

'Yes?'

'He does have a deeper guilt. I could find no basis for it.'

'None?' Kavanagh said. 'Does the fact that the defendant served in Bosnia bring anything to mind?'

The doctor inclined his head. 'Combat stress is an area I suggest be explored.'

'Thank you.' Kavanagh sat down and Alex passed a note to him as Miss Haddon was called and rose to her feet.

'Surely the shock of killing his brother . . . ?' she began.

Kavanagh jumped up. 'My Lord?'

'Indeed.' Mr Justice Carteris nodded. 'Miss Haddon?'

Miss Haddon bowed. 'Grateful, my Lord. Now, Dr Cole, if the defendant had killed his brother, or seen his brother die, would that be shock enough to render him mute?'

'I think it is, dare I say, as I said . . . deeper . . .'

'Yes, but could it?' Miss Haddon interrupted.

'It could,' Dr Cole said, and Kavanagh sighed. 'Hysteria can be brought on by any emotional shock. It's just the . . .'

'Yes, thank you,' Miss Haddon said swiftly. 'Dr Cole, will the defendant ever speak again?'

'Oh yes,' the doctor said confidently. 'One day he will.'

'And how will this happen?'

Edgar roused himself and gazed over at Dr Cole with interest as he said: 'When he feels he can, he will.'

'I see,' Miss Haddon said crisply. 'Thank you.' She turned to the Bench. 'I have no more questions, my Lord.'

Kavanagh leaned towards Alex. 'Where is he?'

'Dartwood is looking for him,' Alex said.

Kavanagh nodded, took off his spectacles and stood up. 'Dr Cole, is my client about to speak now?'

'He is not.'

'No.' Kavanagh looked at the jury. 'Thank you.'

Edgar leaned on the dock rail, with his chin resting on his hand, and watched interestedly as Mr Justice Carteris summed up. 'Members of the jury, consider this: is the defendant mute of malice or mute by visitation of God? You may convince yourselves of the reasons for this. But I must tell you that "visitation" does not not have any mystical connotation. It simply means a person is mute from birth, or has become mute since and cannot reply when a question is put to him. Until it was reformed, the law allowed for such a person who refused question to be liable to the *peine forte et dure*, that is pressed under weights until dead – or pleads.'

Alex rolled her eyes at Kanavagh, who smiled at her. Edgar sat back and glanced idly around the court-room.

The jury returned in under an hour. Mr Justice Carteris

150

resumed his seat and one of the guards standing on either side of Edgar nudged him and told him to rise.

Mr Justice Carteris addressed Edgar directly. 'Edgar Beddoes, the jury has found you mute of malice. You may be put on the country for trial.' He looked towards the clerk. 'A plea of "Not Guilty" will be entered to the indictment alleging murder. Let a fresh jury be sworn.'

The clerk bade the court rise, and a guard moved to take Edgar's arm. As he did so, Edgar shook him off violently and turned towards the judge, his eyes desperate, his mouth working as though he were trying to speak. There was a further struggle before the guards overpowered him.

'He wants to plead guilty,' Alex said to Kavanagh, as they watched Edgar being led away. 'He wants to be found guilty.'

Kavanagh gazed at her, puzzled. 'Why would that be, Alex?'

They had been in the cell since the court rose at four. Kavanagh looked at his watch. It was half past nine. He looked round at Dartwood. His head was slumped on his chest. Edgar, enigmatically silent as ever, was pale and haggard. Only Alex remained interested and alert.

'Come on, Alex,' he said. 'Let's go home.' He stood up and picked up his briefcase. 'Edgar, we're going home. We'll see you tomorrow.'

Alex touched his arm. 'Let me stay.'

'No,' Kavanagh said firmly.

'Please. I can understand a great deal . . . I think.'

Kavanagh shook his head. 'No, Alex, you're not staying.'

Alex looked over at Edgar, who was rubbing his eyes. 'He's tired. You're right.' She stood up and Colin Dartwood, at the back, rose heavily from his hard chair.

'Yes, we're all tired,' Kavanagh said. 'Will you talk, Edgar? I'm sorry. Please forgive me. I mean, can Alex help you? Can you help her see? Edgar, I know it's big and it hurts, this guilt you're heavy with. Alex can come back tomorrow if you like, early in the morning, fresh. Will you, Alex?'

'Of course.' Alex smiled at Edgar. 'Is that all right, Edgar? Yes?'

Edgar gazed back at her blankly. Colin Dartwood tapped on the door and a guard came and opened it. They all looked at Edgar as they filed out. He had slumped on to the table with his head on his arms. 'What strikes me,' said Kavanagh, 'is the thought that our client is in the wrong court for the wrong crime. But where he thinks he is or what he fears he's done . . . well, it's beyond me.'

'I wonder,' Alex said. 'Does he know himself?'

17

Kavanagh paid off the taxi. 'What . . . ?' He turned to look at his house, which glowed and throbbed in the dark, quiet street. Lights blazed from every window, and there was an indescribable din of music and loud voices. His instant reaction was that Matt had come back and was hosting some sort of rave.

He dashed in. There was nobody in the hall. Racing up the stairs into the drawing room, he called out 'Hello!' and noticed that the television was on full blast. He switched off Jeremy Paxman and assorted guests shouting at each other and looked around. 'Lizzie?' There was no reply. The stereo was turned up to full volume, something noisy and magnificent and Wagnerian. James turned it off. 'Anyone home?'

He moved around, clicking off lights, and was bending to deal with the table lamp by the sofa when he noticed Lizzie. She was curled up in a corner of the sofa, wrapped up in a blanket, fast asleep. He touched her shoulder gently. 'Lizzie?'

She woke and looked up at him. Pushing her hair back out of her eyes, she struggled up. 'It was like a morgue when I came in,' she said. 'You know . . .' There was a tremor in her voice. 'You know this house is too big for just us, now.'

Kavanagh sat down beside her and held her close. 'Is it?' He gazed around at the elegant entrance hall, the stairs leading up to this big, comfortable room where he'd spent so many happy hours. 'I suppose you're right,' he said regretfully.

'When I came back this evening . . . I almost didn't want to come in,' Lizzie said, clasping his hand.

She looked like a forlorn child. 'What do you want us to do, Lizzie?' Kavanagh said. 'Find another house, a smaller one?'

'Perhaps we ought to.'

'Well, couldn't we keep it until I retire?' he said.

Lizzie sighed. 'Oh, that'll be years yet.'

'The point is, they'll want somewhere in London, all their friends are here.' He smiled encouragingly. 'We never had enough room before.'

'No,' Lizzie said. 'It didn't take much to fill this house, did it? Matt could do it on his own, when he's . . .'

'When he's here. Quite,' Kavanagh said. He'd been on the go since dawn and he wasn't sure he could cope with the familiar Matt discussion at this late hour. 'Right, let's turn off a few more lights. Must be costing the earth.'

He wandered around the house, flicking switches, and when he returned to the drawing room and sat down again next to Lizzie he was relieved to see that she seemed more her usual, sensible self. 'You all right, love?'

Lizzie nodded. 'Silly of me. Sorry. Just couldn't stand the silence.' She saw the lines of tiredness etched under his eyes. 'And you're obviously knocked out. Did it go all right?'

Kavanagh described the day's happenings. '. . . and the bottom line is that he still won't utter a word. What was

154

he like when he came back from Bosnia, Lizzie? Did you see him?'

Lizzie nodded. 'Mmm, pleased to be back. They both were.'

'Was he changed?'

'He was thinner. He'd been ill, I think.'

'Nothing else?' Kavanagh said. 'Moody . . . ?'

'No,' Lizzie said, 'I didn't notice anything . . .' She thought for a moment. 'There was one thing, though . . .'

'Yes?'

'It was something Angela said when we were down the other weekend. "You know how jolly and silly Edgar's always been?" she said, and looked a bit worried. "Well, he seems to be turning into something of a solitary. Keeps disappearing into his room for hours at a time. Mrs Jenkins can hardly get in there to clean."'

Kavanagh called in at chambers before meeting up with Alex the following morning.

'Didn't expect to see you, sir,' Tom Buckley said. 'Hear you've had a few late nights.'

'Not so late or so many as poor old Dartwood,' Kavanagh said. 'And nothing to eat except stale cheese sandwiches, he tells me.'

'Do him good,' Tom said. 'Got a message for you, sir . . .'

'Oh?'

'A lady,' Tom said. 'Told me to tell you that if you were ever in the vicinity of Cobham and needing something in the soft fruit line, you should drop in. Meadows' Soft Fruits and Culinary Roots, she calls it. It's a sort of garden centre.'

'Sarah Meadows,' Kavanagh said. 'Well, good for her.' Being a barrister, he'd always thought, was rather like being a psychiatrist. You became, briefly, so closely and intensely involved in people's lives that they often found it difficult to let you go. He still had clients from his early days at the Bar who wrote to him out of the past to tell him how their grandchildren were getting on. Sarah Meadows . . . he'd really admired that woman's courage. Maybe he and Lizzie would call in one day. 'She was keen on gardening, I seem to remember,' he said. 'One of the things she resented most about that dreadful husband of hers was that he once trod on one of her precious plants.' He took a handful of letters out of his pigeonhole and picked up his morning papers. 'Well, well,' he said. 'A garden centre . . .'

'No, Mr Kavanagh,' Tom said. 'Not a garden centre. She was most particular you wouldn't be able to buy a rosebush there, we'll say, or a daff or anything except soft fruit and culinary roots, whatever they might be when they're at home.'

'Thanks, Tom,' Kavanagh said. 'I'll remember that.'

'And another thing,' Tom said.

Kavanagh looked at his watch. 'I do have to be in court . . .'

'Just thought you'd be interested,' Tom said, 'that's all . . .'

'Well, go on, then,' Kavanagh said.

'It's the other lady in that case, Mr Aldermarten's client, the one who killed Mrs Meadows' husband . . .'

'Hilary Jameson,' James said. 'The one who *didn't* kill Mrs Meadows' husband . . .'

'Seems they've kept in touch,' Tom said. 'Mrs Meadows says she's gone back to her old man. Italian bloke, as I understand it, lives in Syracuse. She said she thought you'd like to know that.'

James picked up at taxi outside chambers, shut the communicating window, and sat back. He hoped Hilary Jameson had not returned to her husband by default, as it were, because she'd been unable to get another hospital post in England. It seemed unlikely. Like Sarah Meadows she was a strong woman and quite capable of running her life without a man. He dug into his pocket for his wallet and thought, I'm doing it again. Thinking about past clients when I should be concentrating on the current case.

He paid off the taxi and met up with Alex outside the courtroom. 'Any progress?'

Alex shook her head. 'I have an idea but I can't be sure. Nobody can tell us if he can't.'

'Or won't,' Kavanagh said. 'There's always that.'

'No, no, I don't think so,' Alex said slowly. 'But the scenario as I see it, and it really is only an impression I've got from watching his subtle reactions to my questions and suggestions, is that his brother was going to shoot himself, Edgar tried to stop him, they struggled over the gun and it went off.'

'And we don't know who pulled the trigger?'

Alex shook her head.

'Cole says he could start to talk at any time,' Kavanagh said grimly. 'We must hope that he doesn't because he'll confess to something I'm sure we both know he didn't do.'

They entered the courtroom. It was the same cast as for the previous trial, except for the jury. As Alex and Kavanagh took their seats, the clerk read out the murder charge to the new jurors. And then Miss Haddon stood and addressed the judge.

'May it please you, my Lord?'

Mr Justice Carteris nodded. 'Yes, Miss Haddon.'

'The two brothers went rook-shooting together at approximately eleven o'clock . . .' she began.

Kavanagh glanced over at Edgar, who was leaning on the rail, listening intently.

157

'. . . while their father, the Reverend Beddoes, was conducting a service attended by his daughter, Angela. Gemma, the wife of the victim, was alone in the house preparing lunch. She will tell you she saw the two brothers leave the house and, so it appeared to her, arguing vehemently . . .'

Angela Beddoes and her father were sitting on a bench outside the court. Angela was trying very hard not to look at Gemma, who was sitting on another bench across the corridor from them. Angela was hoping, with every fibre of her being, that her father would show the same restraint. Luckily, his attention had been sidetracked by Inspector Judd and Sergeant Spiridion, who were sitting next to him, and he was far too busy giving them his opinion on sloppy police procedures to bother with his daughter-in-law. Angela assumed that the man at her side was also a witness. He had extremely short fair hair, and a pugnacious, fascist look to him which she found unattractive.

She watched with interest as a large black man in a leather bomber jacket and jeans bounded up the stairs, looked around and then made straight for them.

He stopped in front of her neighbour. 'Sarn't-Major?'

The fascist character, who, Angela now realised, was a member of the armed forces, leaped up in surprise. 'Adams?'

'S'right.' Dave beamed. 'Private Adams, witness for the defence.'

The sergeant-major scowled at him. 'You can call me "sir". Must be all up with the padre if he's asked you to give him a character.'

'Saved my life, didn't he, Sarn't-Major?' Dave said.

'Well, there really is no accounting for taste, is there?' the sergeant-major said sourly.

At that moment Inspector Judd was called away from

Matthew Beddoes' harangue into the relative sanctuary of the witness box.

Miss Haddon questioned him about Edgar's alleged confession, he described the circumstances leading up to Edgar writing 'Guilty' on a piece of paper, and Exhibit 5, an evidence bag containing the piece of paper, was waved around the court for everyone to see before it was positively identified by the inspector.

The inspector had an easy ride until James Kavanagh got up to cross-examine him. 'Inspector, how did my client behave when you questioned him?'

'He resolutely said nothing.'

'Resolutely? Do you suggest he was simply refusing questions?'

The inspector, standing stiffly to attention, said: 'I'm not qualified to say, sir.'

'Come now, Inspector,' Kavanagh said in a deceptively gentle tone, 'you've had people refuse to answer questions, surely? How do they refuse?'

'They usually say "No comment" or something like that. Or they give you a "look".'

'Ah.' Kavanagh glanced over at Edgar and then back at the inspector. 'Did my client give you a "look"?'

'He did not,' the inspector replied.

'Not any kind of a look?'

'Not a knowing look, I have to say that, no.'

Kavanagh took a deep breath. 'You first thought the deceased had killed himself, didn't you?'

Miss Haddon was instantly alert, as the inspector agreed that yes, that was so.

'Did you know that the deceased was facing trial?'

'Yes, sir.'

'A long, complicated trial with the possibility of prison if he were to be found guilty?'

'I believe so,' the inspector said, 'although I've no knowledge of the case.'

Kavanagh stared around the courtroom disbelievingly. 'You must be one of very few in the country who could say that. Don't you read the newspapers?'

'That appears to be so,' the inspector answered stoutly.

'It does,' Kavanagh agreed. 'Everybody else had my client's brother hanged, drawn, quartered and sequestrate – by way of informed comment in newspapers. I don't wonder you thought he might have taken his own life.'

On the same morning, in another courtroom on the other side of London, Jeremy Aldermarten was expounding on the morality of his client. 'My . . . my client comes before you *rectus in curia*, upright with . . . with . . .' He faltered. Mr Justice Way was shifting in his seat, darting looks around the room, giving little dry coughs. It was clear to Aldermarten that he had lost Way J's attention.

The judge looked at his watch and then at the barrister. 'I think we might adjourn . . . until tomorrow at half past ten, Mr Aldermarten.'

Aldermarten glanced quickly at the wall clock which read twenty past ten. The court had been sitting for only twenty minutes. 'Oh,' he said, nonplussed, and sat down.

'Court rise,' called the clerk, and Aldermarten jumped up. As Mr Justice Way exited, he turned to Charles Beaufort. 'Tomorrow? Did he say tomorrow?' Charles nodded and Aldermarten sank back in his seat.

'Court rise.' The clerk, a professional to his fingertips, had spotted Mr Justice Way re-entering the courtroom. They all stood and bowed as the judge resumed his seat on the bench. He bowed back to them graciously. They sat down again tentatively.

'Mr Aldermarten?'

Aldermarten leaped to his feet. 'My Lord.'

'Do you prosecute?'

'I do, my Lord . . .' Aldermarten began, and then groaned. No, no, that was the other case. 'N-no . . . n-no,' he stammered. 'I mean, no.'

Mr Justice Way smiled down at him kindly. 'I am delighted to welcome you in Silk, Mr Aldermarten.'

Aldermarten turned to Charles Beaufort, who appeared to be choking behind him. 'This can't go on,' he said.

'This can't go on, Peter,' Aldermarten said. He had told Peter Foxcott about his undignified and baffling half-hour in court, and they were now sharing a pre-luncheon dry sherry in Foxcott's room and discussing the matter. 'It brings the court into disrepute.'

'This was beyond a joke, then?' Foxcott sipped his sherry and clutched at a possible straw.

'Joke?' Aldermarten said. 'It was a farce. The court jumping up and down like a Bluebelle troupe. As Head of Chambers it really is up to you to take the matter in hand.'

'One had rather hoped to avoid this sort of thing when they brought in the age limit,' Foxcott said.

'Oh, Way J isn't *old*.' Aldermarten was still quivering resentfully. 'Way J is off his perch, out to lunch.'

'Lunch,' Foxcott said. 'That's a thought. Perhaps I could invite him to lunch, we could have a little chat . . .'

'Yes, yes,' Aldermarten said. 'Do it now. Ring him. See if he's free tomorrow.'

'Oh, come now,' Foxcott said, anxious to postpone the ordeal for as long as he could, possibly for ever. 'One mustn't be too hasty.'

'One can't be hasty enough,' Aldermarten insisted. 'Not unless you want to make a laughing-stock of the whole legal profession. What if the press gets to hear of it?'

Foxcott put a hand to his head. 'The media . . .' He looked sideways at Aldermarten. 'You wouldn't?'

'No, well, of course not,' Aldermarten said. 'But things do have a way of leaking out . . .'

Foxcott picked up the telephone.

Inspector Judd had stood down and Sergeant Spiridion had taken his place in the witness box.

Miss Haddon addressed him. 'As a man of experience, as both policeman and countryman, what is the weapon of choice in suicide?'

'Often a shotgun, ma'am. A twelve-bore.'

'Yes.' Miss Haddon glanced over at the jury. 'If the jury care to look at Exhibit Seven, they will see a twelve-bore shotgun left on a chair.' The jurors passed along a photograph of the shotgun Miles had left on the study chair in the Old Rectory. 'What would have happened had the weapon used been a shotgun, Sergeant Spiridion?'

The sergeant chuckled. 'Well, we'd be looking up in the rookery for his brains.'

'Thank you, Sergeant Spiridion,' Miss Haddon said, sitting down.

Kavanagh stood up and gazed at Sergeant Spiridion with mock courtesy. 'I, too, thank you for your graphic description of a shotgun blast. Was the weapon used to actually kill Miles Beddoes any less effective?'

'Obviously not, sir,' the sergeant said.

Kavanagh gave Miss Haddon a challenging glance. 'Quite,' he said.

Gemma thought it had been the loneliest day of her life. Sitting by herself on a bench in a bleak corridor, waiting

162

with trepidation to give evidence against a brother-in-law she had always admired; evidence she wasn't sure she wanted to give anyway. But it seemed to her that, for the sake of the boys, it was her duty to discover the truth. Their father was dishonest, definitely. A fraudster, certainly. But he had courage, too, and charm. She hated him for what he'd done to her, the boys, her father . . . but she wouldn't have him wronged. Miles was a fighter, not a quitter. Edgar had admitted his guilt, had actually told her – and Angela – that he had killed Miles. Who, besides Angela, could possibly argue with that? She looked over at Angela, who glanced quickly away. One of the worst things about this whole ghastly business, she thought, was losing Angela's friendship.

There was another reason, too, why she wasn't prepared to connive at the falsehood of Miles's suicide. Money. Not for herself – she didn't give a damn. Her father would make sure that she always had enough to get by. But what about the boys? Miles had always lived life to the hilt, spending as much as he earned, confident that there would always be new deals to be made, more cash flowing in. By the time she had paid back the pensioners, which she fully intended to do, there wouldn't be much left in the bank. The insurance company, she knew, would be unlikely to pay out for a suicide. Gemma sighed heavily. She loved Angela and Edgar, but she loved her sons more. She didn't see how she could sacrifice their inheritance to save Edgar from what, she truly believed, was a momentary act of madness, fuelled, she was convinced, by a large helping of sibling rivalry and self-preservation.

She looked up as the usher came over to her. 'Mrs Beddoes, they're ready for you now.'

Gemma got up with a heavy heart and followed the usher into the courtroom. She was sworn in and Miss Haddon began the cross-examination by asking her why she had gone to the police.

Gemma smiled nervously. 'We got Edgar up to his room after . . . well, after, and they said he was to see a doctor because he was too shocked to speak.' She knew exactly what she wanted to say, but for some strange reason it came out in a whisper. 'I then realised that nothing had been said by any of us when he came back with the bloody gun . . . I mean, there was blood on it.'

Mr Justice Carteris eyed Gemma sternly. 'Please speak up, Mrs Beddoes.'

Miss Haddon inclined her head to the judge – 'Grateful, my Lord' – and turned to Gemma. 'Yes, so what did you do then, Mrs Beddoes?'

'I went to the police and told them what Edgar had said.'

'Yes.' Miss Haddon looked down at her notes and read aloud: ' "He's dead. I just shot him, dead. Miles, I mean. I killed him. Dead." ' She looked up.

'Yes,' Gemma said.

'Yes,' Miss Haddon repeated. 'Mrs Beddoes, do you recognise this manuscript?' A clerk hurried over to Gemma and handed her Miles's manuscript, and Miss Haddon turned to the judge. 'Exhibit Six, my Lord.'

'It is a book written by my husband,' Gemma said.

'Will you read the marked passage on page one hundred and two.'

Mr Justice Carteris reached for his copy of the script and said to Gemma, 'Yes, and, er, will you speak up?'

Gemma cleared her throat. 'Yes.'

'Yes?' Miss Haddon queried.

'Yes, I will speak up.' Gemma turned to page one hundred and two, cleared her throat again and began reading. ' "The delicious irony is that Edgar very nearly got the Military

Cross for rescuing us from a watery grave and leading us through a minefield. Poor old, dear old Edgar needed it more than I did, seconded as he was from the TA and a total misfit as a padre . . ."' Kavanagh looked over at Edgar to see how he was taking this. He appeared to be smiling. ' ". . . wrong background entirely amongst a bunch of thugs like us. We need priests who have more cred than we have, not less; won't listen else."' Gemma smiled slightly. She could almost hear Miles saying that. ' "As it happened,"' she continued, ' "when he got his mention in despatches, he shot up in estimation and ended his tour in fat glory and acceptance, so it was well worth doing. Only Edgar and I know the truth of it."'

'What did you do when you read that for the first time, Mrs Beddoes?' Miss Haddon asked.

'I went to the police,' Gemma said.

'Why?'

Gemma looked down at the manuscript in her hand. 'Because Edgar had written in the margin, "You sod, I'll kill you."'

Miss Haddon smiled. 'Thank you, Mrs Beddoes.'

Mr Justice Carteris gestured to Gemma to stay where she was.

'If you will just wait, er, Mrs Beddoes.' He turned to Kavanagh.

'Mr Kavanagh?'

Kavanagh got to his feet, put on his spectacles and nodded to the judge. 'Thank you, my Lord.' He studied Gemma Beddoes in the witness box. She seemed a decent woman and would probably have been better off married to Edgar Beddoes than to his duplicitous brother. He glanced over at Edgar, upright and clean-shaven in the dock, and then back at Gemma, all tumbling auburn hair and freckles. He'd lost count of the number of villains he'd defended who turned out to be married to charming, kind, good women . . . and it worked the other way, too. He'd once defended a triple murderess whose husband, on his days off, regularly drove under-privileged kids to the seaside in a Sunshine bus. 'Now, Mrs Beddoes,' he said. 'You say the defendant said . . .' He glanced at a piece of paper in his hand. '. . . "He's dead, I just shot him, dead. Miles, I mean. I killed him. Dead." Is that correct?'

Gemma nodded. 'Yes.'

'Do you think he meant it?'

'Of course. I saw the body.'

'No,' Kavanagh said. 'Do you think he meant he had murdered his brother?'

Gemma shrugged. 'It seems the same to me.'

'I see.' Kavanagh paused long enough to make Gemma feel uneasy.

'Mrs Beddoes, do you have children?'

'Yes,' Gemma said. 'Two boys.'

'Brothers. Do they fight?'

Gemma smiled. 'Yes, of course. They're normal, healthy children.'

'Do they hurl insults at each other? Say things like, "I'll kill you for that."'

Miss Haddon looked sharply at Gemma who said: 'No. No, I mean they don't *mean* it.'

Kavanagh chuckled. 'No . . . they don't, I'm sure, mean that they will commit murder.' He smiled at Gemma, content with the exchange. 'Thank you, Mrs Beddoes.'

Miss Haddon sprang to her feet. 'Mrs Beddoes, your husband is killed and somebody tells you he killed him. Would you not know what he meant, and would you not remember every word used for the rest of your life . . . ?'

'My Lord,' Kavanagh protested.

166

'Would you remember that or not?' Miss Haddon persisted.

Gemma nodded. 'Yes, I would. I did.'

'Would this be a convenient moment, Miss Haddon?' Mr Justice Carteris enquired. Miss Haddon indicated that it would, and the court rose.

'*Most* convenient for Miss Haddon,' Kavanagh said to Alex as they came out into the corridor. 'I was hoping to call David Adams.'

'Tomorrow, then,' Alex said.

Kavanagh sighed. 'Yes, tomorrow. Did you notice Edgar's expression when that passage from the book was read out?'

'He was smiling,' Alex said. 'He thought it was funny.'

'He didn't give a damn,' Kavanagh said.

Alex stepped aside as the crowd surged out of the courtroom.

'He wants guilt heaped on him,' she said. 'He twists it in his heart. He wants to be punished for something.'

'Yes,' Kavanagh said, 'but it's not this, Alex. He's using this to scourge himself. It's not this. He's not the least affected by this, by any of us. No, he'll go to prison because he wants to – and not for killing his brother.'

At that moment, Miss Haddon and her junior, Robert Turner, passed by them. 'I hear Miss Wilson has your client talking to her nineteen to the dozen,' Miss Haddon said.

Alex smiled at her. 'Not quite.'

Turner nudged her. 'Does he speak in tongues, Alex?'

Alex regarded him coldly. 'Are you a Christian, Robert?'

Turner shifted uneasily. 'Well . . . yes, I . . . I suppose so.'

'I don't suppose so, I am,' Alex said.

Turner grinned at Miss Haddon. 'Sorry,' he said to Alex, but she had already swept off.

Miss Haddon and her junior nodded to Kavanagh and disappeared down the corridor. Kavanagh looked at his watch. Nice and early, for once. He wandered off towards the barristers' room to disrobe. If Lizzie's home, he thought, we might go to that new thing at the Odeon, and then go on somewhere afterwards for a bite to eat. She'd enjoy that.

18

Jeremy Aldermarten was having a most pleasant morning. His case had been adjourned until the following week. Mr Justice Way, Tom Buckley had informed him, with a wink, was indisposed and a new judge had to be found and sworn in.

He dropped in on Peter Foxcott for coffee, first thing, and was relieved to hear that Foxcott and Way J were lunching that very day.

'I got the impression he was quite anxious to talk to someone,' Foxcott said gloomily. His quiet, old-fashioned courtesy and gentle smile encouraged people to confide in him. He wished it weren't so. 'I understand he told the Clerk of the Court that he was a bit under the weather and, in the circumstances, didn't feel he could continue with the case.'

'On this occasion, he was correct,' Aldermarten said.

'I thought Simpsons in the Strand,' Foxcott said. 'Discreet. There's always a quiet corner where one can talk in peace.'

'Most appropriate,' Aldermarten said.

They discussed chambers matters for half an hour or so. 'How is Miss Ames coming along?' Foxcott said. 'I seem to recall that you wanted me to have a word with her . . . what was it? Something about her not fitting in at River Court?'

'No, no,' Aldermarten said quickly. 'All in the past, Peter. She's doing splendidly.' Helen Ames had not only arranged for one of her solicitors to pass him a plum job, she'd spotted him outside court yesterday and been most complimentary about his new wig. Funny thing about women. They noticed things like that. None of his male colleagues had made reference to it at all.

Leaving Foxcott, he returned to his office and went conscientiously through his papers and correspondence and upcoming briefs; it wasn't often he had time for such an indulgence. He glanced at the Beddoes files in the corner and was just considering that he might well call Gary and make another attempt at disposing of them when, by a curious coincidence, he received a phone call from the really quite distinguished publishers who had been about to publish Miles Beddoes' book, before his unfortunate demise.

'We had a meeting here yesterday, Mr Aldermarten, and decided to go ahead with publication,' the editor said. 'There's a feeling we might be able to cash in . . . well, take advantage of the public interest in his brother's trial . . .'

'Quite,' Aldermarten said. 'I'm sure Mrs Beddoes will be absolutely delighted to know you're still of a mind to publish her husband's book. She does need the money.'

'There's just one small problem,' the editor said. 'I've been taking another look at the manuscript and we don't seem to have the final chapter. We've looked around here. We wondered if perhaps you . . . ?'

Aldermarten thought for a moment. 'Um . . .' He remembered the envelope he'd lightly tossed aside. 'Mmm, yes, I do recall him sending me the last chapter. I'll send it on to you.'

'Splendid,' the editor said. 'We'll look forward to receiving it, then.'

Aldermarten was just about to murmur something suitable and put down the phone when the editor said: 'Is there anything dramatic or, er, controversial in that last chapter? Only I was reading Chapter Nine yesterday and it did seem to be leading up to some sort of intriguing dénouement.'

'Well,' Aldermarten said. 'I haven't actually read it all ... just skipped through it for libel and so on ...' It wouldn't do to admit that he had barely turned a page. He thought for a moment. He hadn't read the rest of the book, either. Perhaps ...? 'Um, am I referred to, um, by any chance at all?'

The editor told him to hold on a sec, and then read him out a passage that Aldermarten considered highly inaccurate if not actually libellous.

'I see,' he said coldly. 'Well, thank you. I did my best.'

He slammed down the phone. Bloody nerve, he said to himself. Now where did I put that envelope? It took him some time to find it. He went through each of the box files twice and then remembered that when Gary was trolleying them to and fro it had been lying on the top. He peered down behind the trolley and there it was, lying on the floor by the wall. He picked it up, took it over to his desk, opened the envelope and read the contents carefully.

He arrived at the final page, and Miles' handwritten note at the bottom. The writing was appalling but, when Aldermarten eventually managed to decipher it, he sat back in his chair, his eyes widening in astonishment. 'Good Lord!' He lowered the manuscript and considered the matter. Now what, he asked himself, has Kavanagh ever done for me?

He studied his gold cuff links, an uncharacteristically witty birthday present from his mother. The left cuff link had 'Yes' engraved upon it, the right had 'No'. He looked from one to the other. '*Yes*.'

Aldermarten dashed along to the clerks' office, where Tom was sitting reading an early edition of the *Evening Standard*. He tapped one of the pages and looked up at Aldermarten. 'Looks as though Mr Kavanagh's up the creek without a paddle on this one, sir.'

'Never mind about that,' Aldermarten said. 'Where's Gary?'

'Just gone out, sir, this minute, to purchase some sandwiches . . .'

Aldermarten darted into the courtyard and caught up with Gary as he was disappearing through the arch. 'Gary.' He thrust the envelope into his hands. 'I want you to go and deliver this to Mr Kavanagh or Miss Wilson. Now. Go as fast as you possibly can. It's really extremely urgent.' Gary looked at the envelope and then looked open-mouthed at Mr Aldermarten. He'd never seen him in such a stew. Aldermarten gave him a shove in the back. 'Run, run. What are you waiting for? Chop-chop . . .'

Gary sped on his way and Aldermarten turned to go back to his office. He did a double-take and dived into a doorway as he saw Peter Foxcott and Mr Justice Way approaching him across the courtyard. He remained there until they were safely out of sight.

'I think Simpsons in the Strand . . . don't you?' Foxcott said to Mr Justice Way, as they strolled along.

'Very kind, Peter,' the judge said. 'Nice thought. We have to eat meat when we can and there, I declare, they positively flaunt it.'

'Mmm.' Foxcott nodded. 'My lot won't have it in the house. They think of me, they tell me.'

'It's a damned disease ... vegetable-ism,' the judge said.

Foxcott chuckled. 'Indeed. Taxi or ... ?'

'Oh, Shanks' pony, I think.'

It took them about a quarter of an hour to get to Simpsons, where the head waiter led them to a quiet table in a corner. He settled them in, pushed the table about a bit to please, and swathed their knees in damask napkins. Then he stepped back and addressed them. 'Good afternoon, gentlemen. I have toad-in-the-hole, I have bubble and squeak, I have Dover sole, very special today.'

Foxcott looked at John Way. 'What do you say to that?'

He thought he discerned a glint of devilment in the judge's eye as he looked up at the head waiter. 'I say lamb chops.'

'I say lamb chops as well,' Foxcott said.

The waiter narrowed his eyes and thinned his lips. 'Very good. And how do you like your lamb?'

'Medium rare, I think,' John Way said.

Foxcott nodded. 'And medium rare for me, too.'

They chatted idly about this and that and then the judge suddenly gazed at Foxcott across the table, in a way that made him shift slightly in his chair, and said: 'Why are we here?'

'You're a friend, John,' Foxcott said.

'What else?'

No good prevaricating, Foxcott thought to himself. Frankness is always the most prudent course in these matters. 'Are you quite ... well?'

John Way hesitated only briefly. 'No, Peter, I am not well.'

173

'Ah.' Foxcott looked up gratefully at the sommelier, who had appeared at his elbow with the wine list. 'Will you have some wine?'

Mr Justice Way didn't prevaricate either. 'Yes,' he said.

Foxcott turned to the sommelier. 'Then we'll have the claret you gave me yesterday.'

The sommelier bowed, left them and returned almost immediately with a bottle of claret. He made rather a performance of pulling the cork and sniffing it. Foxcott noticed that John Way appeared to be getting agitated. And when the sommelier poured some wine into the spoon around his neck and then sipped it and rolled it around his mouth in a knowing sort of way, he was alarmed to see Way taking off his spectacles, leaning back and closing his eyes. Almost as though, Foxcott thought, he wanted to disassociate himself from the charade.

The sommelier filled their glasses and Foxcott picked his up. 'John?' he said tentatively.

John Way opened his eyes. 'I think I'm becoming obsessed, Peter.'

'Ah?' Foxcott ventured.

'It was as much as I could do not to knock that pompous waiter down. All part of the same thing, you know, the furbelows. That damn silly spoon thing – the accoutrements and the rituals are everywhere becoming tedious, irritating and painful to me.'

'I see,' Foxcott said, not seeing at all.

'Is that true of you?' Way put on his spectacles and gazed at him. 'In which case it is simply a question of age. Or are you still content to sport your wig and your conceit and let that be that?'

Foxcott chuckled. 'Ah, there you are. An argument.' He sighed with relief; he knew where he was with an argument. 'I thought it might be.'

He looked up and nodded appreciatively at the head waiter as he placed a plate of medium-rare lamb chops in front of each of them. They looked jolly good to him. He was astonished when John Way leaped to his feet and glared at the chops as though he'd been slipped a dish of poison.

'That is not what I ordered,' he said.

'It *is* the lamb, sir,' the waiter said.

Foxcott looked at the chops and then at John Way. 'It *is* the lamb, yes,' he confirmed.

'It is not what I ordered. Not at all.' John Way threw down his napkin and stormed off.

Foxcott looked apologetically at the waiter. 'So sorry,' he said. 'Er . . . my friend . . . not well. Just put it on my bill, will you . . . I'll settle up . . .'

The head waiter gave him a small smile. He was unaccustomed to this sort of behaviour in his restaurant. 'No problem, sir,' he said.

Foxcott gave his lamb chops a fond, lingering look and then put down his napkin, rose and followed John Way out into the street. They walked in silence back towards the Temple. In a small courtyard Mr Justice Way paused in front of an empty bench. 'Shall we?'

'By all means,' Foxcott said.

They sat down next to each other, and John Way said slowly and thoughtfully: 'Every time an innocent man is convicted, a guilty man goes free. Two kinds of people are injured by crime – the victim and those who are innocent but accused, who face damning evidence against them which has been constructed, cooked up. And to their horror they may find that their lawyers are either useless or completely indifferent . . .'

Foxcott demurred. 'Oh, come, John, these are strong words.'

'And I mean them,' John Way said. 'The huge numbers caught up in the mill of the law mean that nobody has the time to seek out, to test, to present any *real* argument. Hmm?' He looked for confirmation, but Peter was keeping his head well down. 'Nobody cares about lying any more,' the judge continued. 'It's done with a smile, a smirk, and catch me out if you can. Nobody gives a damn. The police certainly don't care about doing it. And it is more and more obvious to me that we are following on, some of us, lawyers . . . judges, even . . .'

Foxcott thought this was going a bit far. 'But . . .' he began.

John Way held up a hand. 'No, Peter. Hear me out. I look at them, us, we, them, me, them, in their intimidating wigs, robes. At mountebanks like Aldermarten.'

'Ah . . .' Now Foxcott felt he must intervene.

'Oh, he's in your chambers, isn't he?'

'He's a very good barrister,' Foxcott said loyally. 'I have a lot of time for him. He's also a friend. I can't let you say that, John.'

John Way gave a kind of hrrmph of acknowledgment. 'You may be right, he's no worse than the rest of you, them, us. He glares so and shoots his cuffs, all that, all of it, and their ritual, our ritual.' His voice rose as he said: 'This is no way to find truth. This is no way to reward evil and virtue.' He looked at Foxcott questioningly and added quietly, 'We're getting it all wrong, you know.'

'Not all of it, surely?' Foxcott said mildly.

John Way got up abruptly and turned to Foxcott as he rose to follow him. 'What?'

'Not everything?'

'Oh, yes,' John Way said. 'Everything. Mr Foxcott, I would be grateful for your help.'

They walked on together towards River Court. 'What can I do to help?' Foxcott asked.

'Will you tell people . . .'

It was a request but Foxcott interpreted it as a question. 'Yes,' he said regretfully, 'I shall have to, John.'

'Good,' said John Way. 'I want you to. I know what's happening to me and I hate it.' He turned to Foxcott. 'I hate it because it means that nobody will listen when I talk about my worries. You *have* listened. Do you take me seriously, Peter?'

Foxcott was profoundly moved. 'I have, John,' he said. 'I do.'

19

It occurred to James Kavanagh that Edgar Beddoes disliked
Regimental Sergeant-Major Brown as much as he was
capable of disliking any human being. He didn't scowl
or frown at the RSM standing to attention in the witness
box. His reactions were more oblique. During the trial,
Kavanagh had seen Edgar bored, disengaged, interested and,
occasionally, absorbed. Now, as RSM Brown responded
to questions in the traditional military manner, his back
straightening briskly and his head jerking back as he
released a volley of short, clipped sentences, Edgar was
fidgeting restlessly in his seat and darting quick glances
around the ceiling cornice as though seeking an escape
from the sergeant's rasping voice.

Kavanagh wondered whether it was the sergeant or what
he represented which caused Edgar such disquiet.

He turned back to RSM Brown. 'Can you tell us,
Sergeant, how the padre got on with his men? How they
regarded him?'

RSM Brown loosened up; his voice became confidential
and matey. 'Well, to be honest, sir, he wasn't the best
liked of padres. He was apt to be disliked by the men.
Like many Territorial Army secondments, he was far too

interested in playing at soldiers.' The sergeant glanced at Edgar and pursed his lips. 'Very eager, very warry. It's not on for a padre. It wasn't till after he got his citation that he came into his own, as it were. Well, he was accepted. He did some very good work. It was the making of him.'

Kavanagh had been keeping an eye on Edgar during this exchange and noticed that although he did not seem at all put out at being labelled unpopular, he appeared to resent the RSM's final, grudging approval.

Brown then left the witness box and Private David Adams took his place. He gazed at Edgar devotedly as he was sworn in and put through the formal preliminary questions.

Kavanagh asked him if he recognised the man in the dock and Private Adams looked back at him open-mouthed, as though he'd like to reply, 'What a daft question.' Instead he said: 'He saved my life.'

Kavanagh smiled encouragingly. 'And how did he do that?'

'He got me out of a river. They were firing at us, the bank was mined. He just dragged me out.'

'Private Adams,' Kavanagh said, 'will you tell the jury how it came to happen that you were in the river?'

'Yeah.' Dave looked admiringly at Edgar again. 'It was night, we were going over a bridge which was mined. The vehicle was blown into the river. I was thrown clear, the padre as well ... all of us. The driver got it. Drowned.'

Kavanagh took a deep breath. 'And where was Miles Beddoes?'

'The padre got him out, too.'

Kavanagh relaxed and, glancing around the courtroom, caught the disbelieving eye of Gemma Beddoes. 'What happened then?'

'We all went up to the village.'

'What happened there?'

'Well, it was winter, wasn't it. I was cold, I got pneumonia. Nearly died. I'd have died a lot sooner if he hadn't got me out.'

'What did you do in the village?'

Dave grinned. 'Shiver.'

'What did Edgar Beddoes do?' Kavanagh looked briefly at the accused. He was so still he might almost have stopped breathing.

'Well, he shouldn't have done it,' Dave said. 'They tried to stop him. He looked into the cellar. Not something we hadn't seen before but, er . . .' He nodded towards Edgar, who had closed his eyes. '. . . he hadn't.'

'And what was it he saw?' Kavanagh said.

'Oh, you know,' Dave said. 'Bodies. You've seen it on the telly. Happened all the time.'

'What did he do?'

'Went down on his knees and prayed,' Dave said. 'Then he just fainted . . . clean away . . . toppled into the cellar.'

'Thank you, Mr Adams,' Kavanagh said. As he sat down he saw Colin Dartwood come in and tap Alex on the shoulder. Mystified, he watched her react with surprise and then follow Dartwood out of the courtroom.

Mr Justice Carteris made some notes on his pad, and nodded to Miss Haddon to cross-examine.

'Are you certain it was Edgar Beddoes who pulled you from the water and then pulled out his brother?'

'He pulled us out together,' Dave said. 'We all ended up on the bank, together.'

'In the dark?'

'Yeah.'

Miss Haddon said drily: 'Half drowned, cold, dark, but you're certain it was him?'

'Absolutely.'

'Why?'

'Well, it said so in the citation,' Dave said.

Miss Haddon smirked. 'Oh, yes. It did, didn't it? Thank you very much, Mr Adams.'

The clerk gestured for Dave to stand down, and he looked around hesitantly before grinning at Edgar and walking jauntily out of the courtroom.

Kavanagh maintained a façade of cool confidence. Clearly Adams was unaware that he'd blown it. He hoped the jury were equally unaware. In fact, he had not been surprised by Miss Haddon's line of questioning. He'd been more surprised when the soldier had appeared out of nowhere with an apparently cast-iron eye-witness account of Edgar's heroic actions. From what he had learned about the disparate characters of the two brothers, he had already concluded that it would be more like Miles to react swiftly and courageously in such an emergency.

'Poor old, dear old Edgar needed it more than I did . . .' Miles had written. Kavanagh sighed. The wrong brother might have got the citation but that didn't make him a murderer. It was obvious that Edgar Beddoes didn't give a damn about the citation or his reputation.

Dave stepped out into the corridor and ran into Alex, who had just received Jeremy Aldermarten's package.

She waved at him. 'All right, Dave?'

Dave gave her the thumbs-up. 'Never better, Miss Wilson.'

'Great.' Alex smiled, went over to an empty bench, sat down and tore open the package. Attached to an envelope inside it was a sheet torn from a memo pad. 'Kavanagh – you owe me one. J.A.' She opened the envelope and pulled out Miles Beddoes's final chapter. She read it slowly and carefully, and when she came to the final handwritten message she rose swiftly and returned to the courtroom.

She saw that Matthew Beddoes was already in the witness box, once again behaving as though he were in charge of the proceedings. He was waving away the clerk, who was trying to hand him the Bible. 'I wish to affirm.'

Mr Justice Carteris glared at him. 'What religion is it that permits you to wear a clerical collar yet not take an oath on the Holy Bible?'

'I've lost my belief in God,' Matthew boomed. Angela, sitting near by, groaned audibly. 'Might I respectfully point out that, in my opinion, a clerical collar, like a uniform or a judge's wig, is not necessarily evidence of faith, courage or justice.'

Mr Justice Carteris regarded Matthew Beddoes with dislike and was about to call him to order when he saw Kavanagh rising to his feet. 'Mr Kavanagh?'

'My Lord, there has been an unusual development,' Kavanagh said. 'I ask Your Lordship's leave not to examine the Reverend Matthew Beddoes at this time.'

Matthew scourged the court with his gaze, as though they were his parishioners. 'Nevertheless, I shall speak.'

Mr Justice Carteris leaned towards him. 'You shall *not*, Mr Beddoes,' he hissed.

Angela almost cheered. She looked across to the dock to share the moment with Edgar, but he seemed bemused. Mr James Carteris adjourned the court and indicated to

Kavanagh and Miss Haddon that he wished them to follow him into his antechamber. Edgar gazed anxiously after them. Whatever the 'unusual development' might be, it seemed to Angela that her brother didn't welcome it.

Ten minutes later, the court resumed proceedings. Mr Justice Carteris picked up Miles's final chapter and handed it to a clerk, who handed it to a second clerk, who handed it to Miss Haddon. She put on her spectacles and studied the handwritten footnote.

'Miss Haddon,' the judge said, 'does the prosecution accept that this evidence is in the handwriting of the deceased?'

'Yes, my Lord.' Miss Haddon removed her spectacles and passed the chapter on to Kavanagh.

Kavanagh put on his spectacles. 'The envelope is date-stamped June the ninth. Postmarked Oxford. The day Miles Beddoes died.' He turned to the jury. 'This is what he wrote. "I hope those who read this will understand that I have no intention of being around when they read it. Their faces, I can see their faces. The shock, anger, fear. But I am gone. I am dead. A victim of self-murder."' Kavanagh looked up. '"Bang. Signed, Miles."'

There was a stunned silence and then a sudden babble of excitement in the court. Angela looked to see how Edgar had taken it, but he was slumped in his chair, his face buried in his hands.

The jury were out for no longer than half an hour. Just long enough, Angela thought, as she took her seat in court, for them to drink a cup of coffee, go to the loo and have a sandwich or a cigarette. They wouldn't have needed much discussion – the verdict was a foregone conclusion. She'd brought a book with her, the one

184

Edgar had been reading the day Miles died. Angela had read it, too, and by the time she'd reached page eighty, she had come to the conclusion that Edgar, who, she felt sure, wanted to be found guilty, had used the book as a crib. It contained a vivid, almost textbook description of catatonic shock. Now, however, she wasn't so sure. She'd been watching him in court. She'd seen him opening and shutting his mouth, trying to get the words out. Edgar simply wasn't up to such a depth of deception. When they were children he had been incapable of telling even the whitest of lies. It had always been Edgar who blabbed unwittingly to the grown-ups.

He was standing now, gazing impassively into space, waiting for the jury to decide his fate.

'Members of the jury, have you reached a verdict upon which you are all agreed?'

The foreman of the jury rose. 'Yes.'

'On the charge of murder, how do you find the defendant, Edgar James Beddoes – guilty or not guilty?'

'Not guilty,' the foreman said.

Angela breathed a sigh of relief and quickly left the court. She found her father already outside, talking animatedly to David Adams. Gemma was walking away down the corridor, and Angela wondered whether or not to follow her and say something conciliatory. By the time she'd decided maybe she would, Gemma had disappeared and her father was at her side, ebulliently, appallingly over the top.

'The black chap, Angela. The black chap, he told me . . .' His voice crackled with emotion. '. . . Edgar forgave them, down on his knees in Bosnia, he forgave his enemies. The boy's a saint.'

Angela touched his arm. 'Please, Father, it's over now.'

185

'What stuff he's made of.' Matthew ignored the interruption as he usually did. 'He sought punishment. On *his* shoulders he's taken the guilt, all of it. Who else did that, eh? In this world, who?'

'Father, please . . .'

Angela paused as she saw Edgar coming out of the courtroom. Matthew went to meet him, sobbing, and gripped his arms. 'The church is a battlefield, you know. Enemies are fought there by young men . . . who still have faith.' He enveloped Edgar in a smothering hug.

Angela turned away and saw James Kavanagh standing further along the corridor, passing files and papers to Alex Wilson. She went over to him and handed him a Waterstone bag. 'It's by way of being a present, James. A copy of a book Edgar's been reading.'

'Why, thank you.' Kavanagh opened the bag, took out the book and glanced at the title. '*Regeneration.* Is it good?'

'Mmm, very,' Angela said. 'A character in it comes back from the war, the trenches, to find he's unable to speak for something he's seen. Something so dreadful that it struck him dumb.'

'I see . . .' Kavanagh didn't notice Edgar walking falteringly towards them. 'And . . . er . . . what happens?'

They stopped, stunned, as Edgar said quietly, 'One day . . . I'll be able to speak. It'll happen . . . just like that.'

Kavanagh glanced down at the book, looked speculatively at Edgar and then at Angela. 'Is it possible . . . ?' he began.

Angela recognised the quiet intensity in Edgar's eyes from when they were children. It had always been Edgar who let on to the grown-ups, she thought again. She smiled at Kavanagh and shook her head.

Edgar seemed unaware of the noise and bustle in the corridor. He closed his eyes and heard, instead, the whimper of an abandoned child, smelled the rotting flesh, saw again the mangled bodies. 'I left my guide and lost my way,' he said softly, 'but now I love . . . and keep thy word.' Slowly, he opened his eyes and looked up.

PART THREE

Ancient History

20

'What's that terrible racket?' the old lady said querulously. 'I can hardly hear myself speak. What's going on out there?'

Her daughter twitched aside the net curtain and gazed across the street. There were half a dozen or so vans parked outside Dr Beck's large, comfortable Victorian house opposite. It was the grandest house in the road, with double-lined burgundy-red velvet curtains at the windows and a flight of marble steps up to the front door; the aspiration of all the other long-time residents. Just the right sort of house for an important man like the doctor, the old lady and her friends agreed.

It was a quiet tree-lined street and, during the afternoons, Jennifer, the old lady's daughter, could feel herself being suffocated by a palpable smog of boredom, which was only accentuated by the occasional echo of solitary footsteps. Today, however, it was vividly alive with laughing, chattering groups of people ferrying armfuls of expensive flowers, crates of champagne and stacks of gold-painted chairs up the marble steps. Jennifer could just see, inside the front door, Marian Beck, the doctor's wife, dishevelled and distracted, attempting to direct operations.

191

'It's delivery vans,' she said. 'The Becks must be having a party.'

'A party?' the old lady said, from the depths of her chintz armchair. 'That's not like the doctor. Such a quiet man . . . dignified. He's not a one for parties.'

Another van drew up and a woman emerged, ran round the back, opened the double doors and carefully picked up a large, white-iced cake which she carried into the house with the intense concentration of somebody in charge of an infinitely precious *objet d'art*. Jennifer Shaw squinted through the gap in the net curtain. The message on the cake read: 'Happy Ruby Wedding Alexander and Marian'. 'It's their ruby wedding,' she said.

'Ruby?' the old lady repeated. 'It can't be . . . it seems like only yesterday Dr and Mrs Beck moved in. The best doctor in Highgate . . .'

'Muswell Hill,' her daughter corrected her. 'He's been retired for ages, Mother. You've been going to Dr Sandman down at the Medical Centre for at least eight years.' She glanced along the street, where an old man, wearing a black Jewish skullcap, shabby grey trousers, and an even shabbier blue jacket over a dusty brown knitted pullover and collarless shirt, stood under a plane tree, staring at Dr Beck's house. 'He's there again,' she said. 'The old man in the skullcap.'

'Oh, him,' her mother said dismissively. 'He's just an old tramp. I'm surprised they allow it.'

A dark saloon car drew up and an official-looking man in a rather ill-fitting brown suit jumped out, followed by a younger man in a grey suit and raincoat. They climbed the doctor's steps, empty-handed. Jennifer thought they had the look of men from the council. 'Two men . . .' she began, but her mother, who was ready now for her tea, waved an impatient hand.

192

'Come away from that window, Jennifer. What if anyone saw you? Dr Beck ... what would he think of us?'

Jennifer sighed and took a final glance across the road. It seemed she was not the only surreptitious watcher. Dr Beck was also gazing out through a chink in his nets. He was standing very still, and there was something curious in his expression. She couldn't be sure whether it was melancholy, fear, impatience ... or even anger. She let the curtain drop discreetly and backed away from the window. But he wasn't looking at her; he was looking at the old man in the skullcap.

Well, he's done all right for himself, Detective Inspector Grover thought as he took in the big leather armchair, the comfortable furnishings, and the dark red antique rug. He went over to a mahogany side table and picked up a photograph of a tall, upright man receiving an award. 'This you, sir?'

Dr Beck, standing by his desk, nodded. 'Must you have it?' he said. 'Is it really necessary?'

''Fraid so, sir,' the detective replied. 'Take it just as a formality.'

Dr Beck sighed. 'Right.' He reached into the top drawer of his desk, took out his passport and handed it to Detective Inspector Grover.

'Thanks.' The detective studied the passport for a moment. 'I like these old ones. Pity they went out.'

'Is it still valid?'

'Of course.' The detective read aloud. '"Renewed to 1999. Born Cracow, Poland."'

The doctor smiled and nodded. 'That is correct.'

He felt a chill of foreboding as the Detective Inspector said grimly: 'We know.'

While his inspector had been interviewing the doctor, Detective Sergeant Hudson had been wandering around the room, looking at photographs, picking up ornaments and putting them down again, and generally snooping around in a way Dr Beck found both distracting and impertinent. Now the sergeant took a notepad out of his pocket, wrote out a receipt for the passport, and gave it to the doctor. 'Nice room, this,' he said.

The doctor bowed his head, accepting the compliment. 'It used to be my surgery before I retired.'

'Oh, right.'

'What happens now?'

The inspector looked away. 'We . . . just report.'

He looked up again, unwillingly, as Dr Beck asked him the question he was hoping to avoid. 'But should there be a charge . . . what will it be?'

'Well . . .' Detective Inspector Grover said, trying not to catch the doctor's eye. 'Technically . . . murder.'

Dr Beck nodded. 'I see.' He went over to the window, pulled aside the net curtain and gestured angrily. 'Ah, you see, there he is.' The two detectives came over and stood next to him by the window. 'Is that my accuser, out there, watching?'

The inspector looked with dismay at the old man in his skullcap. 'He's a potential witness,' he hissed at the sergeant.

Sergeant Hudson did a double-take: 'How the hell did . . . ?'

'He's often there,' Dr Beck said. 'He hangs about. His name is Rypin, as you obviously know. He's pestered me for years . . .'

Inspector Grover turned to the sergeant and said angrily, 'Pack him off home – and tell him to stay there.'

Dr Beck was still gazing out of the window. '. . . abusive

194

letters, phone calls.' He shrugged. 'If he's the best you've got . . .'

Sergeant Hudson nodded to the doctor and dashed out of the room. 'Excuse me, excuse me, sorry,' he said, bumping straight into a woman carrying an elaborate floral arrangement. 'Sorry.'

'I say, steady,' she said, attempting to straighten a couple of bent blooms. 'What's the hurry?'

Lucy Beck, who was standing in the hallway counter-manding her mother-in-law's ineffectual instructions – 'No, no, the caterers go through *there*, and the flowers should be left *here* . . .' – was almost at breaking point. 'This is ridiculous,' she said. 'What on earth's happening, Mother? Don't you know?'

Marian Beck picked up a sheaf of flowers Lucy had just carefully placed next to the other bouquets and carried them off towards the kitchen. 'They're still in there,' she said. 'I think it's just some legal thing.' She sighed. 'What a time to pick.'

Lucy followed her. 'Well, I'm going to get Charlie to come over here,' she said. 'He'll deal with them.'

'Oh, no, don't bother Charlie,' Marian said anxiously. 'He's got such a lot on his plate.'

Lucy picked up her mobile and dialled her husband's number. The way Marian went on about her son's work, you'd think he was running the country rather than a software company. 'Charlie?'

'Bloody hell! Bloody halfwit!' Charlie Beck shouted back down his mobile. 'Sorry, darling, some idiot just pulled out in front without any warning . . .'

Lucy sighed wearily. Any journey with Charlie involved hurling abuse at all the other bloody halfwits on the road. She told him about the chaos at his parents' house, and the final straw, the two men who'd come to see his father and were crashing about all over the house, knocking into florists and caterers.

'Look, Lucy,' Charlie said, 'I'm on my way to see a supplier. Can't you deal with it?'

Lucy said that she had her work cut out dealing with his mother already, without having to cope with a couple of strangers as well. 'I could tell, when they arrived, your father didn't want to see them. Look, I don't know who they are, Charlie, but they've been closeted with him for the past hour.'

'Well, throw them out. If they're upsetting Mum and Dad on their big day, I'll . . .'

'You'll come right over,' Lucy finished for him. 'Charlie, please.'

She put her mobile down on the kitchen table. 'He's coming,' she said.

As Charlie Beck pulled up in front of the house in his red Ford Sierra Cosworth, Detective Sergeant Hudson was still struggling with Rypin on the other side of the road.

He'd begun, civilly enough, by enquiring after the old man's health, and explaining that if he wanted to be a witness for the prosecution he must go away and leave the doctor alone. Rypin had then refused to budge, and the sergeant had put a hand on his arm to kind of ease him along, and Rypin had shaken him off angrily. It had gone on from there.

Charlie got out of the car, glanced at his parents' house, and then at the two men scuffling on the other side of the street. 'What the hell's going on?'

He heard the younger man saying 'This could be construed as intimidation . . .' and the old man replying 'Please, please leave me alone.'

Charlie, bounding up the steps, turned to have another look, as the young man said: 'You mustn't pester Dr Beck,

Mr Rypin. I've told you . . .' He saw the young man linking his arm, rather forcefully, through the older man's arm. Hold it, he said to himself, isn't that the loony who's always hanging around? Rypin, the bloody stalker?

'This way . . .' the young man said, tugging at the other man's arm.

So, the police are on the move at last, Charlie said to himself. And about time, too. He watched Rypin struggling to free himself, and heard him say, in a dignified manner which went strangely with his shabby appearance: 'Excuse me, don't put your arm . . . take your hands off me.' After another brief tussle the policeman manhandled Rypin into a black car and drove off with him.

'Well, that's got rid of him, then,' Charlie thought, and, entering the hallway, he looked challengingly at the throng of strangers milling about. Eventually, he spotted his mother. 'Who are all these people, Mother? Did you let them in?'

Marian Beck could see that Charlie was going to be difficult. She had put a conciliatory hand on his arm and begun 'Well, dear, your father . . .' when Detective Inspector Grover emerged from the study, followed by her husband.

Charlie scowled at the inspector. 'What's all this about? And who the hell are you?'

'Charlie, it's all right,' Dr Beck said in a voice Charlie should have recognised, from his childhood, as ominously quiet.

He ignored the interruption and, thrusting his face close to the inspector's, said pugnaciously: 'What do you want with my father?'

The inspector backed away. 'I think it would be best if . . .'

Charlie snapped open his mobile. 'I think *I'll* call the police.'

The inspector reached into his pocket for his ID card and flashed it. The gesture gave him some satisfaction. 'Talk to him,' he said, nodding towards the doctor, and went swiftly out of the front door.

Charlie turned off his mobile and, looking around for someone to shout at, saw a cluster of caterers in the dining-room doorway. 'All right, all right,' he said. 'Show's over. Carry on with what you were doing.'

The caterers retreated. Charlie gave his father a brief, questioning look, and called out for Lucy and his mother to follow him into the study. He ushered them in and slammed the door firmly. 'Now, what's all this nonsense about, Father?'

Marian Beck walked straight past Charlie and, going over to her husband, who was standing very still in the centre of the room, took his hand. 'Alexander, my dear, they've upset you.'

Alexander looked down at her. She was a short, plump woman with unmanageable grey hair and the unlined face and open expression of a trusting child. He feared how this might change her. 'I'm being investigated as a war criminal,' he said quietly.

'You *what*?' Charlie cried as he and Lucy looked up in shocked disbelief.

Marian stepped back. 'I'm sorry . . . ?'

'They're trying to say you never knew me, my dear . . .' Alexander put his hands on her shoulders. '. . . all this time.'

'Alexander . . .' Marian gazed up at him, unwilling to accept what he was saying.

'That during the war I was not a victim of the Nazis, but a perpetrator.'

'Stop it. Stop it.' She moved away from him and put her hands over her ears to block out the terrible words.

Alexander smiled consolingly. 'It's a mistake, of course. There's some ancient muddle in the records.'

Marian rallied. 'Then they'll have to sort it out.'

'Of course they will.'

Charlie walked over to the window. 'This is all down to old Rypin, isn't it? I saw him outside.'

Lucy went over to her father-in-law and gripped his hand. 'The mad creature?' she said. 'Well, surely he's harmless.'

'He's back,' Charlie said grimly, opening the window.

Marian rushed across the room. 'Go away, go away,' she shouted. 'Leave us alone. Why don't you go?'

The old man gazed up at the window, mumbling rhythmically: '. . . O-seh sha-lom bim-ro-mav . . .'

'What's he saying?' Marian turned to Alexander. 'I can't make it out.'

'It's a prayer,' Alexander said. 'The Hebrew Kaddish. A prayer for the dead.'

Lucy shivered. 'At *us*? It's like a curse.'

Dr Beck shook his head. 'No,' he said. 'I heard it often enough in the camp. It's for *their* dead.'

21

'Are you going to take it, sir?' Tom Buckley said, as he handed James Kavanagh his morning papers. 'I had the CPS on to me this morning, very keen. You've got fans in high places.'

'Thank you, Tom.' Kavanagh took the newspapers and tucked them under his arm. 'That's most consoling.' He glanced at the file of papers in his hand, headed 'Crown versus Dr Alexander Beck'. 'I don't know, Tom, it's a nasty business . . . those old men . . .'

'They were nasty people, the Nazis,' Tom said. 'Let them get what they deserve, I say.'

'If they've got the right man,' Kavanagh said. 'The Crown Prosecution Service is not currently famed for its investigative skills.'

Tom grinned. 'True enough, sir, but this one's cast-iron. I was talking to Miss Ames about it, and she thinks like I do.'

'Does she indeed,' Kavanagh said.

As he wandered along the corridor towards Peter Foxcott's office, he thought how unlikely it would have been, only a few months ago, for River Court's senior clerk and River Court's most successful junior to agree on anything. Ever since the awkward evening in the wine bar, when he'd advised Helen Ames to ease up on her feminist spikiness, she'd been spreading charm around chambers like confetti. She'd won over Aldermarten and now she'd conquered Tom Buckley. Kavanagh chuckled to himself. Why, he even called her Miss Ames these days, instead of Ms with a hostile hiss.

He'd asked Helen to be his junior on this case – if he took it. She had a first-class mind and had already amassed a formidable battery of information and legal precedents.

She was sitting in Foxcott's office when he went in, and Kavanagh was amused to see Aldermarten pouring out coffee and taking a cup over to her. One of the things that had enraged Helen, she'd once confided, was Aldermarten's bland assumption that women were there to serve. He helped himself to a coffee and nodded to the group.

'I was just saying to Helen,' Foxcott said, 'that the Bar Council meeting last night was unusually stimulating.'

'Good Lord,' Kavanagh said. 'Dancing girls?'

Foxcott gave a thin smile. 'Mr Justice Way,' he said, 'trouncing us all up hill and down dale over our professional ethics.'

Aldermarten, who had just spent a fortune on tickets for his favourite ballet, only to find that all the girls were played by chaps, decided that perhaps it hadn't been such a bad evening, after all. 'Fees?' he said.

'Amongst other things, yes,' Foxcott said. 'I must admit that at that point I did rather regret encouraging the President to give Way J the floor.'

'Oh, it was your doing, was it?' Kavanagh said. 'Good for you. We lawyers ought to have our knuckles rapped every now and again, just to know what it feels like.'

'The whole charging system is archaic,' Helen said, with

feeling. 'Unless they get involved in a flashy case, ordinary people can't afford a top barrister, and unless you're a top barrister you can't afford to go into Tesco while you're hanging about, waiting for your fees to be paid.'

Aldermarten looked over at Helen with a puzzled frown. 'Tesco?' Surely, that was the place where one bought the Weetabix and so on?

Before Helen had a chance to react, Kavanagh said quickly: 'Why didn't you tell me Way J was putting the cat amongst the pigeons, Peter? I'd have been there.'

Foxcott smiled apologetically. 'I didn't think. You were so caught up in this Nazi business. And I must say, James, I'm none too happy about the War Crimes Act.'

'Yes.' Aldermarten nodded. 'It should never have been passed.'

'But it was,' Kavanagh said. 'Now it is the law of the land. Surely . . .'

'Retrospective legislation.' Foxcott pursed his lips disapprovingly.

'It's against all our traditions,' Aldermarten said.

'Reaching back fifty years to accuse people of crimes committed in some other country?' Foxcott shook his head. 'I don't think so.'

'Of course, it was forced through by the Jewish lobby,' Aldermarten said, helping himself to another spoonful of sugar.

Foxcott shifted uneasily. 'Ah . . . now you lose me.'

'No, I don't mean . . .' Aldermarten hurried to correct himself, and Helen Ames shot Kavanagh an amused glance. 'I mean . . . you know, you know what I mean. I'm not. Quite emphatically.'

'Some of your best friends . . .' Kavanagh suggested.

'Well, yes, actually,' Aldermarten said. 'Voices raised in favour, most eloquently and . . . er . . . colourfully.'

203

'As you would expect of them,' Kavanagh said.

'Yes,' Aldermarten said defiantly. 'Since you put it like that.'

'I don't, but you do.' Kavanagh resisted the rising desire to say something he'd later regret concerning bigotry. 'Don't dig yourself any deeper, Jeremy.'

'Surely,' Helen said, 'it was to punish crimes against humanity?'

'It's bad law,' Aldermarten said. He put his cup down firmly on the table and went towards the door. 'Thank you, Peter.'

''Bye, Jeremy,' Foxcott said. He turned to Kavanagh. 'So are you going to, er, accept this brief?'

'Not until I've done a bit more homework,' Kavanagh said.

Foxcott sipped his coffee thoughtfully. 'Ancient history, James?'

Kavanagh returned to his office and began going through the papers. He'd only got halfway through the witness statements when he sat back in his chair, took off his spectacles and sighed heavily. They were almost too terrible to comprehend, like reading a dispassionate account of medieval tortures. And the shocking fact he found hard to accept was that these horrors were perpetrated in his own lifetime and some of the torturers were still alive. He shook his head, half disbelieving, half not wanting to believe what he had just read. He was relieved when the phone rang.

It was Lizzie wanting to know when he'd be home. Her father, Lord Probyn, was coming to dinner. 'What time's he coming?' Kavanagh said. 'Eight o'clock? No, no, I'll be there. Actually, there's something I want to ask the old boy.'

*   *   *

204

pay him half the rent which was fair enough, but one day I got a sighting of the rent book, and found out that I was paying the whole bloody lot.'

Lizzie had shaken her head sympathetically. 'So, what did you do?'

'I thumped him,' Matt had said. 'And here I am.'

'I don't like to think of Matt hitting people,' Lizzie had said to James later, as they were getting ready for bed.

'Sounds to me as if Pete deserved it,' James had said. 'I tell you what pleases me, Lizzie. He went out and earned. That's the first time our son has shown any inclination to get off his butt and do something.'

'And it seems he became acquainted with the Jif bottle.'

Lizzie smiled at the memory of this extraordinary happening, finished in the kitchen and went upstairs to shower and change. 'Dad just phoned,' she called up to Matt. 'He'll be back for dinner.'

'Great,' Matt shouted back. 'Anything I can do?'

She clutched the banister rail for support. This, she said to herself, is too good to last.

Lizzie beamed fondly at her father over the dinner table. He must be around seventy now, but he looked younger and happier than he had ten years ago, when he and her mother split up. She'd never asked him about the divorce, or anything else personal, for that matter. He was not a man to talk about 'feelings' or 'relationships', but Lizzie guessed that being married to her feckless, glamorous mother must have put a heavy strain on his British reserve. She'd been famed around the shires as 'the bolter', and when she finally bolted for good with the interior designer who'd been doing up the Manor, or 'turning the old place into an out-of-town Hilton', as her father had put it, he had seemed, after the initial shock, really rather relieved.

'Funny thing is, Lizzie,' he'd said, making a joke of the tragedy, 'I had the fellow down as a poofter. Shows how wrong you can be.'

He was always immaculately turned out, and this evening he was wearing a well-cut sports jacket with a Jermyn Street label and crisply pressed grey flannels. Lizzie often wondered if her father's capable housekeeper, who had a distinct twinkle in her eye, did more than put the creases in his trousers, but she wouldn't think of asking about that, either.

She had a moment of anxiety when they got on to politics over the chicken. 'Bring back Maggie Thatcher, that's what we need,' her father said. 'Put a bit of backbone into the country.'

Lizzie gave Matt a look that signalled 'Don't even think of saying what I think you're going to say', but all he did was grin. 'You know what you are, Gramps, an old fascist.'

Goodness, Lizzie thought to herself, he really is growing up. It was when she went off to get the biscuits and cheese that Kavanagh started to tackle her father about his role in the war; a subject he was always happy to expound on at length.

'Do I remember the end of the war?' Lord Probyn said. 'I'll say I do, rather vividly, as it happens. Swanning through Germany as a young subaltern.' He looked at his grandson with mock severity. 'Don't grin, Matt. That's what I was. In an armoured car, too.'

'You told me once how you got to Belsen,' Kavanagh said.

'The camp?' Lord Probyn said. 'I liberated it.'

Kavanagh smiled. 'Did you indeed?'

'Oh, those poor creatures. They were so grateful. All starving, in a pitiful condition. There were corpses stacked high.'

Lizzie dropped her napkin on to her plate and stood up. 'Let's have coffee,' she said.

They moved into the sitting room and Kavanagh turned to Matt. 'Will you do something for me, Matt? Trawl the Internet. Just try the word holocaust.'

'Okay, Dad.' Matt wandered off upstairs and Lizzie poured out the coffee.

'When did you get into Belsen?' Kavanagh asked his father-in-law.

'April 1945. I can't be sure of the exact date.' He looked a bit shamefaced. 'Actually ... it wasn't just me. I ... I lay it on a bit, I'm afraid. Awful habit.'

Lizzie felt a surge of love and gave her father's hand an affectionate squeeze as she put his coffee down on the table in front of him.

Kavanagh raised an eyebrow. 'There were other chaps?'

'Of course,' Lord Probyn said. 'Quite a bunch of us. We were stopped at the gate by the bloody commandant, would you believe.'

'He wouldn't let you in?' Lizzie enquired.

Her father nodded. 'That's right. Kramer, his name was. Josef Kramer. Horrible thug with jackboots and medals. So we shot him.'

Lizzie gave an involuntary shudder and Kavanagh, putting down his cup, looked searchingly at his father-in-law. 'Didn't you tell me once before that Kramer was run all round the camp in a Jeep?'

Lord Probyn thought for a moment. 'A Jeep ... ah, now.'

'As a prisoner,' Kavanagh continued, 'with a gun at his head, for them all to see?'

209

'So he was. I remember now,' Lord Probyn said. 'Yes, it must have been some other chap.'

'Wasn't Kramer put on trial and eventually hanged?'

'Could be.' Lord Probyn nodded. 'It's a long time ago.'

'I expect you've told the story so many times,' Lizzie said, 'with embellishments.'

'That's true,' her father said. 'I can't stop myself.'

'Anyway . . .' Lizzie turned to Kavanagh '. . . You're not doing Belsen, are you.'

'No, no,' Kavanagh said. 'My man was in Dachau.'

'Oh,' Lord Probyn said, 'the Yanks got that one. Then there was Auschwitz – the Russians got it. The death camp with the gas chambers and crematoria. I never saw that. Belsen was enough for me.'

After his father-in-law had left, Kavanagh went up to the playroom. Matt was sitting at the computer and Kavanagh came over and stood behind him. Matt tapped at the keyboard and a horrific image of emaciated bodies came up on the screen. They were piled high along the length of a yard enclosed by barbed wire and, in the forefront, a pathetic figure made up of rags and bones seemed to be reaching out a hand towards the photographer. Kavanagh winced and turned away.

'I could go on all night,' Matt said. 'I just picked out bits.' He looked grey and shaken. Kavanagh put a hand on his shoulder.

'Thanks, Matt.'

Matt shook his head. 'It's all unbelievable, of course.'

'Yeah.'

'So some people choose not to believe it. There's a lot of that, too, on the Internet – stuff saying it never happened.'

'Holocaust denial.'

'In Germany they've made it a crime.'

'Oh, they've got something right, then,' Kavanagh said. 'Matt . . . your grandfather saw it.'

Matt looked up at him. 'I know.'

Lizzie came out of the bathroom as Kavanagh began undressing. 'You were testing him, of course . . . his memory?'

Kavanagh nodded. 'Do you think he minded?'

Lizzie got into bed. 'Not really. And he's always been careless.' She sighed. 'He knows that . . . admits it.'

He sat down next to her on the bed. 'I've been wondering, you see, what I'd be up against. Witnesses of his age.'

'You'd have to put them through it?'

'Oh, yes.'

'Will it be worthwhile?'

Kavanagh thought of the harrowing witness statements he'd been reading that day. 'Lizzie . . . if this man really did what they say he did . . . no, no, if he only did a tenth of it, a hundredth . . . I would want him never to have been born.'

22

Charlie Beck, sitting at his office desk, surrounded by shelves of computer components, couldn't believe what he was seeing on his screen. He tapped the keyboard venomously. The image of an enemy alien in an odd sort of helmet zapping a heroic figure padded up like a hunky American baseball player kept flickering and fading before his eyes. 'Look at it,' Charlie shouted. 'Just look at it.'

It had been a bloody awful week in every possible respect. His mother crying all over the place, his father thin-lipped and silent, and the party, which had cost him a fortune . . . the party – Charlie shuddered at the memory – had been a right fiasco.

They'd all tried to act as if nothing had happened, of course, but it *had* happened and some of the guests had obviously got wind of it. When he'd said all that stuff in the speech – which, incidentally, he'd sweated over for days – about wonderful parents . . . happy couple . . . admired and respected doctor, et cetera, et cetera, there'd been a distinctly dodgy atmosphere. Not helped, in Charlie's view, by his mother, who had sat there, red-eyed, picking at her food and, for God's sake, actually breaking up and sobbing during the cake-cutting ceremony. Lucy had said that everyone would put it down to the emotion of the occasion, but Charlie had his doubts.

And now *this*. Charlie looked around for Dave, his senior manager. Nowhere to be seen, of course. 'Dave!' he shouted.

Dave came over just as Charlie's mobile rang. He raised his eyes to the ceiling. 'Je-sus Christ. Hang on a minute, Dave.' It was his father telling him that he'd been down the high street and briefed William Boothroyd of Boothroyd Boyd and Sons to represent him. Charlie took a deep breath. 'Father, I know he's been a decent, reliable old stick for all these years. Give him some conveyancing to do, by all means, or a will or . . .' He clapped his hand over the mouthpiece as his father went into a long rigmarole about how conscientious Mr Boothroyd had always been . . . a loyal friend . . .

'I can't accept this crap,' he said to Dave. 'Send it back, all of it.'

'But they made it a condition . . .'

'A what?' Charlie gazed at him, astonished.

'If you want the twelve thousand new chips at the price stipulated, we've got to take this poxy stuff.'

'And you agreed to that?'

Dave shifted his feet. 'I said it'd be down to you.'

Charlie prided himself on his instant decisions. 'Right,' he said. 'Well, stick the old labels on it. *Not* Beck Components. Got that?' He removed his hand from the mobile. 'Father? No, nothing, nothing, just idiots. Now listen, I've got somebody else lined up for you . . .' He held the mobile away from his ear as his father explained that he had complete confidence in Mr Boothroyd, and anyway, it was only a simple matter of stating the facts and . . . 'I know, I know,' Charlie said patiently. 'But, Dad, when they start waving pieces of paper around, you're going to

214

need to be ready. Now, he's a solicitor named Salthouse. Guy Salthouse. And he's big-time.'

'So, it comes down to the crucial matter of identification,' Guy Salthouse said in a voice Dr Beck suspected was what people meant when they talked about Estuary English. He certainly had the look of a man who'd be happier shouting the odds on the Stock Exchange trading floor, or even in Berwick Street Market, than as the tenant of this ultra-modern office in Canary Wharf. It was all glass and chrome and brutal modern statuary, very expensive. He dreaded to think how much all this nonsense was going to cost. He became aware that Charlie was looking at him.

'Identification, Dad. Mr Salthouse was just saying . . .'

'It's a malicious fabrication,' Alexander said. 'Mr Salthouse, that is all it is. Started by that crazy man.'

'Rypin?' Mr Salthouse enquired.

'We took out an injunction against him,' Charlie said.

'Stopped him,' Alexander said. 'Bound over to keep the peace. That should have been the end of it.'

Guy Salthouse leaned back in his chair and fiddled with his gold Mont Blanc pencil. 'I'm afraid this is a new law, Dr Beck.'

Alexander shrugged his shoulders irritably. 'So that they can throw their dirt at me?'

'They have three principal witnesses,' Guy Salthouse said. 'One, this fellow Rypin.'

'Forget him,' Alexander said.

'Secondly, a man named Shapiro – from Israel?'

'Never heard of him.'

'Third, a Pole named Somper. Karol Somper.'

Alexander shook his head. 'No.'

Guy looked at the old man opposite him, sitting straight

in his chair, exuding defiance rather than evil. 'All claiming to have known you in Dachau.'

'Lies.'

'If so,' Guy said, 'they will be faced with them. Now, there'll have to be an identity parade.'

Charlie leaned forward aggressively. 'A what?'

'Parade?' his father said, disbelievingly.

'I'm afraid you'll have to submit yourself. But, right now, I've got one or two questions . . .'

'I have answered your questions,' Alexander said.

Guy Salthouse narrowed his eyes, which were quite small already. Awkward old cuss, he thought. He turned to Charlie. 'So far we have only discussed the witnesses. I obviously can't proceed unless I'm in possession of the relevant facts.'

Charlie nodded. 'Right. Answer the questions, Dad.'

Alexander sighed as Guy Salthouse pulled a pad towards him and unwound his propelling pencil. 'You were born Aleksander Tad . . . is that Tadoise?'

'Pronounced Tad-ay-oosh,' Alexander said. 'I changed to Thaddeus when I was naturalised, to sound more English.'

'Well, there's no harm in that.' Guy Salthouse sniffed and smiled briefly at his client. 'So . . .' He jotted down the name. 'Alexander Thaddeus Beck. While the Germans occupied Poland, you were picked up as a suspected partisan. Were you one?'

'I wish I had been.'

'And you were sent to Auschwitz?'

'That is correct.' Alexander inclined his head. 'I was later transferred to Dachau.'

'Why?'

Charlie looked over at his father. He hadn't known that.

'They never . . .' Alexander hesitated. 'They don't tell you. They put me in labour gangs, all kinds – digging in the sand quarry, construction work and for the SS. They ran their own factories for their own profit.'

'Will there be any records?'

'No. Everything was destroyed.'

The solicitor gave Dr Beck a piercing look. 'You're sure?'

Alexander shrugged and glanced at Charlie. 'It's what I've read.'

'Who's prosecuting?' Charlie said. 'Do you know?'

'Yes,' Guy Salthouse said. 'A Q.C. named Kavanagh.'

'Any good?'

'Yes, he is. He's rather an interesting choice. It's not the kind of case he usually . . .'

'So we need the best,' Charlie interrupted. 'Any ideas?'

'I could suggest a few names.'

'Who's the top man?' Charlie said.

'Well . . .' Guy paused to consider. An elderly retired doctor – he hadn't expected to get into the big league with this one. 'We might try Giles Culpepper. Now, be warned, he's very pricey.'

'I'll pay,' Charlie said.

'Charlie,' Alexander remonstrated. 'You mustn't think of it.'

Charlie turned to his father. 'It's my name as well, don't forget. And the firm's name.'

'Leave it to me,' Guy Salthouse said. Charlie Beck's manner was beginning to get on his wick. 'I'll make the approaches.'

Charlie got up and said belligerently: 'I do a lot of trade with the Germans, you know.'

'What we may need to prove, Mr Beck,' Guy Salthouse said sharply, 'is that your father *didn't*.'

Alexander and Charlie drove back to Muswell Hill in silence. Charlie wanted to ask his father if there was any truth in all these allegations. Naturally, he didn't believe any of it, it was all rubbish ... still, the horse's mouth and all that. But one look at the old boy, thin-lipped and ramrod straight, made him decide that this was one time when he'd do well to keep his mouth shut.

He pulled up in front of his parents' house and leaned over to open the passenger door.

Alexander climbed out, stiffly and awkwardly. 'Aren't you coming in, Charlie?'

Charlie, irritated by his father's painfully slow movements, and with no desire to become further embroiled in his mother's misery, shook his head. 'Got to get back to the office, Dad. I'll be in touch.'

He swerved off at speed and Alexander went slowly into his study and poured himself out a whisky. It was halfway to his lips when Marian came in, carrying a large brown paper parcel. 'Supper won't be long,' she said. 'I expect you're hungry.'

'Yes.' Alexander downed the whisky in one gulp. 'It's been a trying day. That lawyer of Charlie's ...'

'Will he be any help?'

'He's very sharp.' Alexander looked questioningly at the parcel. 'What have you got there?'

Marian hugged the parcel to her, wondering if, once again, she was making an awful mistake. 'Just ... some things.'

'Show me.'

Unwillingly now, she unwrapped the parcel. They both gazed at the cheap calico, the telltale stripes of a concentration camp uniform. Marian looked at Alexander. She couldn't imagine him in such a thing. 'They made you wear these?'

She watched him anxiously as he said: 'Where did you find them?'

'At the bottom of a trunk . . . oh, ages ago. I was looking for jumble. And just now I remembered . . .'

Alexander seemed incapable of taking his eyes off the uniform. 'I thought I had destroyed them.'

'It was in case the lawyers wanted to see them.' Marian sighed. 'Oh, I didn't think . . . I'm so sorry. I'll take them away.'

'Leave them,' her husband said.

Marian's lip quivered. 'Oh, I always do the wrong thing.'

Alexander was still looking at the uniform. 'They're shaming,' he said quietly.

'Of course they are.' She moved to bundle the uniform back into the paper. 'I'm so sorry.'

Alexander put out a hand to stop her. 'No, it doesn't matter.'

'Now I've upset you,' Marian said. 'Oh, Alexander, I'm so stupid. You've got such a stupid wife.'

Alexander came towards her, smiling. 'You're not stupid.'

'I am,' Marian sobbed. 'I am.'

'Would I ever have married anyone stupid?' He put his hands on her shoulders.

'Perhaps you did.'

'And never noticed all this time?'

'You always say that.' Marian's voice was muffled by his jacket.

Alexander put a hand under her chin so that she was forced to look up at him. 'Listen to me. You have made a perfect home. You've done all those things a doctor's wife should do. Haven't you?'

She turned away from him. 'I'll burn these.'

219

'No.'

'But . . . they've upset you.'

'Not yet, anyway,' he said thoughtfully.

'They're dirty.'

He nodded. 'Perhaps you were right.'

She looked at him in surprise. 'How?'

'Well . . . they prove that I was a prisoner.'

Marian's lips quivered again as Alexander smiled at her and murmured, as though it were an endearment, 'Little Marian.'

Kavanagh straightened his back and moved his shoulders around. He and Helen had been poring over the Beck papers for hours. Exhausting, distressing work.

He sighed. 'And our next hurdle, Helen – the identification parade and the classic confusions of witnesses. "The man was running, Your Honour. No, no, he was walking – slowly. He was, er, he had brown hair. No . . . he was bald."' Helen grinned. ' "Middle-aged. No, he was a teenager." Even recent memories. Ours have to think back fifty years.'

Helen drew in her breath. 'I know, and . . .'

She stopped when there was a knock on the door and a portly middle-aged man with a small ginger moustache came in, carrying a large briefcase. Kavanagh waved him to a chair. 'Come in, Arnold. Arnold Westrope of the CPS. Helen Ames, who is my junior.'

Helen rose and put out her hand. 'Hello.'

'Hello.' Arnold Westrope gripped her hand, and because he knew what ladies liked and expected, added, 'We haven't met. I'd have remembered.'

Kavanagh chuckled inwardly, waiting for Helen's response, but she just smiled back sweetly. 'Found us any more witnesses?' he asked Westrope.

He shook his head. 'I'm afraid our enquiries in the Czech Republic have run into the sand.'

'Ah,' Kavanagh murmured. 'All we need.'

Westrope reached into his briefcase and produced a pile of documents. 'But I do have the charges in specimen form.'

'Why specimen?' Helen enquired.

Westrope turned to her. 'Well, we can't be sure on what date or to whom.'

'Yes, of course,' she said.

Westrope picked up the top document and began reading. '"One: murder of a Jew, unknown, between April and May the fifth 1944."' He looked up. 'There'd been a large intake of test persons at this time. "Two: murder of a Jewess, unknown, between March the seventh and April the twenty-ninth 1945." Both in Dachau camp.'

'April '45,' Helen said. 'So, the war was nearly over.'

'Yes.' Westrope laid the documents on Kavanagh's desk. 'Well, that didn't stop them.'

'I don't like "Jewess",' Kavanagh said. 'It sounds animal, somehow.'

'It is, er, correct usage,' Westrope said.

'Whoever she was, she was a person,' Kavanagh said. 'Even when she was unknown.'

Westrope had no inclination to get involved in a semantic discussion. 'It's just terminology,' he said, closing his briefcase with a sharp click.

'Don't you see,' Kavanagh said, 'it's what they tried to destroy. They were the experts. They took away your clothes ... and your name ... even your hair ... till you forgot who you'd been.'

'Right,' Westrope said. 'Well, I'll be on to you if anything else turns up.'

Kavanagh saw him out and returned to his desk. Helen

was still sitting, gazing sorrowfully into space. 'You *are* right, James. We mustn't let them down.'

They spent the remainder of the afternoon going painstakingly through the pile of documents. Eventually, Kavanagh stretched. 'I've had it for today, Helen. Fancy a pint?'

Helen smiled. 'Not another lecture, James?'

'Not needed,' Kavanagh said. 'I was most impressed by your reaction to Mr Westrope's old-world courtesy.'

'He meant well,' Helen said. 'No to the drink, thanks. I think I'll just sift through this lot again.' She might have added, but didn't, that Rupert was staying overnight with a schoolfriend, and she didn't relish the thought of spending the evening with her mother, who had one of her migraines again.

'Well, don't overdo it,' Kavanagh said. 'Conserve your energy. This is just the beginning, remember.'

When he arrived home, he found Lizzie looking pleased. 'Kate's been on the phone,' she said, kissing him. 'She's over the moon. According to her tutor, her essay on the transfer of power in India is the best exposition on the subject he has ever read.'

Kavanagh took off his coat and hung it on the peg. 'Well done, her.'

'And he insisted on reading it out aloud to the rest of the group in the tutorial.' Lizzie chuckled. 'That included Caro.'

'Kate's best friend?'

'Exactly. Apparently, she was green with envy, which added to Kate's pleasure. She's coming home in a couple of weeks. Says she's longing to see Matt.'

'Excellent.' Kavanagh missed his daughter. He loved both the children equally, of course, but Kate . . . well, he had to admit it, maybe she was his favourite. She was just so much easier to have around. Although Matt recently had been totally different. And he was getting really involved in this holocaust research. 'Where is Matt?' he said.

'Upstairs,' Lizzie said. 'On the computer.'

'I'll just have a word, then.'

'Well, don't be too long, either of you,' Lizzie said. 'Dinner's about ready.' She smiled after him as he climbed the stairs. This case had really brought the two of them together.

'You still at it?' Kavanagh said, coming into the play-room.

Matt turned around. 'Do you know, Dad, your Dachau wasn't the worst camp. They killed thirty thousand.' He glanced back at the screen, showing details of the different concentration camps. 'In Auschwitz they could gas more than ten thousand in one day. They got through more than a million. Mostly Jews.' He sighed. 'Why?'

Kavanagh shrugged, seeking an answer. 'Obeying orders?'

'That was just the excuse,' Matt said.

'They thought they were the best. The *Ubermenschen*. That set them free to do anything . . . to anybody.'

'Are you going to win?'

Kavanagh smiled. 'Now that, if you ever go to the Bar, is known as a leading question.'

23

The Rypin family – Avram, his wife Miriam, their two sons and their three grandchildren – were standing together in the observation lounge at Heathrow Airport, noses and hands pressed to the glass, eyes glittering with excitement.

Avram was unrecognisable as the sad old man who kept his daily vigil outside Dr Beck's house in Melrose Avenue, N10. He was dressed in a chunky black overcoat and wearing a Homburg instead of his yarmulke. Surrounded by his family, and radiating happy anticipation, he seemed years younger.

They were waiting to meet Avram's old friend Lev Shapiro, who was coming over to testify at Dr Beck's trial. Avram had no doubt that when he and Lev told the court what they knew, the doctor would be finally punished and his victims – among them too many of their own friends and relatives – avenged.

'He's here!' Avram had no trouble recognising Lev. Sure, he looked older, but, although sickness had shrunk the flesh on his bones, he was not as thin as the emaciated young man who had shared his precious pot of laurel-flavoured potato peelings with Avram in Dachau. He was first off the back of the plane and, as he was being pushed across the tarmac in a wheelchair, Avram hustled his family down to the arrivals lounge to meet him. 'Lev! You're here!'

The stewardess, pushing the wheelchair, stepped back as Avram rushed forward to embrace Lev.

'Avram.' Lev Shapiro's eyes misted over. His arms were weak, but he summoned up enough strength to reach out and grip Avram's shoulders. 'It's so good to see you.'

'You're looking well,' Avram said. 'Better than I ever . . .'

'Huh.' Lev smiled at him. 'For a dying man . . . I am in exceptional rude health.'

'Tsk, tsk . . .' Avram shook his head. 'Please don't say that.'

Lev chuckled. 'They were so good on the plane. They gave me oxygen.'

Avram stepped back, shrugging and gesturing to his family. 'Oxygen they gave him.'

'You should try it. All due to this young man.' Lev indicated the dark, handsome twenty-four-year-old standing at his side. 'My grandson, Yitzak. Born in Israel,' he said proudly. 'A sabra.'

They shook hands. '*Shalom aleichem*,' Avram said.

'*Aleichem shalom*,' Yitzak replied.

Avram grinned at him. 'I've heard all about you.'

'I'm sent by the family to look after him,' Yitzak said. 'He is difficult, I needn't tell you.'

Avram pinched Yitzak's cheek, beamed at his old friend and said, in Hebrew, 'He's a good-looking boy. Come, meet the family. Please.' He ushered Miriam, his children and his grandchildren forward; he'd dreamed often of this moment. 'Everybody, this is Lev Shapiro, my very good friend I haven't seen for years. He's looking well, thank God. Here is Yitzak, that's his grandson . . . a sabra.'

The Rypins clustered around Lev and Yitzak, hugging,

226

shaking hands, laughing. Paul, Avram's ten-year-old grandson, tugged at his hand, looking over at Yitzak. 'What's a sabra, Grandpapa?'

Lev, overhearing the question, smiled at the boy. 'A desert cactus, prickly on the outside, soft on the inside.' He nodded to Avram and Miriam. 'A good name for the Israelis, wouldn't you say?'

They escorted Lev out of the building towards an ambulance where Detective Inspector Grover was waiting to greet him. 'I did not expect such luxury, Inspector,' Lev said.

The inspector nodded to Yitzak and shook Lev's hand. 'You're an important guest, Mr Shapiro.'

The driver came around to fix a ramp to the ambulance, and Yitzak took a folded newspaper cutting out of his wallet and gave it to the inspector. 'By the way, we found that photograph. It's from a local newspaper. English.'

'It wouldn't be evidence,' Grover said, glancing at the faded photograph. 'Just a matter of interest.'

'Avram sent it to me years ago,' Lev said. 'He said, "Do you recognise anybody?"'

Inspector Grover read out the caption under the picture. '"Colleagues celebrating the retirement of the popular Dr Alexander Beck."'

'And there he is.' Lev Shapiro stabbed a finger at the face in the photograph. 'Balinski.'

The inspector saw the old man into the ambulance. He thanked God that He had spared one of his principal witnesses. He knew that Shapiro was terminally ill, and had spent sleepless nights worrying about whether he'd peg out or be too sick to survive the journey. Yitzak followed his grandfather into the ambulance and the Rypin family said their farewells, assuring Lev that they would follow in their car and meet up with him later.

One up, two to come. The inspector wondered if his sergeant, over at Terminal 4, had managed to locate Colonel Brennan. He flicked up his mobile and dialled. 'Toby?'

'Flight arrived fifteen minutes ago,' Toby Hudson said. 'They're coming through now.' He was holding up a placard with Brennan's name on it and, as he was speaking, a man with a crew cut and a military bearing came towards him, pushing a luggage trolley. 'Got him,' he said.

He went over. 'Colonel Brennan?'

'Sergeant Hudson.' They shook hands. 'How are you?'

'Very well, sir, very well.' The sergeant reached for the luggage trolley. 'I'll take that. Did you have a good flight?'

'Thanks.' The colonel handed over his luggage trolley. 'I slept through it, so I'm all ready for action. Which is . . . um . . . remind me, is this something like our Grand Jury?'

They walked towards the exit. 'Not exactly,' the sergeant said. 'It's a preliminary, to test out the charges.' He paused as his mobile rang again.

'Ah, to see if they stick?'

'Right.' Sergeant Hudson reached into his pocket for his mobile phone.

'And if they do?'

'Then it goes to the Old Bailey.'

'The old what?'

Sergeant Hudson stopped. 'Excuse me, sir.' He put the phone to his ear. 'Hello, Inspector, yes, I'm with the colonel now. An earlier flight? Right, I'll see you there.'

He turned to the colonel. 'Forgive me, Colonel. Another witness. Seems he arrived early and he's been hanging around the airport for a couple of hours . . .'

'Don't you worry about me, young man,' the colonel said. 'I'll get a cab at the rank over there . . .' He waved towards a sign saying 'Taxis-Coaches' and retrieved his luggage trolley. 'I'm staying at the Churchill, if you need to get hold of me.'

'Great.' Sergeant Hudson raised a hand in acknowledgment and dashed over to the arrivals board. He checked on the flight numbers and moved through the crowds, searching for Karol Somper. He'd seen him only once, in Cracow, a scruffy old boy, on the tubby side, with unkempt dark hair, and he hoped he'd recognise him. He gazed around anxiously, accosted a couple of elderly foreigners who, on closer inspection, proved not to be his man, and eventually spotted Somper, standing forlornly in a corner with a steward, holding a small battered suitcase. He went over. 'Hello, there. Mr Somper?'

'Somper, yes.' The old man didn't smile as he shook Sergeant Hudson's hand.

'We met in Poland,' the sergeant said. 'Toby Hudson.' He turned to the steward. 'Thanks very much, I'll take charge now. Is that the only bag he's got?'

'Yup.' The steward handed over the case and smiled at Karol Somper. 'Right, then, sir.' Mr Somper looked back at him morosely.

As they were leaving, Sergeant Hudson saw Inspector Grover coming towards them. 'Look what I've found.'

'Thank God,' the inspector said.

Charlie and his father had been kept waiting for about twenty minutes to see Giles Culpepper, Q.C. Charlie, stubbing out one cigarette and lighting another, was nervous. Events appeared to be moving on at a cracking pace and he wasn't sure he'd got a grip on them. Where was Salthouse, for a start? Surely, for the money he was getting out of them, he should be here holding Dad's hand, so to speak. He looked over at his father, quietly contained, sitting on a leather sofa, and had to admire his dignity. Really, the whole thing was a bloody disgrace . . . a man like that being put through this. He stubbed out his cigarette and rose as Guy Salthouse came in.

'Sorry to hold you up.' He shook their hands. 'Another client . . . bit of an emergency.' He gestured towards Culpepper's office. 'Shall we go through?'

Charlie was impressed. Not just by the office, which was stuffed with old law books and – he could tell – genuine antiques, but by Mr Culpepper, who had the languid, distinguished look of a man born into the right class – used to running the show and commanding respect.

They were introduced to Mr Culpepper and served coffee in delicate porcelain cups. Guy Salthouse helped himself to cream and sugar and took a document out of his briefcase. 'So, finally we have the actual charges. "Murder of an unknown Jew. Murder of an unknown Jewess." Both between some very vague dates. Both counts in the name of Alexander Thaddeus Beck, also known as Aleksander Balinski.'

'I am not Balinski,' Dr Beck said.

Charlie exploded. 'It's a bloody joke. Unknown victims on unknown dates. I bet this Balinski was bloody unknown as well.'

Guy Salthouse scowled. 'Mr Beck, please.'

'I do understand your concern for your father,' Giles Culpepper said. 'Believe me, I share it. And it's time to hand over to me.' He nodded dismissively at the solicitor who, trying not to look as affronted as he felt, sat back and made a lot of noise stirring his coffee.

'Yeah, I'm sorry, Mr Culpepper,' Charlie said.

'I shall guard his interests.'

'Of course.'

Culpepper looked over at Dr Beck. 'Back in Poland, before the war, you had begun your medical studies?'

230

'A year, year and a half.' Dr Beck shrugged. 'It was merely a beginning.'

'I'm sure it was. As bad as the law.' Giles Culpepper chuckled disarmingly. 'Dr Beck, I must put this to you. In Dachau were you ever in the medical block where these experiments were carried out?'

'No,' Dr Beck said.

'So you were never a subject of any of these experiments?'

'No.'

'Could there have been any occasion for you to be in there wearing a white coat?'

'You mean like a doctor?' Dr Beck queried.

'Yes.'

'Never. Quite impossible.'

Culpepper glanced briefly at Guy Salthouse, who nodded imperceptibly, aware of the tricky questions coming up.

'What did you know about the special unit – the freezing experiment?'

Dr Beck frowned. 'Freezing?'

'Conducted on the prisoners to test their endurance.'

'Ah,' the doctor said. 'To find the survival limits of the Luftwaffe pilots shot down in the sea.'

'You knew about that?' Culpepper said quickly, and glanced again at the solicitor.

'I read about it since,' Dr Beck said.

'And you saw nothing?'

'How could I? I was never in that place.'

Guy leaned forward. 'These men were tortured to death,' he said. 'And according to what I've read, there was so much screaming it disturbed people living in the vicinity.'

Charlie flinched, but there was no change in his father's expression as he said: 'Oh, there was always screaming. I

231

screamed myself many times. To be beaten after standing for twelve hours in the heavy rain.'

Charlie was appalled. His father had never talked to him about his wartime experiences, and Charlie had never wanted to ask. 'Is all this really necessary?' he said. 'You're really putting him through it.'

'As he most certainly will be, Mr Beck, by Mr Kavanagh,' Guy Salthouse said.

The following morning, Charlie drove his mother and father to the police station for the identification parade. He pulled up outside and opened the passenger door. 'Right, Dad,' he said. 'We'll hang around.'

Marian started to open her door at the back. 'Alexander, wait ... I'm coming with ...'

Charlie turned around. 'No, Mother. His solicitor is in there. That's all they allow.'

Marian looked back at him, red-eyed; she hadn't slept properly for three nights, worrying about this parade. 'But his family?'

'Particularly his family,' Charlie said. 'He's on his own.'

On his own? Marian looked back at Charlie bleakly.

Dr Beck walked into the police station without a backward glance at his wife and son. He was ushered into a room, and joined a line-up of five other men who looked around the same age as himself and were sitting on individual chairs, each under a different number. The doctor was placed under '5'. He found the experience unbelievably humiliating, and sat rigidly upright staring at a sand-blasted glass panel behind which, he understood from Mr Salthouse, who was up there with them, the witnesses were to carry out their identification.

The first man in was Avram Rypin. Considering he'd

spent years standing outside Dr Beck's house watching his every move, Guy Salthouse thought, he was making a bit of a production of it. He studied each man carefully and then pointed to Dr Beck. 'That's him. Number five.' He nodded. 'Yes.'

Lev Avram was then pushed along the length of the glass panel in his wheelchair. To and fro he went, looking at each man and shaking his head, obviously desperate to get it right. Guy watched him hopefully. 'It has been so long,' Lev said to the police officer in charge. 'Once I would have sworn number two but . . . not now. Maybe . . . five?'

'Take your time,' the police officer said. He nodded to the policeman pushing the wheelchair and Lev was wheeled slowly along the line-up again. He stopped and pointed as he got to Dr Beck. 'Yes,' he said with a slow intake of breath. 'Five.'

Lev Shapiro was wheeled out to where Yitzak was waiting in the corridor. 'You saw him?' Yitzak asked.

Lev's eyes blazed with triumph. 'Yes!'

A policeman walked past them towards the room where the identification parade was being held. 'This way, Mr Somper,' he said. 'It's all right, they won't be able to see you.'

Lev raised a shaking finger and pointed. 'That man!'

Yitzak followed his gaze. 'Who is he?'

'He was inside the place,' Lev said.

While Somper was being brought in, Guy Salthouse was down amongst the suspects, reorganising the line-up. He was quite pleased with himself; this was not something the police were always prepared to do. He put a hand on Dr Beck's arm. 'If I can move you to . . .'

'This is stupid,' Dr Beck snapped, moving unwillingly to his new place and allowing the solicitor to place him under '2' instead of '5'.

'Thanks, Sergeant,' Guy Salthouse said.

'Not taking any chances, eh?' the sergeant said.

Dr Beck sighed and Guy Salthouse gave the sergeant the thumbs-up. 'We can go on now, thank you.'

He went up to the viewing room where Karol Somper was standing next to the police officer.

'Now,' the officer said quietly. 'Will you please look at each man carefully and then if, and only if, you can identify the man you call Aleksander Balinski, give me his number.'

Karol Somper looked at the line-up and, without hesitation, pointed out Dr Beck. 'There he is.'

'Just say his number,' the inspector said.

'Two. Number two. Balinski.'

'Are you sure?'

Karol Somper nodded. 'I knew him in Dachau.'

Guy Salthouse stepped forward quickly. 'I think that's quite enough.'

Looking around the room, Karol Somper said: 'I carried bodies he had killed.'

Salthouse escorted Dr Beck out of the police station to where Marian and Charlie were waiting in the car. 'It'll be the magistrates' court now, I'm afraid,' he said.

Dr Beck didn't look at his solicitor. 'It's ridiculous,' he said. 'A ridiculous farce.'

As they approached the car, Charlie and his mother got out. 'How ...?' Charlie began, and then saw the expression on the solicitor's face. His father, as usual, was giving nothing away.

'They're old men,' he said contemptuously. 'Probably too old to recognise their own children.'

Marian, distraught, put her hands to her face. 'What does it mean?' she sobbed. 'What happens now?'

Alexander put a hand on her shoulder. 'Be calm,

234

Marian. It is a foolish mistake, as they will discover in the magistrates' court.'

Charlie sighed. 'It's going on, then?'

''Fraid so,' Guy Salthouse said.

Helen Ames had picked Colonel Brennan up in Portman Square and brought him along to the court.

'Thank you, my dear,' he said. 'And where do I go now?'

An usher came up to them. 'He's just been called,' he said. He gestured towards Colonel Brennan. 'This way, please. Follow me.'

He led the colonel into the witness box and handed him the Bible. The colonel took the oath and then cleared his throat. 'Colonel, er ... John D. Brennan, United States Army, retired ...'

James Kavanagh stood up. 'Colonel Brennan, I believe you were with the American forces that liberated Dachau concentration camp?'

'Yes, sir, I was. Er, April twenty-ninth, 1945. I was then serving with the United States Seventh Army.'

'What were the conditions like inside the camp?'

'A nightmare. The whole Nazi organisation had collapsed and they were trying to hide what they'd done by sending all the people away in trains. About ... er ... two days before they'd marched out about six thousand men and shot 'em. About half of them were Jewish.'

The colonel continued delivering his evidence in the matter-of-fact tones of an old soldier describing an everyday military manoeuvre. Marian, sitting between Lucy and Charlie, clutched Charlie's hand and tried to close her ears to the horrific facts which were totally beyond her understanding. She knew about the concentration camps, of course. She'd seen the newsreels at the time; in fact, those

235

newsreels had remained so vividly in her mind that she had never questioned Alexander about his time in Dachau, afraid the memories would be too painful, that she would upset him unnecessarily. She was always nervous about upsetting him.

A clerk came in carrying a large board and Marian whispered: 'What is it?'

'Some kind of map,' Charlie said. 'I don't know, for God's sake.' Anxiety made him more sharp-tempered than ever.

The map was propped up in the witness box next to the colonel. He studied it carefully for a minute and then pointed to a corner on the left. 'Over here they had their, er, medical block and "special unit". I found water tanks about, let's say, two yards wide, two yards deep. That's where they did their freezing experiments.'

Giles Culpepper stood up, and the magistrate acknowledged him. 'Mr Culpepper?'

'Sir.' Giles bowed. 'As I said before, I do not intend to carry out cross-examinations at this hearing, but, um . . . ?'

The magistrate gestured for him to sit down. 'Thank you, Mr Culpepper. If you'd continue, Mr Kavanagh . . .'

Kavanagh nodded. 'Now, Colonel, I take it that you saw no evidence of these experiments?'

'No,' the colonel said, 'but I heard about 'em. That was enough, believe me. In the blockhouses the naked bodies were stacked up ten feet high. Some of 'em were even still alive. We managed to save a few.'

'Did anyone run out of the camp?'

The colonel shook his head. 'Nobody *ran* out of that place. Except we caught a few SS guards trying to disguise themselves in prison uniform.'

'Would it have been possible, in the confusion, to get away, to escape?'

Culpepper looked thoughtfully at the colonel as he said: 'Well . . . it might have been *possible* but . . .'

Marian was feeling sick. 'I want to go home, Charlie. I don't want to stay in this place, listening . . .'

Charlie nodded to Lucy who took Marian's arm and stood up. 'Come on, Mother. I'll go with you. We'll see you later, Charlie.'

'Right.' Charlie watched them go. He would have liked to have gone with them. One, he was still having a hassle over the lousy computer game software and he didn't trust Dave to deal with it. Two, he didn't like the way things were going. Why hadn't Culpepper forced the magistrates' arm on that circumstantial stuff about the freezer tanks? He couldn't believe his old man was mixed up in all these grisly goings-on, but even if he had been, there was a war on and it was history now, wasn't it? He sighed heavily. For Dad's sake, he'd have to sit it out. There was an archivist in the witness box now, handing the magistrate some folder described as 'exhibits JS44 and JS45, file number three'. The lady barrister, sitting next to Kavanagh, was bobbing about taking them from the usher, who'd taken them from the magistrate, and was handing them back to the guy in the dock who gave them a swift butcher's.

'These are correct,' the archivist said. 'They are records that have been held at the police archives in Potsdam. They refer to the Polish family Beck. I mean, one family Beck. All of them received . . . "special treatment". That is, they were exterminated. All except one – Aleksander Tadeusz.'

Charlie sat up, instantly alert. 'What happened to him?' Kavanagh asked.

There was an expectant silence as the archivist paused for a moment. 'He was transferred from Auschwitz to Dachau. For experimental purposes.'

There was hushed chatter in the court, which fell silent as

Avram Rypin was led into the witness box. The jury watched him closely as he took the oath. This was the first eye-witness account from somebody who had actually been a prisoner in Dachau. Charlie regarded him with loathing.

'Mr Rypin,' Kavanagh said. 'You are a Jew?'

'Oh yes.' Avram chuckled.

'How did you manage to survive so long in Dachau?'

Charlie was pleased to see that Culpepper was taking notes, as the old fool said: 'I was, er . . . skilled. A bootmaker. I had to make boots for the SS men. That way I was . . . spared from the selection.'

'What selection?'

'Selection to be killed.'

Kavanagh nodded. 'And did you know Alexander Beck?'

'Oh yes,' Avram Rypin said.

'Do you see him here?'

Avram shook his head and a rustle of interest went through the court. 'No,' he said. 'No, the real Mr Beck was . . . he was brought from Auschwitz . . . they made experiments with him. Yes. They cut every day from his leg a piece . . . to see if that will heal, you know, to heal up properly. Yes. I saw him many times in the hut. He died . . . very, very slowly.'

Charlie turned his head away and shuddered. God, this was disgusting. Only a madman could believe that his father would be involved in anything so . . . *disgusting*.

'I believe you have already identified the defendant?' Kavanagh said.

'Oh yes . . .' Rypin pointed across the court at Dr Beck. 'He is . . . Aleksander Balinski.' Dr Beck slowly shook his head. 'You see, sometimes I made boots for the SS men that were in the . . . the medical block. I take them there. And I saw him . . . passing through in his white coat.'

'Where was he going?' Kavanagh said. 'Any idea?'

'Yes,' Avram said. 'To the special unit – where they freeze people.'

As Avram left the witness box he heard Lev Shapiro's name being called and was amazed to see his old friend actually walking into the courtroom. True, he was supported by a nurse on one side and the usher on the other, but it was a brave gesture, and brought tears to Avram's eyes.

They propped Lev up in the witness box and, clinging to the wooden bar in front of him, he took the oath on the Bible which the usher was holding up for him.

'If you choose to be seated, you may,' the magistrate said.

'No,' Lev said. 'I am Lev Shapiro, citizen of the State of Israel.'

He looked around in short-sighted confusion as Kavanagh said: 'Mr Shapiro, do you remember your time in the medical block?'

Locating Kavanagh in the body of the court, Lev focused and said: 'Yes. I was a TP.'

'A TP was a test person?'

'I was not one of Balinski's,' Lev said. 'I had to drink seawater. Litres of it every day. It was to do with the air pilots falling in, to test for madness.' He straightened his bent body and said with pride: 'I kept sane. I stole water from the fire buckets.'

'But . . . Balinski?' Kavanagh reminded him.

'He would hurry through to the special unit – to the freezing tanks where he killed people.' Lev looked accusingly at Dr Beck.

'Did you see that happen?'

Lev seemed confused. 'I . . . I heard about it.'

'Mr Shapiro,' Kavanagh said. 'Did you ever see Balinski kill?'

Lev was confident now. 'Yes. Yes, I did.'

'In the special unit? You were there?'

'No, no,' Lev said. 'No, it . . . it was after the camp was liberated. I saw him running.'

'Where was this?'

Lev looked down. 'I . . . I can't remember,' he mumbled. 'I do not know . . . maybe the parade ground or so. He shot a man who tried to stop him, with a gun.' He raised his voice. 'He shot him.'

'Was it one of the guards?'

'How could it be? All the Nazi guards were long gone. It had to be one of us.'

'A prisoner?' Kavanagh queried.

Lev shrugged. 'It was just a shooting. There were always shootings. Shootings didn't matter any more.' His voice faltered and he began to tremble. 'You could be killed just for the way you looked at somebody.'

The magistrate raised his hand. 'Er, Mr Kavanagh . . . perhaps it's time for a short adjournment.'

Kavanagh nodded and prepared to sit down but Lev Shapiro, raising his voice, said: 'No, let me speak. For fifty years I have struggled with the question – why? Why would they do it?'

'Mr Shapiro,' the magistrate said, 'if you wish to compose yourself . . .'

But Lev Shapiro would not be silenced. 'I wish to tell you, sir, about Nazi science. It was never to discover any truths. It never came to anything. It was just an excuse to torture and torment human beings.' He pointed a shaking finger at Dr Beck. 'And that is what *he* was doing.'

Kavanagh interrupted. 'Mr Shapiro, I think . . .'

'Every day in that camp you had to say to yourself, "I will survive." The only reason to survive was that one day the evil would end, then we would tell. And all the world would know what the evil had been.'

Avram nodded his head, and Yitzak shot a warning glance at the nurse and the usher as his grandfather's trembling became uncontrollable.

The magistrate nodded to the usher. 'Take him outside ... help him.' Lev held his side, groaning, and together the usher and the nurse supported the old man out of the court and laid him down on a bench in the magistrates' antechamber. Helen Ames and Yitzak hurried in and Lev looked up at his grandson.

'Yitzak, did I tell them?' There were tears in his eyes. 'I can't remember.'

Yitzak took his grandfather's hand. 'You did well, *Zayde*.'

'Is that so?' Lev wiped away the tears with his other hand. 'I . . . I think I failed. There was so much more . . .'

'You did fine,' Helen said. She nodded to Yitzak. 'I must go back.'

'Okay,' Yitzak said softly, as his grandfather fell back and closed his eyes.

When Helen arrived back in court, Karol Somper was in the box and Kavanagh was asking him about the special unit.

'I had to go there as a prison orderly.' Somper looked over at Dr Beck. '*He* was my boss.'

'You mean the defendant?' Kavanagh said.

'Yes.' Karol Somper nodded towards the doctor. 'Him. Dr Balinski.'

Beck raised his eyes resignedly and Kavanagh said: 'When was this?'

'Mmm . . . Christmas 1943. Before that I was on freezing experiments with Dr Rascher.'

'You were transferred?'

'Yes, when Dr Balinski got permission to set up his own outfit. The Todesengel programme. That's, er, German. It means Death Angel . . .' He looked straight at Dr Beck. 'Isn't that right?'

Dr Beck turned his head away and Kavanagh said: 'Address the court, please.'

'Well,' Karol Somper continued, 'in the spring of 1944 there were a lot of fresh TPs brought in. Some Russian prisoners, but mostly Hungarian Jews – for his programme.'

'And what was that?' Kavanagh asked quietly.

'Making people slowly die by freezing, and then trying to bring them back to life.'

Somper spoke in a flat monotone and seemed unaware of the electric effect his words were having on the court. There was a ripple of hushed chatter, and Avram gazed challengingly across the court at Dr Beck, who stared ahead into space, without moving a muscle.

'Did that ever happen?' Kavanagh asked.

'Oh yes,' Karol Somper said. 'Sometimes. And then he would make them die again. There were women, too. He said young Jewish women responded best – "They keep coming back."'

'And if they didn't finally die?'

'They got shot.'

'Who did it?'

Karol Somper looked over at Dr Beck. 'He did.'

Is it possible? Charlie asked himself. My father . . . Dad . . . he'd always been in the business of saving lives, not killing people. How many times had he been stopped in the street by some old crone telling him how his father had saved her life or her husband's life, or how wonderful he'd been with her grandchildren? He gazed over at the dock, disbelievingly, and was pleased to see that his father had not lost his cool, but was slowly shaking his head in denial.

The magistrate glanced down at his notes and then at the scruffy old man in the witness box. 'Mr Somper, what part did *you* play?'

'I got the bodies out of the ice,' he replied. 'They were heavy . . . I was strong. That was all I did. I never killed. Not a single one.'

'What was done with the bodies?' Kavanagh asked.

'Sent away to be cut up. To test the theory that being communists and Jews affected the structure of a skeleton.' Karol Somper lifted his head. 'I am not a Jew.'

Jennifer Shaw and her mother had been watching an afternoon quiz programme. When the local news came on afterwards, there was a whole lot about Dr Beck. They showed an elderly Polish man and the disreputable old tramp from down the road leaving the court, then out came the doctor, smiling and nodding at reporters and looking unconcerned, as well he might, Jennifer thought.

'Just look at all those disreputable-looking old men,' her mother said. 'Not fit to wipe the doctor's boots. You remember how kind he was when I had the sciatica, came round twice a day?'

'And the massage,' Jennifer reminded her mother. 'He was never too busy to give you the massage.'

'Will I ever forget?' the old lady said. 'Such gentle hands.' She watched the poor doctor struggling through the reporters to his son's red car. 'He'll be on his way back now, Jennifer. You get over there and tell him we're right behind him.'

Jennifer waited until the car came around the corner and then she went out into the street, which was already full of people jostling each other on the pavement outside Dr Beck's house. Some of them were reporters, but most of them she recognised as locals, including a number she'd seen in Dr Beck's waiting room.

They all pushed forward as Charlie opened the door and the doctor got out. 'Good on you, Doctor!' a man called out. 'Don't you worry, Dr Beck, we'll tell them . . .' a woman shouted. There were cries of support and encouragement and a young woman grabbed his arm, saying: 'I'll never forget what you done for our Jeannie . . .'

Jennifer couldn't get close enough to say anything, but she smiled at Dr Beck, who smiled back at her as he hurried up the steps. 'Thank you,' he was saying to everyone. 'Thank you for your support. Thank you. Thank you all.'

Jennifer looked up at the house as the doctor went through the front door, and saw Marian Beck gazing out into the street. How strange, Jennifer thought. She wasn't in court to back him up. I would have been. They wouldn't have been able to keep me away.

24

Detective Inspector Grover and Karol Somper waited by the LOT desk, while Sergeant Hudson checked in Somper's suitcase.

'We'll try to give you plenty of warning,' the inspector said.

Mr Somper seemed puzzled. 'Warning?'

'Of the date . . . when we need you for the trial.'

'But it's all happened,' Karol Somper said. 'He's guilty. The judge, he said . . .'

'The magistrate,' the inspector corrected. 'The magistrate found there was a case to answer. Dr Beck . . . er, Balinski . . . has been committed for trial and released on bail.'

'But, sir,' Karol Somper said, 'I did not understand . . .'

'Never mind,' the inspector said. 'Ah, here comes the sergeant with your ticket.'

'Ticket and passport,' Sergeant Hudson said, handing them to Karol Somper.

'Well . . .' Somper shook them both by the hand. 'I say goodbye.'

'Take care, Mr Somper,' the inspector said.

They went back to the car and, as they got in, the phone rang. The inspector picked it up. 'Grover . . .' He

245

groaned. 'Oh my God. Right, I'll come straight along.' He hung up the phone. 'It's Shapiro,' he said. 'Heart attack. Look, drop me off at St Mary's and then get back to the station a.s.a.p.'

Sergeant Hudson whirled up the M4 with his sirens blaring. He always enjoyed setting off the siren and weaving through the traffic like one of those American cops in *NYPD Blue*. He blazed along Praed Street, causing the late commuter traffic and the taxis heading for Paddington Station to cower in the gutter, and, in record time, deposited the inspector at the main door of St Mary's.

'Thank you, Toby,' the inspector said, getting out of the car swiftly. He was not surprised to find that his legs were distinctly wobbly as he went up to Reception, and reminded himself not to share a car with the sergeant during any future emergency.

He was directed up to a private room on the fourth floor, where he found Lev Shapiro lying in bed, attached by tubes to a heart monitor, and looking extremely shaky. The grandson, Yitzak, and Avram Rypin were on either side of the bed.

Lev put out a hand as the inspector came in. 'Inspector . . .'

The inspector went towards the bed. 'How are you now?'

'Come close . . . come close,' Mr Shapiro said, 'and listen. *He* must speak for *me* in court.' He gestured towards Yitzak. 'My grandson.'

'I've told him I can't,' Yitzak said.

'He's not a witness, you see,' the inspector said.

Lev grabbed the inspector's sleeve. 'But he must. He must. He knows. We have studied together. He knows it all.'

Grover bent over the old man. 'Give me something I can pass on to the lawyers. When you saw Balinski shoot this man, how was he dressed?'

Lev appeared distressed. 'I don't know . . . prison stripes, maybe.'

'Could he have been wearing them as a disguise?' the inspector suggested.

Lev shook his head from side to side. 'Don't ask me these things. They do not matter.'

'No, no,' the inspector insisted. 'They might be vitally important.'

Yitzak stood up and said quietly, 'That's enough, now.'

Lev groaned and, with an effort of will, turned to Avram Rypin. 'Avi . . . you were in Dachau. You know. You must tell them.'

'I will,' Avram said. 'I will, I promise.'

'You must tell the whole world otherwise they will do it again . . .' Lev shuddered. '. . . someone will do it again.'

Yitzak took his grandfather's hand. '*Zayde* . . . ?'

The inspector looked up at the heart monitor and saw that it had stopped.

Marian Beck was standing in the garden dead-heading her roses. She enjoyed gardening; it took your mind off things. Sometimes she felt that it was the only thing she was any good at. She looked up as Alexander came out of the back door and down the steps.

'I've just had a phone call from Guy Salthouse,' he said. 'Old Shapiro's dead.'

Marian snapped off another rose with her secateurs. 'Good riddance,' she said.

Lizzie was trying to sleep, something she always found difficult when James was lying awake beside her. She turned over towards him. 'I don't think you've been asleep at all.'

247

'Not much,' he said.

'What is it?' Lizzie said. 'Worries?'

'Images,' Kavanagh said. Every time he closed his eyes he saw raggedly attired scarecrows, their hair brutally cropped, reaching out to him, or the pleading eyes of frozen men and women trapped in a bed of ice.

Lizzie put her arms around him. 'Do you want a pill?'

'No.' As Kavanagh turned to her, gratefully absorbing her warmth and her strength, the telephone rang.

'Oh, no,' Lizzie said, as Kavanagh reached over to pick it up.

'Kavanagh,' he said. There was a pause. 'Who? When? Right. Well, thanks for letting me know.' He sighed and put down the phone.

'What . . . ?' Lizzie began.

'Old Shapiro. Dead. He's just had a massive heart attack.'

'Oh God,' Lizzie said. 'I'm sorry.'

'One of our chief witnesses, too,' Kavanagh said.

'What will this do?'

'I'm not sure.' He shook his head sadly. 'Lizzie, I was trying to make him tell me how one man shot another. But what was in his mind was something far bigger. A logic bereft of humanity, a whole philosophy gone bad.'

The following morning there was a meeting in Kavanagh's office in River Court. Helen Ames had called up Arnold Westrope and Inspector Grover to see if there was any evidence they could retrieve from Yitzak before he returned to Israel.

They had been through all Lev Shapiro's testimony and decided that the most useful contribution was probably his final description of the shooting.

248

'Did your grandfather ever go into any detail about that shooting he witnessed?' Kavanagh asked Yitzak.

Yitzak shook his head regretfully. 'No. It didn't interest him. Only the lessons of history.'

'I understand that,' Kavanagh said.

Westrope looked around the room. 'You could see it either way. A guilty man shooting his way out, or an innocent inmate in terror.'

'Either way,' Kavanagh said, 'I'll have to forget it.' He looked across at Yitzak. 'When are you flying him back?'

'Tomorrow,' Yitzak said. 'By freight . . . so . . . I have much to arrange.'

'Of course,' Kavanagh said. 'Helen will see you out, and . . . once again, I'm so sorry.'

At the door, Yitzak turned to Helen. 'Miss Ames, I would like to see this through to the end. Can I come back and be there . . . at the Old Bailey?'

'Yes, of course.' Helen smiled. 'We'll see you then.'

Marian would never know how she got through those weeks before the trial. Sitting across from Alexander at breakfast and dinner, trying to pretend they were leading perfectly normal lives, listening to Charlie ranting and raving about 'bloody Jews' and what all this was doing to his business, and putting up with the sudden silences and prurient stares as she went into the corner shop to buy a pint of milk.

Alexander spent most of the time locked in his study, refusing to speak, except when Guy Salthouse, the flash young solicitor, came around for meetings, and then she could hear her husband raising his voice defiantly and arguing his corner.

Lucy had been kind. She came around quite often and helped Marian in the garden; she hadn't seemed to want to talk to Alexander, though, which Marian had found rather hurtful.

She didn't know what she'd have done, really, if it hadn't been for the Shaws opposite. They had been so friendly, asking her around for coffee and cups of tea and never putting any pressure on her to say anything about Alexander or The Case – she always thought of it in capital letters – unlike some of the neighbours who, under the guise of friendliness, had been frankly inquisitive. Not that she could have told them anything. Marian had always believed in the old saying that the less you knew the better. It hadn't occurred to her to ask Alexander if any of the dreadful things they had said about him were true. Most days, anyway, she didn't – couldn't – believe it. On the days when she wasn't quite so sure, she was too afraid of his answers to ask.

'It probably seems odd to you,' she'd said to Jennifer, the day before the trial, 'but I'm glad it's going to happen at last.'

'Of course you are,' Jennifer said. 'Soonest done, soonest over. And then we'll be opening the champagne, won't we, Mother?'

'We've got a bottle of Bollinger in the cabinet,' Mrs Shaw said. 'Daddy was keeping it for a special occasion.' She smiled at Marian. 'We'll crack it open the day Dr Beck walks out of that court a free man.'

25

Lizzie looked around the court anxiously. There was a murmur of expectancy in the air. Everyone was seated except for the judge and the defendant – and Matt, who'd gone off to look for Yitzak Shapiro.

An usher called for quiet as Matt and Yitzak crept in and took their seats next to her.

'They'd shown him into the wrong courtroom,' Matt whispered.

'Oh, right.' Lizzie smiled and nodded to Yitzak. 'Hi,' she said quietly. 'Lizzie Kavanagh. It was tragic about your grandfather . . .'

Yitzak leaned over Matt and shook her hand. 'He was very old. I am here for him.'

'Of course,' Lizzie said.

Matt turned to Yitzak. 'You were saying, as we came up the stairs, that he was not just an old man, but a great man.'

Yitzak nodded. 'In Israel, yes. His funeral was quite remarkable. Even I was surprised.'

Dr Beck walked into the dock, his head held high. Matt touched Yitzak's arm. 'Here's Beck.'

Yitzak corrected him. 'Balinski!'

The clerk asked the court to rise and Mr Justice McMinn took his seat on the bench. He smiled at the clerk, who read out the indictment – that in the concentration camp at Dachau, Dr Beck, also known as Aleksander Balinski, had murdered a Jew and a Jewess, both unknown.

He pleaded 'Not guilty' to both charges, and Marian, sitting between Lucy and Charlie, was not surprised to hear the firm confidence in his voice. It was his confidence which had first attracted her all those years ago.

They had met at a Young Conservatives dance at Pauls in Ealing. Pauls was *the* teatime place for fancy cakes stuffed with mock cream and all sorts of other rich goodies which were a luxury in those austerity days. They also had a banqueting suite, much sought after for masonic dos, wedding receptions and dances. Marian had lived with her parents, not far away, in a quiet road facing the tennis club. She was not a very good tennis player, but she was pretty and undemanding and was a favourite with the young men who frequented the club. One of them, Peter Barton, had invited her to the YC dance. Marian quite liked him. She'd been out with him often, to the pictures, for walks on the common, to friends' parties. She'd allowed him to kiss her a few times, and there had been several clumsy fumbles in the back of his father's Morris, but that had been as far as it went. Marian was definitely not That Sort of Girl – as Deirdre McArthur had been known in the club. Until that evening, she'd supposed she would probably end up marrying Peter. He was nice-looking and had prospects – he was training to be something in the City. She was nearly twenty-one and her mother had started saying: 'You'd better get a move on, Marian, or you'll be left on the shelf.' And then Alexander had come over during the Excuse Me dance – the band had been playing 'The Very Thought Of You', she'd never forget it – and that had been it, really. He was so good-looking – tall, slim with grey eyes that somehow seemed to see right into her mind and know what she was thinking. He had the most beautiful voice, an accent like Anton Walbrook, the film star, and when he held her strongly and firmly close in that dance, he'd aroused feelings inside her that had melted away any resistance she might have made that night, or for many nights over many years to come, for that matter. She had never known what he'd seen in her; she was aware that she was quite pretty, but so were lots of girls, and she wasn't at all clever – not like Alexander, who knew all about cultural things like books and art, as well as politics and medicine. He even read the financial pages in the newspapers and seemed to understand them. Her parents had disapproved of the match at the beginning – he was fifteen years older than she was, he was a foreigner, he had no family background – but Alexander had just finished his finals and qualified and they enjoyed telling their friends: 'Oh, Marian's marrying a doctor, you know.'

She looked at him now, still so handsome, sitting in the dock of the Old Bailey, and wanted to weep for the happy young couple who had cut the white tiered cake together in Pauls. She groped for Lucy's hand and forced herself to listen to what was going on.

'In short,' James Kavanagh was saying, 'I intend to demonstrate that in 1945, Aleksander Balinski escaped from Dachau camp and punishment for his murderous experiments there by assuming the identity of a prisoner he knew to be dead, Aleksander Tadeusz Beck. And that he was able to come to England and eventually settle down here, turning his considerable medical skills to a proper use as a general practitioner.'

*   *   *

Later that morning, Kavanagh questioned Colonel Brennan about reports of a prisoner being shot around the time when the US forces reached Dachau.

The colonel was outraged at the suggestion that one of his men might have done the shooting.

'No, no, no,' Kavanagh said quickly. 'By someone trying to escape. Perhaps one of the SS?'

'Sir,' Colonel Brennan said, 'we had thousands of people on our hands. We were trying to save their lives before they turned into Mussulmen. That's what the Nazis called them when they just gave up and died.'

Giles Culpepper then asked the colonel what he'd found when he opened up the special medical unit where the alleged experiments had supposedly been carried out.

The colonel grimaced and cleared his throat. 'Er ... some filth and human debris in the water tanks.'

Were there any records? the defence counsel wanted to know. Lists of names, staff rotas?

'All carefully burned,' the colonel said.

Avram Rypin appeared just before the lunch break and Kavanagh put him through much the same questions he'd answered in the magistrates' court. And then he asked Avram how often he had seen Dr Beck in the camp.

Avram looked over at the dock. 'Balinski? Not many times. Thank God. Once he got you into the special unit you were kaput – done for.'

'Did people know his name?'

'Oh, yes, yes, yes,' Avram said. 'You hear them whispering one to the other. "Balinski ... Balinski this ... Balinski that ... Balinski." And where are these people now? Mmm? All dead. Only me to speak for them ...' He choked and paused. '... and I do.' Avram put his hands to his head and sobbed.

Culpepper rose and smiled reassuringly. 'Calm yourself, Mr Rypin, I have very few questions.'

Avram sniffed. 'That's good.'

'In, er, Dachau you were given work as a bootmaker?'

'Oh yes. For the SS. That is why they don't kill me.'

'Special boots with much fine detail?'

'Oh yes.' Avram chuckled. 'For them, sure. Yes, of course. It had to be.'

'And so you needed glasses as you do now?'

'No,' Avram said.

'Surely, for such fine close work?'

Avram fingered his glasses. 'No, I don't wear glasses for this. You see, I've got, um, what is it, er, short sight, you see. For this work it . . . that's . . . that comes in very useful, that.'

'But for all other purposes?'

'Oh yes. Yes, glasses, sure.'

'Strong ones?'

'Yes, very strong.'

'Did you wear them round the camp? When, as you've told us, you stood for hours on the parade ground? In the huts and out of the huts? Did you?'

'Yes,' Avram said.

'Oh no you didn't. Or you'd have had them smashed in your face by one of the guards.' There was a harshness in Culpepper's normally bland voice. 'You were *ein Dreckjude*. And you *never* wore them when you were near the medical block, for example.'

Avram raised a hand. 'Please . . .'

'And if you'd seen anybody wearing a white coat, you couldn't have told who it was.'

Mr Justice McMinn did not approve of defending counsel hectoring the witness in this way and called Culpepper to order.

255

'Don't worry, it's all right,' Avram said to the judge. 'It's . . . er . . . I don't mind. He's right. Yes, they break my glasses. Those guards beat you all the time for no reason but, you see, there were always more glasses, any sort that I want. Any prescription.'

'Where?' Mr Justice McMinn asked.

'Where they stored them,' Avram said. 'Where they keep them . . . where they take them from the dead people. There were shoes, too.' He sighed. 'Those I could mend.'

The judge managed not to show his satisfaction at this swift reversal. 'Mr Culpepper? Any further questions?'

Culpepper glanced quickly over at the doctor, who shook his head. 'No, my Lord,' he said.

James Kavanagh, who had thought, a few moments earlier, that Avram Rypin was walking innocently into the pit that had been cunningly dug for him, stood up. 'No re-examination,' he said. 'Thank you, Mr Rypin.'

A new witness appeared on the stand after the lunch break. Her name was Miss Dodd, a slim, well-preserved woman in her late sixties, wearing a trim brown woollen dress with a brown-and-cream silk scarf elegantly twisted at her neck.

'Miss Dodd,' Kavanagh said, 'can you tell the court about your involvement in relief work after the war?'

'I volunteered when I was eighteen,' Miss Dodd said in a clear Home Counties accent. 'I'd learnt German at school so . . . I was sent to help in, um, some of the camps for displaced persons. Um . . . d'you know . . .'

Kavanagh nodded. 'We understand the term, Miss Dodd.'

'It wasn't just a matter of feeding them,' Miss Dodd said. 'We had to provide, er, cultural rehabilitation whenever we could. I was working in a camp near Stuttgart when I met Alexander Beck.'

'The defendant?'

Miss Dodd glanced briefly at the doctor. 'Yes. He told me about his time in Dachau. His suffering in the labour *kommandos*. He wanted to become a doctor and I was able to obtain some books for him to study.'

'I believe you did more than that?'

'I . . . I tried to help him come to England.'

'With you?' Kavanagh said.

'Oh, no. No. Er, I had work to do.' Marian caught the fleeting expression on Miss Dodd's face as she glanced again at Alexander. It was an expression she had grown used to intercepting over the years on the faces of Alexander's more attractive or susceptible women patients. She saw Lucy looking at her sympathetically and tried not to betray what she refused to admit, even to herself – that this woman was another of Alexander's conquests.

'How did you help him?' Kavanagh asked.

'I wrote a recommendation to the authorities . . . in rather glowing terms.'

Kavanagh smiled. 'It seems to have worked.'

'Well,' Miss Dodd said, 'things were very confused at the time. There were so many . . . well, thousands of people, actually . . . on the move. Er . . . I have sometimes worried that I might have exceeded my duties.'

'You were instrumental in the defendant's coming here?'

'Yes,' Miss Dodd said. 'I believe I was.'

Kavanagh sat down and Culpepper rose. 'Miss Dodd, when you first met Alexander Beck, what was he wearing?'

'Oh, those terrible striped things . . . like all the prisoners,' Miss Dodd said. 'But I found him some better clothes.'

'And what opinion did you form of his character?'

There was a catch in Miss Dodd's voice as she said: 'I

257

found him . . . quite remarkable. He stood out from . . . all the others.'

'And if you could have accompanied him to England . . . ?'

'No, no,' Miss Dodd said quickly. Too quickly, Marian felt. 'I . . . I never saw him again.'

While Culpepper was still cross-examining, Helen Ames tapped Kavanagh on the shoulder and whispered. 'I've just been handed a note. Arnold Westrope's outside. Wants to speak to you urgently.'

Kavanagh bowed to the judge and darted out of the courtroom. Westrope was standing just outside the door. He grabbed Kavanagh as he came out. 'Somper's disappeared,' he said.

'My next witness?' Kavanagh was appalled. 'What's happened? Where is he?'

'They're looking for him now,' Westrope said.

Kavanagh looked at him sourly. 'Well, that's a comfort.'

'He's got lost, that's all,' Westrope said. 'It's happened before.'

Kavanagh got back into court just as Miss Dodd was standing down. 'Er, no re-examination, my Lord,' he said, 'but I would ask your indulgence in calling my next witness. There seems to be some delay.'

Detective Inspector Grover presented himself at River Court at 7.45 a.m. the following morning. He and Sergeant Hudson had spent the previous evening at Heathrow. 'I'm beginning to feel we might as well book into one of the airport hotels,' the inspector had remarked dryly to his sergeant, as they'd hurried towards the LOT desk.

He'd flashed his ID at the girl in charge and said: 'Right. I need to see passenger lists of all the incoming flights from Poland. This is very urgent and extremely important. Please hurry.'

There was no Somper on any of the lists. The two policemen had then separated, and checked on all the airlines with flights that connected with even the obscurest towns in Poland. Again, they drew a blank.

They had ended up, eventually, back in front of the LOT desk.

The girl had stamped a couple of passports, attached tickets to half a dozen suitcases and had then looked up and given them her air hostess smile. 'Did you say police?'

'Yes,' the inspector had said impatiently. 'I showed you my ID.'

'Oh, well, then,' she'd said, 'this may be for you. It says "Police at airport. To collect." It came by courier service two days ago.'

'And this was the letter she gave us,' the inspector said, handing it to Kavanagh. 'You can imagine how we felt.'

'"I will not go back to London. I do not trust English justice,"' Kavanagh read. '"Signed, Karol Somper."'

'Oh my God,' Helen said.

'Was it made clear to him that he has immunity?' Westrope asked the inspector.

'Perfectly, sir.'

'And he understood?' Kavanagh said.

'He seemed to.'

'Perhaps he didn't,' Kavanagh snapped.

'James, please . . .' Arnold Westrope raised both hands, but Kavanagh was not to be placated.

'This is my only substantial witness and you've lost him. He worked with Beck, saw him every day . . .'

'I've got Toby Hudson and his team on it,' the inspector said. 'They'll do all they can, but . . .'

'"But" sounds the appropriate word,' Kavanagh said.

Westrope looked worriedly at the inspector. 'And if he's gone to ground . . . ?'

'We'll be starting from scratch,' the inspector said. 'It's essential to liaise with the Polish authorities, set up enquiries . . .'

'How long?' Kavanagh said.

'Ten days . . .' The inspector shrugged. 'Maybe fourteen.'

'I'll try for a week,' Kavanagh said. 'I won't get it.'

In the end, by stressing the vital significance of the witness, and the exceptional circumstances surrounding his non-appearance, Kavanagh managed to persuade Mr Justice McMinn to give him five days to find Somper. 'If the witness is not here first thing Monday morning, you must continue as best you can,' the judge said.

Kavanagh hurried back to River Court, where Helen Ames was waiting for him in Tom Buckley's room. 'Yitzak is in your office now,' she said. 'He says he can help us.'

'Yitzak Shapiro?' Kavanagh said. 'I don't think so.'

'Well, just talk to him,' said Helen, who had already done so.

Kavanagh went into his office, followed by Helen, and dumped his briefcase on the desk. Yitzak jumped up from where he'd been sitting and shook his hand.

Kavanagh looked at him curiously. 'Helen tells me you can help us find Karol Somper.'

'I can,' Yitzak said. 'Your men are English, they have to do everything the correct way. I do not.'

'Oh, no,' Kavanagh said, thinking of all the illegal Israeli groups, societies and terrorist organisations he had become familiar with in the preparation of the case. 'Oh, no. You are asking me to approve something that is possibly illegal?'

'I'm just telling you,' Yitzak said. 'I can go to Poland. I

know the country. I've researched there on Auschwitz and on other places.'

'He speaks the language,' Helen said.

'And I have friends.'

Kavanagh looked at Yitzak. He suddenly seemed much, much older than Matt, with a cynical worldliness Kavanagh hoped his son would never need to acquire. 'Your friends,' he said. 'Are they in Poland.'

'No,' Yitzak said.

Giles Culpepper met up with Guy Salthouse in the Ebury Wine Bar, a favourite haunt. He came over with two large glasses of claret. 'Try this, Guy. Great year.'

'Good health,' Guy said, taking a sip. 'Ooh, yes.'

'Mmm. Mmm,' Giles murmured appreciatively. 'What have you got there?'

Salthouse laid a pile of letters on the table. 'Rejects, most of them. Dozens of letters from grateful patients. Here's one from an ex-patient, Mrs Anita Buckley.' He held it up and read, "'He saved my unborn baby. I worship that man.'"

Giles swilled another mouthful of wine. 'OTT. No. That Miss Dodd, she fell apart when she saw him again. You know what my guess is? Beck's been a notable lecher in his time – shagged half the neighbourhood, I wouldn't wonder, and the missus turned a blind eye. It happens.' He put down his glass, and glanced admiringly at a pretty girl walking past the table in a very short skirt.

'Okay, then,' Guy said. 'How about this one? Halina Birnbaum. Claims to have known Beck in Dachau.'

Giles raised an eyebrow. 'Girlfriend?'

Even Guy looked pained. 'Giles, hardly, in a concentration camp.'

'Birnbaum. Jewish . . .' Giles held his glass up to the light and admired the pleasing colour of the wine. 'Might make a good character witness.'

'Well, she's been in a charity home since the end of the war,' Guy said. 'It was they who wrote to us. She's physically very frail. Oh, and mentally . . .'

'Oh dear,' Culpepper said. 'Far too risky, then.' He studied his glass again. 'You know, this really is remarkably good.'

'Mmm,' Guy agreed.

'In fact, we may not be putting anyone at all in the box.'

'You mean if the case collapses?'

'*If?*' Giles smiled confidently. 'Come along, Guy, with their only relevant witness holed up in some obscure Polish slum? Tell you what, cheer your client up . . . take him a bottle of this.'

Dr Beck uncorked the bottle. 'This is very kind of Mr Culpepper,' he said. He poured out three glasses and handed them around. 'Marian . . . Mr Salthouse . . .'

'Cheers!' Guy said. 'So, Dr Beck, I'm very pleased to be able to tell you that I think your worries are over. The case will be stopped.'

Alexander paused, puzzled, with his glass halfway to his lips. He put it down. 'I won't have to give evidence?'

'Nobody will.'

'Why, that's wonderful.' Marian rushed over and put her arms around her husband.

Guy Salthouse raised his glass, 'Well, cheers, again,' he said.

Yitzak Shapiro telephoned Helen Ames on Saturday night. There was a buoyant note in his voice as he said: 'I've got Somper.'

'Brilliant,' Helen said. 'Where?'

'Here. In my hotel room.'

'Oh, Yitzak,' Helen said, 'I'm so grateful. But how . . . ?'

'Someone I know brought him to meet me at a friend's flat, in Cracow,' Yitzak said, 'and I gave him a simple choice.'

'And he chose to come back?'

'There were two flight tickets on the table in front of him. Both made out in his name. "Pick this one," I told him, "and you come with me to London tomorrow. Pick the other and you go with my friends to Israel." Helen, I have to say that I looked then at my friend who is standing behind Mr Somper, and Mr Somper turns around and looks at him, too. My friend is a very large man, an ex-boxer, actually. Yes, he chose to come back.'

'I see,' Helen said. 'Yitzak, on no account mention any of this to Mr Kavanagh.'

26

The phone went as Lizzie and Kavanagh were finishing breakfast. 'I'll get it,' Lizzie said. 'It's probably for you.'

'Tell them I'm not here,' Kavanagh said, looking at his watch. 'I said I'd meet Helen in chambers and we're in court at ten.'

'Right.' Lizzie nodded and picked up the phone. She reacted to what was being said at the other end so dramatically that Kavanagh almost wished he'd answered himself.

'What on earth was that all about?' he said, when Lizzie had hung up and sat down.

'Angela,' Lizzie said. 'Her father had a stroke a couple of days ago; he died last night.'

'Well, I won't pretend I'm sorry,' Kavanagh said. 'But Angela . . . is she very upset?'

'More sorrowful, I think,' Lizzie said. 'You know, wasted life . . . own worst enemy, that sort of thing. And he went out like a light, no pain . . .'

He smiled. 'You're not going to tell me he died peacefully?'

'Oh, no,' Lizzie said. 'On a tirade, as you'd expect. One moment he was shouting at the paper-boy about his

Telegraph arriving late and the next he was flat out on the doorstep.' She looked at him. 'Oh dear, I do sound callous, don't I? But he really was a most un-Christian Christian.'

'That was certainly my view,' Kavanagh said. 'And Edgar? I got the impression when you were on the phone there, running the complete gamut of emotions, that you were being pleased about something to do with Edgar.'

'Yes,' Lizzie said. 'Right. The bishop spoke to him yesterday, said he couldn't promise anything, of course, but dropped a definite hint that Edgar might be offered the living.'

'And would he like that?' Kavanagh said. 'Buried away in a small village, preaching to the elderly converted?'

'Angela says he would like nothing more.' Lizzie grinned. 'She says she and Edgar will be archetypal Jane Austen – the handsome young vicar with the fierce older sister fending off all the hopeful mothers of unmarried daughters.'

Kavanagh grinned. 'And when's the funeral?'

'Friday. You will be able to come?'

'Of course,' he said. 'If this case is finished, which it will be, with any luck, within the next few days.'

'Oh dear,' Lizzie said. 'And I promised Angela I'd go down there in an hour or so. You don't mind?'

'Matt and I will keep you informed,' he said. 'Try stopping us.'

'Where's Somper?' Kavanagh said to Helen, who was waiting for him at River Court.

'In good hands,' she said. 'Yitzak has assured me he will be in court this morning.'

'Don't tell me anything I don't need to know,' Kavanagh said.

'There's nothing you need to know,' Helen assured him.

They strolled together towards the Old Bailey and arrived just as a pale blue Rolls-Royce drew up alongside the kerb. They both watched as Giles Culpepper's chauffeur jumped out and ran to open the rear door for the illustrious Q.C. to alight.

'I wonder why one always alights from a Rolls-Royce and merely gets out of a Ford Mondeo?' Kavanagh mused.

They went up the steps and Giles bounded after them. 'Well, what's it to be, James?' He grinned. 'Are you going to fall on your own sword, or let His Lordship stick it in?' He pushed open the swing doors into the main hall. 'They always say it's better tactics to do it yourself.'

He who laughs . . . et cetera, et cetera, Kavanagh thought, smiling rather smugly as he went to the barristers' room to put on his robe and his wig. Mr Justice McMinn was surprised to hear that Kavanagh had managed to locate his witness and the trial could, therefore, proceed. He was not, however, as surprised as Guy Salthouse when Kavanagh called Karol Somper.

'They've got him,' Giles murmured to Salthouse. 'I never thought he'd turn up.'

'Well, he has,' Guy said. 'And we need a trick or two up our sleeves. What do you suggest?'

'What about that Jewish woman?' Giles said, and was irritated when Guy obviously didn't know which Jewish woman he meant. 'You know,' he said. 'The mad one.'

'But I thought you said . . .'

Giles twirled his pencil. 'Never mind what I said. What I'm suggesting now is that you cut along to that nursing-home place and check her out.'

'Right.' Guy darted out of the courtroom, and Giles concentrated on Somper's testimony. The standard preliminaries were over and Kavanagh had begun questioning him about the freezing programme. Whatever he answers, Guy thought, it's going to be bad news for me and, I suspect, worse news for Beck.

'Who was actually used in the freezing programme?' Kavanagh was saying.

'Prisoners,' Karol Somper said. 'Jews mainly. They were kept in the ice and timed until they died. It was very important to keep measuring their rectal temperature. I . . . I suffered with my hands.'

Charlie, sitting with his wife and mother, shuddered. What kind of monster was this Polish guy that he could stand there and admit doing such a filthy thing? He shot a quick look at Marian and Lucy to see how they were taking it, but couldn't tell, because they were both resolutely studying the ground.

'But you carried out your duties?' Kavanagh continued.

'I was only a *kapo*, a prisoner,' Somper said. 'I had to do what Balinski said.'

'Were they ever revived?'

'Always. I mean, we always tried to bring them back, even after they were clinically dead. He had all sorts of secret drugs.' He looked across at Beck. 'Sometimes he . . . he could do it.'

'And then?' Kavanagh asked. 'Were any spared?'

'Oh, no,' Somper said. 'Soon they would go back in the ice. He said it was to find out what death truly was.'

Guy studied Somper. He was big and shambling and dirty and looked as though he had bad breath. Not a man to endear himself to a jury. Add to that the rectal business and the fact that he was a foreigner, and it was just possible that they might refuse to accept his word against the word of the good doctor from Muswell Hill. No . . . Guy shook his head. Wishful thinking. There was no doubt that the ghastly old Pole in the witness box exuded a sort of brutal honesty. You just knew that what he said went on did go on. So – he sighed heavily – it's down to identification again.

After going through the preliminary questions, Giles said: 'Now think very, very carefully. I put it to you that the Balinski you knew there was a separate person from the defendant, Alexander Beck, and that Beck was a helpless prisoner in the camp who was starved and beaten like all the rest, and sent out on labour gangs. But . . . he had the awful additional misfortune to look like your Balinski.'

Karol Somper tilted his head and looked at Culpepper thoughtfully. 'But not *be* him?'

'That's right.'

'I never saw such a man,' Somper said firmly. 'He'd have had prison clothes and his head all shaved.'

'Nearly two hundred thousand prisoners passed through Dachau,' Giles said slowly. 'Might you not have missed him?'

'But I know Balinski,' Somper insisted. 'Look, I worked for him every day. I knew him.'

'Fifty years ago!' Giles exclaimed.

'I know him now,' Somper said, looking directly at Dr Beck.

Alexander sighed and shook his head again. 'No . . .' he murmured. 'No . . .'

Kavanagh jumped up as Culpepper sat down. 'Did you *like* Balinski?' he asked.

'I didn't mean to but he could make you like him,' Somper said. 'He said we would all get medals from Hitler.'

Guy Salthouse had been sitting on the M25 behind a green-painted Eddie Stobart lorry for fifteen minutes; he sometimes wondered what the point of owning a Porsche that cruised nice and easy at 150 m.p.h. was when the most you could do legit was seventy, even on a totally empty motorway.

It had looked so easy on the map. A quick whirl around the M25, and then off down the A286 to Haslemere. So far he'd been going for an hour and a half.

The place he was after was between Haslemere and Milford. He found the road easily enough, one of those wide, winding avenues with large ugly Edwardian houses hidden behind overgrown trees and rhododendron bushes. No numbers, of course. Nothing as simple as that. The houses all had names like Windyridge and The Pines, written on small wooden signs, cunningly concealed amongst the foliage. They were the sort of houses where, Guy reckoned, quite ordinary elderly couples would have lived comfortably with their maid and their housekeeper some sixty years ago. Now people like his gran paid through the nose to live in just one room in these kinds of places. Not even a whole room, since they'd all been sliced and subdivided and partitioned to fit in as many elderly punters as possible. He slowed down as he spotted a sign reading 'Emanuel Reuben House'. The very one. Parking in the curved drive in front of the front door, he hopped out and rang the bell.

It was quite a decent place, actually, with a nice Turkish carpet on a well-polished wood floor in the hall and comfy chairs arranged around a telly going full blast in the lounge. Just like a hotel, he thought, if it weren't for the residents. The sight of them, sitting there so useless and hopeless, sent a shaft of depression right through him.

The attendant, a middle-aged woman with a kind face, wearing a quality tweed skirt which made Guy think she was a voluntary worker rather than a careworker, led him out to a conservatory (a broken-down old thing, he noted, not one of those smart jobs with twiddly knobs on top they advertised in the Sundays), where he could just see, behind

270

some large-leafed plant, a frail, pale old woman sitting in a wheelchair.

'There she is,' the attendant said.

'Is she up to it?' Guy said.

'You know,' the attendant smiled at Guy, 'it might just help her.' She went over to the chair and turned it round to face Guy. 'Halina,' she said, 'Halina. Someone's come to see you.'

Guy smiled at the old lady. He thought she was smiling back until he realised that the sweet smile never left her face; her eyes, though, were somewhere else. Opening his briefcase, he brought out a photograph of Alexander Beck and, crouching down next to her, held up the picture. 'Miss Birnbaum,' he said. 'Do you know who this is?'

Halina Birnbaum turned very slowly in her chair and looked at the photograph, still smiling. She nodded, equally slowly. 'Ah,' she sighed. 'Ah, it's Aleksander.' She didn't notice Guy taking her photograph with his Polaroid, or see him quietly slip away.

He drove back to London swiftly and arrived at the Old Bailey just after the court had risen. Giles and Dr Beck were coming out.

'Well?' Giles said.

'Okay,' Guy said. 'Can we . . . ?'

'We can go in here,' Giles said, leading the doctor into an anteroom.

They sat down at a wooden table and Guy produced his photographs of Halina Birnbaum and showed them to Dr Beck.

He shook his head. 'I don't remember her.'

'She remembers you,' Guy said. 'Fifty years ago she'd have been quite a pretty girl.'

'Juries are strange creatures,' Giles said. 'Sometimes, without realising it, they need help.'

'To see the truth?' Alexander Beck said.

'Of course to see the truth.' Giles looked sharply at his client. 'Now, at the moment, I think they've found Mr Somper rather bad news.'

'Yes,' Guy said, 'but they *might* go for her.'

Giles nodded. 'Now, Dr Beck, if you *had* encountered this woman, it would have had to have been in the main camp, would it not?'

'Yes,' Dr Beck said. 'Of course.'

'She's very frail,' Guy warned.

'So I'd have to be gentle with her,' Giles replied.

'Yes,' Guy said, 'she's, er, lived mostly away from the world.'

Alexander shook his head again. 'I'm really not convinced.' He took another look at the picture. 'A bit crazy, would you say?'

'Damaged,' Guy said.

'A lot of us were,' Alexander said.

Giles stood up. 'It's a risk. I think we must take it.'

The following morning, Giles Culpepper called Dr Beck, and the doctor, dressed in a shabby raincoat, took the oath. There was a gasp of astonishment in the court as he unbuttoned the coat slowly and took it off, revealing a concentration camp uniform.

Avram Rypin raised his eyes to the ceiling. My God, he said to himself, is there nothing this man wouldn't do to save his filthy skin?

James Kavanagh stood up as Beck clumsily put the matching cap on his head. 'My Lord, is this demonstration to be permitted?'

Mr Justice McMinn looked sharply at defending counsel. 'Mr Culpepper, was this your idea?'

Giles, concealing his own surprise at his client's curious

garb, bowed to the judge. 'I fancy it was the Nazis' idea, my Lord.'

McMinn sighed. 'Very well. Proceed.'

Dr Beck removed the cap as Giles Culpepper began questioning him. 'You were sent out in labour gangs?'

'*Kommandos*, yes,' Dr Beck said.

'And in the camp, where did you live?'

'In barracks. Huts.'

'Did you ever see the witness Karol Somper?'

'Never.'

'Were you ever in the special unit of the medical block?'

'No.'

'So, if there were a man named Balinski working there . . .'

'It was not I . . .' Dr Beck said decisively.

'Now,' Giles said, 'when the camp was liberated . . .'

'I ran away. I lived in fear for so long it was all I could feel.'

'You didn't . . . er . . . shoot anybody?'

'What with?' Dr Beck queried. 'I just kept going . . . and starving. They took me into a DP camp for the displaced, and I met kind people.' For the first time during the questioning, Dr Beck's eyes moved away from Giles Culpepper, and he looked around the court-room. 'They gave me a paper to show who I was, and I went on and I found many making their way to England. Poles, like me. And they made me welcome.'

'Was that when you decided to become a doctor?'

There was passion in Dr Beck's voice as he said: 'I swore it. After all the wickedness I had seen, I only wanted to save lives . . . during the whole of my own.'

'Thank you, Dr Beck,' Giles said, congratulating himself

on what a first-class witness the doctor had turned out to be.

Kavanagh took some time standing up, rearranging his robe and gazing around the court, and then he said benignly: 'It's not easy to become a doctor, is it, Dr Beck? Takes time.'

'In those days I worked at anything,' Alexander replied. 'Labouring . . . whatever I could, but I always studied.'

'As you had studied before you were briefly sent to Auschwitz? Medical studies?'

'I'd hardly begun.'

Kavanagh looked over at him. 'You must have a tattooed number on your arm. It was the Auschwitz practice.'

Dr Beck pulled up his sleeve to reveal a scarred forearm. 'There. None. I burnt it off.'

'Why?'

'It was shaming.'

Kavanagh nodded understandingly. 'But aren't those prison garments you've got on shaming?' He paused, and Marian gripped Lucy's hand. It was terrible, horrible to see Alexander standing before all these people, dressed like that. She should have got rid of those things. 'Dr Beck,' Kavanagh continued, 'why did you keep them? If I were in your place I'd have burnt them long ago.'

Dr Beck, for the first time that morning, seemed confused. 'I . . . don't know,' he said. Marian longed to get up and cry out: 'It was me, I kept them, it was my fault . . .' But she just gripped Lucy's hand even more tightly.

'Let me suggest a reason,' Kavanagh said. ' "They might come in useful one day." Such as now. To back up an alias.'

'My Lord,' Giles Culpepper protested, but Alexander, taking no notice of the interruption, said brokenly, 'I . . . feel . . . so much guilt.'

'Guilt?' Kavanagh queried.

'Yes. It's the feeling any survivor must have, that somehow you were spared while all those others died. All those thousands . . . millions. And here you are still alive. Why? Why?' It was a cry of despair and the doctor began sobbing. 'And that's why I force myself to wear these shaming things . . . to remind me, to relieve the guilt . . . of still being alive.' He put his hands over his eyes to conceal the tears.

Avram Rypin, sitting behind Yitzak and Matt, shook his head vehemently. 'No,' he muttered. 'No, no, no.'

Kavanagh waited for the doctor to control himself and said: 'Dr Beck, when Karol Somper says that he assisted you to perform these obscene experiments . . .'

Dr Beck didn't wait for him to finish. 'He's lying.'

'If he doesn't know you, why should he lie about you?'

'I mean . . . he's mistaken,' Dr Beck said. 'He's most dreadfully mistaken.'

Dr Beck was breathing heavily as Mr Justice McMinn adjourned for lunch.

Marian sat in the canteen ignoring the chicken sandwich Charlie had fetched for her. It was all a dreadful nightmare, anyway, and now she had learned that Mr Kavanagh was going to call her as the next witness. 'I don't want to do it,' she said.

Lucy put her hand on Marian's. 'For Alexander,' she said. 'You must.'

Marian nodded miserably. 'It's not going well, is it?'

'Just wait,' Charlie said. 'I've just had a word with Mr Salthouse. He's got a mystery witness up his sleeve . . . someone who will prove that Dad was nowhere near that disgusting . . . that freezing place.' He pushed the plate with the sandwich towards Marian. 'Come on, Mother, eat up.

You'll need all the strength you can get to cope with that devious old bastard.'

As it turned out, Marian needn't have worried. Mr Kavanagh was quite kind, really, and all she had to do was answer ordinary questions about how she'd met Alexander, when he'd qualified, where they had lived and how they had managed for money. Simple things like that.

He finished up by saying: 'Mrs Beck, when you first met your husband, did he ever talk about his immediate past?'

And she was able to answer honestly: 'Oh, no, hardly at all. He ... he said that he'd put all that behind him. I remember the day that his naturalisation papers came through. He was ...' And then she did remember that day and the tears pricked her eyelids. '... he was so proud. He said, "I'm no longer Polish. I'm an Englishman."' Tears flooded down her cheeks as she looked over at Alexander. 'And now ... I see him there.'

The judge told her she could sit down, and as she took her seat between Lucy and Charlie, she was still too distressed to notice an elderly woman being wheeled into the courtroom. Charlie gave his mother a nudge and whispered, 'This is the one.'

Halina Birnbaum seemed even smaller and frailer than when Guy Salthouse had met her in the charity home. She was still smiling that strange, ethereal smile, and as she was wheeled past Dr Beck, she looked up at him adoringly, and breathed softly, 'Aleksander.'

Dr Beck frowned back at her, and Giles Culpepper got to his feet and said in a softly encouraging voice, 'Your name is Halina Birnbaum.'

She nodded, but she was still smiling at Dr Beck. 'Yes, yes.'

'You were in Dachau concentration camp in Germany.'

'Mmm. Mmm.' Halina nodded.

'You were fifteen years old?'

'Mmm . . . yes.'

Giles gestured towards Dr Beck. 'You know that man?'

Halina, who had still not taken her eyes off the doctor, nodded again. 'Aleksander.'

'Do you remember how you lived in Dachau?' Giles asked her.

Halina gazed into the distance. 'I was in Dachau . . .' She faltered and turned again towards Dr Beck, smiling. 'And . . . he was in Dachau. He was my life . . .'

Marian winced. Another woman . . . she took a deep breath and told herself not to be foolish. This was long before she and Alexander had met, and anyway – she looked at the poor broken creature in the wheelchair – this was no threat.

'You managed to be together, then?' Giles said.

'Together,' Halina breathed. 'Always.'

'Whenever you could,' Giles said briskly. 'He would have been in the men's barracks, and you in the women's. But somehow . . .'

Halina was not listening. 'Aleksander . . .' She savoured the name slowly. 'Aleksander made me safe.'

'You mean,' Giles said, 'that he managed to take care of you? He protected you? From the attentions of the guards, perhaps? Was that it?'

James Kavanagh looked curiously at Halina, at the way she smiled at Beck as she whispered, 'He was . . . my life. My life was his.'

'Until the camp was liberated and you were both free,' Giles said. 'Did you leave together?'

'My life was his,' Halina repeated.

'You loved him?'

Kavanagh felt a chill of horror. He leaned back to Helen Ames, sitting behind him, and said: 'That smile . . . she's not smiling.'

'I know,' Helen said, biting her lip.

Kavanagh looked over at Mr Justice McMinn, indicating that he would like to cross-examine Miss Birnbaum. The judge nodded and he got to his feet.

'Miss Birnbaum . . . Halina.' She turned towards Kavanagh with her strange smile. 'When you say your life was his . . .'

'My life was his,' she repeated.

'Was it his to take?' Kavanagh said slowly. 'And . . . to give back?'

Halina breathed in as though she needed more air to get through what she had to say. 'He made me die. And when I was dead . . . he made me alive again. And then . . . he gave me things, good things, to make me better.' Her head was shaking slightly at the memory. 'And when I was all better it was time to die, again.'

Kavanagh looked at the pathetic woman in front of him. She was still smiling her gentle, vacuous smile. He had to fight back tears as he said quietly, 'You only met him in the special unit in the medical block. He put you in there and he froze you, wasn't that it? He froze you to death. And then he brought you back to life . . . for the Todesengel programme?'

Halina nodded, smiling.

Kavanagh sat down and looked over at Giles. 'Why didn't he shoot her?'

Marian closed her eyes. The crowded courtroom revolved before her eyes; she felt as if she were going to faint. Lucy and Charlie, putting their arms around her to support her, exchanged grim glances.

Mr Justice McMinn leaned over towards Halina's attendant and said softly, 'Take good care of her.'

As Halina was being wheeled out of the courtroom, she looked up at the man in the dock. He was standing to attention, and even in the concentration camp uniform he looked like a soldier. She raised an arm weakly, and waved at him. 'Aleksander . . .'

Aleksander Balinski looked straight ahead and addressed the court. 'It was original,' he said. 'Completely original research into the nature of death. It might have . . . it might . . . I was proud of my work there.'

Charlie and Lucy hurried out of the courtroom, almost carrying Marian between them. They dodged the reporters and the crowds shouting insults and hurriedly clambered into Charlie's Sierra Cosworth. Charlie, revving up for the getaway, looked through his windscreen and saw a figure watching them. It was Avram Rypin. 'Look,' he said to Lucy. 'There's that bloody Jew again. If it hadn't been for him . . .'

Helen Ames, walking down the steps with Arnold Westrope, Matt and Yitzak Shapiro, saw Marian Beck's blotched, bemused face through the car window as she was being driven away. 'Poor woman,' she said. 'She never knew.'

'Or didn't want to,' Westrope said.

Kavanagh came over to join them. 'What will happen to Balinski?' Yitzak asked him.

'Life imprisonment,' he said.

'Ah,' Yitzak said. 'Life.'

That evening, as Halina Birnbaum sat in her wheelchair in the conservatory, she heard a beautiful sound. '*Yit-ga-dal v'yit-ka-dash sh'mei ra-ba b'al-ma di-v'ra chir-u-tei,*

v'yam-lich mal-chu-tei b'cha-yei-chon u-v'yo-mei-chon . . .'
Outside the window Avram Rypin was chanting the Kaddish in memory of his friends; and in memory of the girl Halina used to be.